BEST

WOMEN'S EROTICA

OF THE YEAR

VOLUME SEVEN

BEST
WOMEN'S EROTICA
OF THE YEAR

VOLUME SEVEN

Edited by

RACHEL KRAMER BUSSEL

CLEiS
PRESS

Published in the United States by Cleis Press, an imprint of Start Midnight, LLC, 221 River Street, Ninth Floor, Hoboken, New Jersey 07030.

Printed in the United States
Cover design: Jennifer Do
Cover image: Shutterstock
Text design: Frank Wiedemann

First Edition.
10 9 8 7 6 5 4 3 2 1

Trade paper ISBN: 978-1-62778-311-8
E-book ISBN: 978-1-62778-524-2

CONTENTS

INTRODUCTION: SURPRISINGLY SEXY

I've been editing erotica for over twenty years, so when I chose the theme of surprise for *Best Women's Erotica of the Year, Volume 7*, I admit that part of my motivation was selfishness. After reading thousands of erotic short stories for both work and pleasure, I still love the genre, but sometimes I find myself feeling a sense of, *Haven't I read that before?* I wanted to change that and push authors to try something new, to take readers on a wild journey, to put their character in situations where perhaps they weren't totally sure what to do, or had to push themselves into new territory.

The twenty adult stories you're about to read take the theme of surprise and serve it up in the most enticing, alluring, and sensual of ways. They not only surprised me, which, as I said, isn't the easiest thing to do, they also collectively offer a slice of the erotic world that I think captures so much of what women and people of all genders look for from sex. They offer urgent physical lust and passion, and deep emotional connection, and they navigate how sexuality grows and changes as the specifics of our lives also grow and change.

INTRODUCTION: SURPRISINGLY SEXY

I had a feeling that when most of us think about the idea of surprises, birthday parties where a roomful of guests shout the fateful word at a startled celebrant would leap to mind. I wanted to offer readers different types of surprises. Inside this book you'll find a woman who sees color because she has synesthesia in "Colors" by Velvet Moore. She channels her way of seeing into erotic art that has a very powerful impact on its viewers. You'll enjoy sci-fi erotica in the form of "Gravity" by Gwendolyn J. Bean, about a sex worker who uses gravity in some very interesting and erotic ways.

Whether they're parents looking for a little time to escape their everyday demands, such as in "Hot Pockets" by Angelina M. Lopez, or a woman getting a very erotic education in "Private Lessons" by Penny Howell, these characters find ways to surprise themselves. They do things that are out of the ordinary for them, and discover that often, simply showing up and making oneself available is enough to set off surprises.

What I most wanted to give you, my readers, was the opportunity to be surprised, whether by plot twists, characters unlike ones you've read before, or your own reactions to these stories. You'll find here stories that delve into worlds very different from our own, such as in another sci-fi erotic tale, "Sealing the Treaty" by Ann Castle, and ones that are entwined in everyday challenges, the stuff of, literally, life and death, such as in "Before and After" by Kristine Lynn.

Other stories serve up fun surprises, such as the m/m/f trio attending a movie in "Symmetry" by Angela Kempf. While reading it, I couldn't decide whether I most wanted to be part of such a scenario or watch one. In Lucy Eden's "'Ohana," another m/m/f tale, the protagonist finds true love with two lion shifters. Eden writes, "After years of running from love and almost giving up on my soulmates when they found me, I'm finally in the place where I belong, between my lions." In a tale about not judging hot but nerdy guys based on their appearances, Gabrielle Johnson's "Puzzle" offers a sexy take on strippers, lust, and secrets that gives *Magic Mike* a run for its money.

Sometimes the surprise is about discovering that there's chemistry where one might not have expected, or that the embodiment of that chemistry has the potential to change, such as for Camilla and Lucy who only get it on when they're both in the title city of "Tulsa" in Erin McLellan's racy tale. In "Who Is Like You?" by Sara Taylor Woods, best friends finally give in to the power of their attraction, which they've danced around, lingering on that edge between friendship and something even more sensual, powerful, and all-consuming. Woods writes of the moment before that happens: "I turned my face to hers, too scared to shift my whole body. Too scared to commit to that much. But she was so close already, her breath brushing my mouth, that I thought: *fuck it.*"

In Holley Trent's "The Two of Us," a marriage that began based on convenience grows into an arrangement that's far more intimate, even if it's not the traditional lovey-dovey husband/wife scenario we're all sold as the one and only relationship ideal.

It can be internal changes, the kind that transform our sense of self, that convey the most drama. In "Lioness" by Theo de Langley, the surprise isn't so much about the narrator's relationship with her kinky partner, but her relationship with her own levels of bravery as she pushes herself to the edge of what she can handle, eager to find out the sexy rewards on the other side of the unknown. In Joanna Shaw's "Your Name on My Lips," Lila explores a new way to communicate with Andy that has an explosive effect on their sex life.

In other tales, women push back against the propriety society expects of them, finding the kind of passion and erotic fulfillment that works for them, even if others would disapprove, such as in "Broken Bars" by S.P. Jaffrey and "A Modest Woman" by Lin Devon. In Kim Kuzuri's gender-bending historical tale "Phosphorous," Billy defies the norms of how women are supposed to look and behave, carving out an identity that suits her, rather than refashioning herself to suit society. In "Bitch" by Inga Gardner, Jessica knows that the title word is one her underlings at work call her, but it isn't until she owns the title in her most personal relationship that she and Chris discover how playing with power and even rage can elevate their intimacy and fulfill both of their deepest desires.

You'll read about telekinetic powers in "Wicked Ride" by Corrina Lawson, in which Beth shows Alec exactly how sexy her special skill can be. Lawson writes, "She closed her eyes and reached for his mind. An initial burst of thought, desire, need, love, and ecstasy raced through her, overwhelming all sense of touch, pushing her even closer to the edge of orgasm."

And sometimes, the surprises you'll read about here are pure fun, such as in the sensuous f/f story "Dripping" by Adriana Herrera, in which model Julissa and her lover Freya play with the toys Freya's sent as a surprise, including anal beads. Even though Julissa isn't normally a fan of surprises, she's more than happy to accept this one when personally delivered to her waiting, aching body by such a sexy woman.

I hope these stories surprise, delight, and arouse you, whether you're reading the first time, or over and over again.

Rachel Kramer Bussel

COLORS

Velvet Moore

A bright, pink tongue hung from its mouth, filling space between pointy canines, making its blue and red catlike face more mask-like than human. If it wasn't for the golden pointed helmet atop its head and four human arms, you might think it more animal than man. The artist was clever that way. His fantastic creation wielded spears and swords in its hands, raised high in a stance that looked half dance, half threatening warrior. The figure filled much of the canvas, surrounded only by explosions of color, with crude graffiti peeking through.

Street art and Hispanic heritage melted together and resulted in art that was purely Adam Hernandez. This piece, more than the others on display at the night's exhibit, spoke to me. Adam's work is always bleeding with neon, but there was an ethereal effect that moaned through that one. Ghostly messages that were scribbled, scratched, and sprayed stretched toward the canvas' surface. The colors that faded together, dripped together, pushed and pulled together drew me in.

I have a kinship with color.

I wanted to buy it, but Maria insisted that purchasing a piece from your own gallery guarantees bad luck. I tried to convince her I was buying it from her half, but she rarely appreciates my humor.

I was admiring the piece again when she interrupted me. "Will you take and put these extra price sheets at the front desk," she said, in a tone that conveyed more command than question.

I grabbed the edges of the stack she waved at me and noticed her half-smile as she held her grip a little longer than necessary. We caught eyes and my mood softened. We've spent fourteen years as partners, ten years as business owners, and the past four as mostly just friends. There are moments when words aren't necessary. Time has a language of its own.

I placed the price sheets, attempting to make them more enticing by splaying them out like playing cards, but a glimpse of emerald pulled my attention.

Maria's voice travelled towards me from the rear of the gallery, high-pitched tones singing as she greeted familiar patrons who had proven to be enjoyable company and excellent customers. Her voice can still make me see color.

The green tones aren't as vivid as the first time I met her, eager in her Getty Marrow curatorial internship role. Her mentor had convinced me to participate in their fall exhibition. Maria was my coordinating contact, responsible for visuals and event marketing. The way she spoke rang with appreciation—for me, for her internship, for life—and her voice exploded my vision with swirls of green, draping her shoulders.

Maria's greens were wonderfully stunning the first night we opened the gallery, jade brushes of color flowed from her as she welcomed customers and beamed with pride.

They were deeply intense later that night when we made love on the front desk. We pushed aside sales slips and business cards so they wouldn't get damaged as I buried my face between her legs and she held the desk's edge for leverage to push against my searching tongue.

We've spent years together here in Gallery Rojo, what some call LA's premier gallery for showcasing work from groups under-represented in visual arts. I just call it ours. I feel more myself here with Maria than anywhere else, even though her colors don't capture my attention as often as they used to. Yet, when they do, it's always the same beautiful emerald, my crowning jewel.

What started as a crazy love affair and eventual creative business prospect now feels more like a familiar, languid dance. She promises to charm the customers and run the business if I promise to solicit the artists and keep us afloat financially, which usually involves selling my own art.

We're not traditional, but it works for us—especially when it comes to keeping the business alive. She's much better with people than I am. There's something about being shoved into the spotlight early and often that makes you want to stay out of view more than ever.

I was young when my parents realized I wasn't like all the other kids. Like any typical three-year-old, I could repeat back to you any animal sound; a cow says moo, a dog goes bark. When it came to writing them down, things weren't so clear. Instead of writing the letters m-o-o, I drew shredded brown lines sliced in half with a fling of yellow. No matter how many times they asked, I used color to represent the cow's sound. They thought I was being defiant, considering me more inclined to draw than to practice my letters. The repeated misunderstanding made me cry.

My parents never admitted that they took me to be evaluated because they thought I was impaired. Doctors preferred the word gifted. It wasn't until I was ten that I was able to articulate chrom-esthesia—the technical term for seeing sounds.

By then I had been interviewed, studied, questioned, and judged for years. I came to learn that I am different. I hear sounds just as everyone else does. It just so happens that when I hear certain sounds, I simultaneously and naturally experience a color. The colors remain constant with their specific sounds. To this day, I see shredded brown lines flung with yellow whenever I hear a cow.

"That's interesting," people often respond. What they really mean is, that's odd. Being different makes you stand out when you don't want to.

Maybe it's cliché that I became an artist, but I consider it more of a convenience. Isn't that what everyone does to get by in this world, make the best with what they've got?

So, in my typical way, I was trying to stay away from the crowds that evening. In her typical way, Maria wasn't having it.

"Suck it up, buttercup," she said. "It's time to show off those beautiful tits."

She really knows how to handle me.

An hour into the event, I knew it was going to be a profitable night. Adam Hernandez was aglow, sharing with anyone willing to listen what inspired his art. More price lists were clutched in hands than there were abandoned alongside empty plates and wine glasses. The crowd was at ease and, finally, so was I.

I was tweaking the angle of a light to better highlight one of the paintings when a honey-yellow laugh rose from across the room. Golden spots were suspended around a man I had never seen before. Yellow faded away with his booming laugh, but warmth remained.

It had been a long time since a man had made me see color.

Drawn to the blush, I joined his company.

"It's good to see you again, Paul," I said to the familiar man to

my right. Paul was a supporting member of our local art community, more mouth than money, but he had always been good to
Maria and me. "I wasn't sure tonight's artist would interest you,
considering your penchant for monochrome."

"Ah, hello Sofia," said Paul. "You're right. This work is a little
too colorful for my taste, but Ramiro insisted I come along."

Paul gestured to the man with the honey-yellow laugh, and the
stark difference between the two was notable in age and in style.

Paul's fluffed white beard and glasses, most accurately
described as spectacles, spoke of age and experience. Ramiro's
V-neck, black T-shirt and tattooed tribal work that crept up his
neck suggested youth and exploration.

"Ramiro, this is Sofia Vicario, artist and curator of this lovely
gallery," said Paul, as he placed his hand along my shoulder.

"How do you two know each other?" I asked, my gaze pointed
at Ramiro as though an answer from Paul would be unacceptable.
I needed to hear Ramiro again; I was seeking the light.

Unfortunately, honey didn't drip from his words like I had
hoped. I don't see all sounds, just the ones that sync with my brain
in some unexpected way. It's something I've always considered a
blessing within this curse.

"I'm a grad student at Otis, and Paul and I met at a show at the
college last fall," Ramiro explained. As he smiled, the dark skin
near his eyes crinkled in a manner that made him appear wise for
his age. "Paul told me about your gallery and when I heard Adam
Hernandez's work was being featured, I had to come. I'm undone
by the colors in his art," he said.

I smiled, pleased by his fondness for color, but disappointed in
the lack of it coming from him.

"Maybe tonight you'll find something to take home with you,"
I said. "Adam is right over there if you haven't met him yet. Excuse
me," and I stepped away from the pair.

Maria handed me her glass of white wine, and poured another as I leaned next to her against the desk.

"He's cute," she said as she took a sip and side-eyed me.

"Who, Paul?" I said, trying to sound serious despite my teasing.

Maria rolled her eyes as she downed the wine. "He's cute, but he's young," I replied.

"You had me young."

"You were special," I said. "You had an eye, and a mind, and you put up with my bullshit."

"I still do."

I clinked my glass with her empty one. "Cheers to that!"

I was nearly finished with my wine when she said, "Do you mind mingling a little more and helping to sell some art? I think Joan has her eyes set on the *Goddess of War*."

"The one of the female warrior with her boob out?" I asked, squinting to view that canvas from across the room.

"She said looking at it gives her confidence," Maria explained, shrugging her shoulders with an expression of nonchalance.

A familiar voice came from behind us. "It reminds me of my mother," shared Ramiro.

Maria and I turned in surprise. Ramiro was shaking with his hearty, honeyed laugh before we could fully catch the humor in his comment.

It didn't really matter whether or not his comment was worth laughing at. This man could make me see color, even if it's just with his laugh, and I wondered what more he could do for me.

I took the empty glass from Maria's hand and whispered in her ear before kissing her cheek, "Looks like Joan is all yours."

Ramiro took Maria's spot, leaning next to me against the desk. He filled my glass with wine.

"I Googled you," he said as he handed it back to me.

"Oh, yeah?" I responded, taking an intentional swig. "Did you read the good stuff or the bad stuff?"

"I read that you're known as an innovator in color work and that you were nominated for the Bucksbaum Award a few years ago," he said.

"Nominee, not awardee," I responded and finished my drink.

"You're too modest," he said, and removed the empty glass from my hand using both of his, as fingertips grazed my skin. Suddenly, he made me tingle.

"I'm drawn to color," he said. "Are you selling any originals?"

"Uh, I don't know," I said. I rolled my head back and forth, to try to ease the tension I suddenly felt, as though pulled in separate directions. "This is Adam's show tonight and I need to support him over my work. Wouldn't feel right," I said.

Besides, Maria would kill me if I sold something to a patron over the night's featured artist, I thought. It's bad business to compete against your own gallery.

"Yes, this is Adam's show," he said. "And I've enjoyed it so much that I already purchased a piece from him."

He showed me the sales slip as proof. I recognized Maria's signature at the bottom, so I knew it was authentic. Suddenly, I didn't feel so bad.

"I got what I came here for," he continued, indicating the sales slip. "Now I need a piece of you."

The certainty in his voice triggered the tingle again and his words settled between my legs.

"Do you have anything here in the gallery?" he asked.

I looked at him from the side, squinting a little to size him up, his confidence swaying me to assent.

"Okay," I said sighing. "I have a few pieces in the back room." I stood up and headed toward the rear of the gallery, and he followed.

A click echoed through the room, bouncing off walls toward the high ceilings as I flicked on the light switch. Color came to life as the light found the deeply tinted canvases that lined the walls. I had about twelve in the room, some classic works, many newer pieces.

Ramiro passed by me and walked deep into the room, his head on a swivel as he took in the sights, from wall to wall.

"Wow," he said. "You do like color."

I closed the door behind us as to not disturb the gallery showing. I followed closely behind him, saying nothing as he toured.

"I love the red in this one," he said, pointing to the left and toward the middle of the wall.

He stopped in front of one further on that spread about five feet wide. "What's this one?"

"Tell me what you see," I said.

I wasn't playing coy. It's always interesting to hear an interpretation from someone who is neurotypical. I can only see the sound that triggered the colors.

"I see a spread of yellow plowing its way through a purple landscape. Like a phoenix ignited in flame, blasting through a purple-pink sky, pushing aside stacks of white clouds." Ramiro spoke using his hands, with broad fingers spread wide, pushing imaginary paints this way and that.

He looked over his shoulder toward me, as though seeking confirmation of his description.

"What do you see?" he asked, emboldened by my silence.

"I see the sound of a train, its whistle screaming as it passes by crossing gates," I said. "The first time I saw it was when I was sixteen. I'd only been driving for a few weeks when my first train stopped me. I didn't know it was customary to blow the whistle when passing crossing gates, so it scared me a little, but it was quite a sight to see."

He nodded his head in response, acknowledging my memory with a bit of understanding.

He moved further down the line and stopped at a smaller canvas on the other side of the room. I braced myself.

"What's this one?" he asked, a question that seemed fated to be posed.

I held a pregnant pause before answering. "That one I did about fifteen years ago," I said. "It's titled 'Surprise.'"

"It looks kind of dark, with that black canvas and burst of white, green, and red," he said.

"Well," I said as I rubbed the back of my neck with my hand. "It's my first sexual encounter with a man. More specifically, it's the sound he made when he came in my mouth."

Ramiro spun around and looked at me, his mouth dropping open. Then he laughed. He laughed so hard that it doubled him over, his hands finding his knees to keep balance.

I watched as the honey-colors swirled around him, his laugh getting bigger and filling the space between us. I wanted to bury my face deep in it. Let it intoxicate me.

I walked closer, to settle into his colors. His laughter calmed with my approach, golden swirls fading away.

He looked again at the canvas. "It's awfully small, isn't it?" he asked, a question facetious and truthful. I smiled.

He turned his attention away from the canvas and back to me. He ran his fingers up my arm as he spoke, "I could do better." I believed him.

I leaned in as his hand found my shoulder and pulled my body against his chest. One hand sailed against my neck, finding my chin and tilting my head up for a kiss that started slow, but quickly grew more passionate.

His other hand trailed down my back and gripped my ass, his fingers tickling their way downward and pressing between my legs from behind. I held on to his hips, like the wheel of a ship holding steady in a swirling sea.

Eager to dive in, I pushed up the hem of his black T-shirt, signaling him to take it off. He worked it over his shoulders, and I stared at the calligraphy, Virgin of Guadalupe and other embellishments that stained his skin. I placed a finger over the Virgin's eyes as to signal her not to watch, then drew a line down his stomach, into his waistband, and made quick work of his button and zipper.

He pulled away to rid himself of his pants and returned to me on his knees. He hooked fingers into my black pants and shimmied them down my legs, biting and kissing a path along my thighs. I kicked the pants from my heels, along with my shoes. Then, by gripping the plunging neckline, I yanked my shirt over my head.

He rose, grabbed one full breast, and used his chin to push away the bra's fabric cup, so his tongue could have space to swipe and swirl my nipple. Tingles from my nipple bolted down between my legs, where the palm of his hand was pressing against my crotch. He peeled my panties aside to dip two fingers deep inside me, and trailed slick juices across my clit. My eager hips pressed forward as he painted me.

He pulled his hand from my breast to rub his obvious swelling, and I took the opportunity to remove my bra completely. I watched as his swelling sprang forward, now shed of the underwear that had held it at bay. He grabbed my wrist and placed my hand on him, wrapping my fingers around his stiff shaft. It felt unfamiliar in my hand, but he moaned when I strengthened my grip and spots of color filled my vision again.

He grabbed me by the hips and spun me toward a nearby drafting table. He pressed into me from behind. I sprawled my upper body across the angled surface, pressing my breasts against it. With my hips aligned with the table's edge, he used both hands to tilt them upward, causing my back to arch and my nipples to drag spectacularly across the table.

Light dappled with gold pounced forward as his moan colored my world and his stiff cock slid deep and heavy inside me. I gripped the table's edge and he found a steady rhythm. I watched his moans swirl around me, refusing to close my eyes, the visuals amplifying my pleasure.

He continued trusting and I felt his hand move again to my clit. His weighted fingertips pressed against my slippery, plump clit and swirled and swirled and swirled. With a burst of electric release, I came hard, closing my eyes with the intensity of it.

I opened my eyes as I caught my breath and reconnected with the honeyed swirls of his moans. I felt him tighten his grip and he increased his speed. His groans turned to sharp exhalations. Then the sudden, staccato "ohhhh fuuuuck" of his orgasm poured color everywhere, as violets, yellows, and greens flowed and peaked across the wall in front of me. The sights faded slowly, creeping back into cracks in the walls as Ramiro's breathing normalized.

A comfortable silence settled as we redressed, occasionally glancing up at each other. Ramiro extended an arm to lean against the drafting table, reclaiming his territory.

"How was that? Does it measure up to this guy?" he asked pointedly, as he gestured toward the small, darkened canvas.

I laughed. "It was stunning," I said.

His honeyed laugh now paled in comparison. "If that's what you title the next one, at least give me a heads up."

When I saw Maria again, she was locking the door behind the last visitor. She snatched a forgotten blue napkin from one of the nearby cab tables, balled it up, and threw it at me.

"What did you do tonight?" she asked as I ducked.

"I did what you told me to do," I said.

"Oh, yeah? What's that?"

I removed a sales slip from my pocket handwritten with the words "Surprise" and "Sold," balled it up gently, and tossed it to her.

"I sold some art."

THE TWO OF US

Holley Trent

"Damn it. He would show up now, wouldn't he?"

With the appearance of that ancient pickup truck coming up the wooded path, any hope Faith James had of an uneventful day went down the drain.

Letting the sun-bleached kitchen curtain fall closed, she scraped her riot of coily hair into a precarious bun and scanned the room for pants. She'd discarded them somewhere after that run to the mailbox and hadn't seen them since. She may have lived at the edge of internet access, but her satellite connection was powerful enough for her to teach first-year law students online from the comfort of her kitchen.

Or rather, from her kitchen table. The kitchen wasn't hers to claim.

The kitchen belonged to the owner of those thundering footsteps on the porch.

Shoving her feet into her slacks, she braced herself for the heavy-handed knock.

"Car's out there," she shouted through the locked screen door. "Didn't believe I was here?"

He didn't answer, but that was pretty much expected.

Faith could never tell if Dillon Shaw couldn't be bothered with polite communication or if he just didn't waste words on his wife.

Their arrangement was . . . complicated.

Scoffing, she padded toward the door, glancing at the wall-mounted calendar as she went.

"Couldn't even let me have the week, could you?" she muttered under her breath.

That was all that was left on the contract made under duress. He'd needed a wife so he could soothe his dying grandmother's tormented brain before she passed. *Someone* had to take care of her boy.

Faith had barely known the woman, but old Mrs. Shaw had specifically proclaimed her to be "the one."

There'd been no courtship, just a terse email in her work inbox with a contract attached.

Understandably, Faith had been offended. How could anyone expect a person to disrupt their life without bending over backward to convince them?

Dillon hadn't bent over backward. He hadn't bent at all.

Or even picked up a phone for them to hammer out the details. Everything was detached. Impersonal.

But the deal was hard to refuse.

Her only attachments had been to her law office and the university where she was an adjunct professor. Just one year, and she could go back to her old life, one parcel of property richer. What she was doing was strange and ridiculous, and she knew it, but that land meant something. Her grandparents had worked it for years without being able to own it, just as her great-grandparents had.

Standing in the doorway, she folded her arms over her chest and cleared her throat.

It was like an eclipse had come at midday with no warning, but that was just Dillon blocking all the sunlight.

He stood on the steps, tall, broad, and glowering, carrying a cardboard box under his arm.

She inched her gaze up to his face and the unforgiving expression on it.

In nearly a year, she'd never seen the man crack a smile, and she no longer bothered to try to warm him up enough to get one.

She had at first, though. Fifty-one weeks ago, she'd been obsessed with that picture in her brain of that stern mouth softening and those creases at the corners of his amber eyes deepening.

She pictured him as a charming giant—a roguish Viking whose arrival meant she'd have her breath fucked out of her and not her annoyance spiking toward Valhalla.

Something in his broad chest rumbled, like mallets falling on timpani heads. She supposed he must have cleared his throat.

"Brought this." His voice was scratchy from disuse, but had a beautiful, sonorous deepness that made her clit ache.

Ugh.

She couldn't help what her body liked, even if the *what* was bad for her.

"I told you before not to let the postman give you my packages," she snapped with frustration. "You showed me before exactly how you felt about bringing them up here."

"Not mail. It's . . . things I thought you might want."

Perplexed, she opened the door.

He let himself in without an invitation and set the box atop her table.

He did that seismic throat-clearing again as she pawed through the contents.

They only served to confuse her even more. A ham and bags of fresh cornmeal. Pounds of pecans. Perfectly unblemished pears. They were things from the farm on the other side of the woods.

There were sweets in that odd assortment, too. The sugared peach bud candies seemed a curious choice.

"I don't understand. What is all this?"

He shoved his hand into his pockets, the same way he always did when he had nothing to say.

But this time he drew one right back out.

He turned his palm over and dropped the contents of it into her hand.

"It's just . . . me and you out there," he said, and apparently, that was supposed to explain why he'd given her a strip of condoms.

The red hue of pride unfurled its banner up his neck. With his gaze locked on the open vee of her shirt, he shifted his weight, and the floorboards creaked.

"I figured you'd like that stuff."

Suddenly, it dawned on her that that box of produce and that trio of latex sheathes were the giant's idea of an icebreaker.

Breaking the ice after a year of marriage? And like this?

She let out a strained laugh.

"I . . . *really* don't understand," she said.

Nothing made sense. But again, nothing really had in a year.

He'd combed his hair. He usually had a disheveled look about him with all that dark hair falling into his eyes and onto his neck, but he'd gotten all the gnarls out.

And as he moved, the scent of bergamot laced the air.

He didn't usually smell like that.

"It's just the two of us living out here, Miss James. No one else for a mile."

"*Ms.* James."

"Ms."

The way he softened his voice as he made that small concession stirred something unwelcome in her—something low and deep.

Ugh.

"So, to be perfectly clear," she said, pressing her thighs together tightly to dull the defiant ache forming at their juncture, "you're standing in this kitchen suggesting that since we're both available, we should fuck?"

"Doesn't sound so pretty when you say it like that."

"Then tell me how I should say it, Mr. Shaw. That email you sent me last year sure wasn't pretty, either. How did you expect me to react?"

Wishing to punish him in small ways and large, Faith leaned her ass against the edge of the kitchen table. As she pressed her arms over her chest, she knew exactly the effect the pose had on her body. In her scramble to make herself presentable, she'd neglected that high-up button on her shirt. The see-through lace of her demibra presented a rich brown tease of her exquisite breasts and hints of swollen nipple.

She watched the prominent bulge of his Adam's apple convulse.

He shifted his weight again and attempted to discreetly fold his hands over the tented triangle at his crotch.

There was no way to conceal what he was packing, and the fact that it took so little to boil his blood thrilled and emboldened her.

"You mean to tell me . . ." she said with dare in her voice. She was consuming his discomfort like the richest mousse. "That in all your long trips into town, you didn't find some woman to put on her back for five minutes? Tall, strapping bachelor like you?"

"I'm a married man, Ms. James."

"Only on paper."

"Paper's enough to keep me decent."

"Huh," she uttered, stunned.

He'd hardly spoken to her for a year except in grunts and sighs, but he was apparently a *faithful* caveman. They'd been chaste together.

It seemed fitting that they'd both suffered. Their signatures were side by side on that contract.

She dragged a corner of a condom packet across the heated flesh beneath her collarbones and let out a teasing sigh.

His cheeks mottled with red, and his rugged jaw tensed.

"You had to know I'd be skeptical, Mr. Shaw. We're one week before the end of the agreement. I don't have to be a lawyer to know you're trying to annoy me away."

His dark brows snapped together. "A week from . . . You're talking about this place?"

"Don't act like you didn't know. Calendar's right there." She shifted away from the table to show him the date.

He followed close on her heels.

With every step she took, she could feel the focused intensity of him at her back, and she was walking slowly as though he were nothing more than an animal prone to pouncing.

He studied the calendar, dragging one blunt fingertip across the glossy paper as he counted forward and backward.

Big fingers. Long.

Her pulse quickened and breath caught at the mere thought of those thick digits teasing along her crease and invading her wet places. She bit down hard into her lower lip.

He'd probably launch her into space just by putting a fingertip into her.

Ugh. Stop it!

Too late. He must have noticed where her attention was. He let his hand fall slowly as he turned to her, only to raise it again. He held it in front of her face, spreading his fingers wide, revealing their marvelous span.

"I didn't keep track of that," he said, slowly letting his fingers inch toward her parted lips. "I don't care. You can have whatever you want."

"That's preposterous."

The pad of his index finger was barely an inch from her mouth. It may have been her imagination, but she would have sworn she could feel his heartbeat through it. Or maybe that was her own elevated pulse she was feeling.

"You came here . . . that summer years ago to stay with your grandparents," he said. "You were in a yellow sundress. Made your skin glow."

That finger finally landed against her lip, so softly that she couldn't tell she wasn't in a dream. But his apprehensive caress of the width of it left little doubt that she was awake, and this strange thing was happening.

"Prettiest thing I've ever seen. You make me so nervous, I—"

Reflexively, she grabbed his hand when he tried to steal it away from her.

She'd decided it was hers and she was entitled to it just as much as she was that house and the five acres it stood on.

"I make you nervous, Mr. Shaw?"

"What would you want with a man like me? Why would you want to be married to me if not to get this place?"

"How should I know? You've never given me a chance to find out."

She knew one thing she wouldn't mind having from him, though, and it didn't come in a cardboard box or on five acres of hard clay.

She hooked her fingers into the waistband of his faded jeans and tugged him closer.

He had to be nearly twice her weight, so he moved only because he wanted to and not due to her will.

THE TWO OF US

"If you're standing here telling me this isn't some sick fucking joke—"

"If I wanted you gone, you'd be gone, Ms. James," he said in a husky rasp as she pushed his jeans button free of its hole.

She wanted the heft of his cock on her palm, and on her tongue, perhaps. So much depended on what he said next.

"This seems very convenient, Mr. Shaw."

"*Dillon*. You've got your hand in my pants. If you're gonna play with my dick, you should call me Dillon."

And he could call her Faith, *his* Faith, as he thrust into her from behind and planted kiss-swollen lips against her jaw, her neck, her sensitive shoulders.

As her fingers encircled his dick, she reflexively spread her legs farther apart as if to greet it.

"Nothing convenient about this," he said, rocking his cock onto her palm and growling as she stroked the honeyed end of it. "Convenient would have been doing this a year ago. Do you know how many times I've stroked myself raw after catching a glimpse of you? Gone into the barn and dropped my pants to my ankles 'cause I just couldn't take the pain you put on me? How many times I couldn't wait it out?"

She could hardly make sense of what he was saying, even as his hips found a broken rhythm—shallow thrusts that painted sticky, iridescent swirls across her lifeline.

She didn't need a palm reader to tell her the future. It said clear as day, *"Fucking him."*

"Well. Let's . . . let's not be precious about it," she said with false calmness. She'd never felt so impatient before. "Let's not pretend anything about this is romantic."

The want of her husband's cock inside her, invading her, and stroking her senseless had suddenly become her highest priority.

His fingers were too large and unwieldy to negotiate her shirt buttons. With a feral grunt of frustration, he gave up and started on his own.

As the plaid cloth separated from the center of his chest, Faith's focus locked onto the dark swirls of hair that covered his torso. Her hands followed, sliding over the silken mats, followed by her lips, which she used to trace the paths her fingertips had made.

He shuddered against her as she latched onto one taut nipple and sucked hard.

He hadn't expected that. She could tell by that noise of half fear and half arousal that rumbled in him. It was a *"we don't do that around here"* sound, and she wondered where else she could put her mouth to make him do it again.

"Keep that on," she whispered as he tried to shrug his shirt down his shoulders. "And take off your pants. I like the way that looks."

In spite of the look of deep curiosity on his face, he didn't question her. He disrobed, leaving the plaid shirt on as she'd asked.

She took her time peeling off her pants, socks, and panties, and examined the virile column he made. Powerfully muscled legs and firm ass. Tight abs that arrowed down to his straining, rude cock.

Spreading his legs, he tucked a palm under his heavy balls and hooked his thumb around his cock.

He looked uncomfortable, but wetness gathered even more at his cock's tip.

She unbuttoned her shirt while holding his hungry gaze.

Her bra fastened in the front. One flick of her finger and her breasts greeted him, nipples hard and aching in that urgent way.

"Now we match."

And she cupped herself, too, to show him exactly how much. Brushing her palm across her overstimulated clit, she threw back her head and moaned.

She'd never felt so bold and wanton before. She had never wanted to undo someone so much before.

But he'd arrived at her front door and asked for it. In her mind, she was simply acting in the spirit of marital cooperation.

She could barely get the condom onto him. There was so much nervous energy thrumming through her. Her fingers didn't want to pinch or grasp.

But she managed, and he started to pump into her hand again.

"*Fuck.* You see what you do to me?" he growled. "I think about sitting you on my face when you do that. Tug on my dick while I stick my tongue inside you and drink you up. I'd keep you on me until I couldn't forget what you taste like."

Oh God, yes.

Resisting the urge to grind her palm against her aching clit, Faith swallowed hard and tried to regain control of her faculties. He hadn't said more than a handful of words to her in a year, and he'd suddenly yanked the rug out from under her.

"Fuck, yes, squeeze me hard just like that, Ms. James. *Harder.* You won't break me, ma'am."

"Oh . . . I hadn't meant to . . ." She cleared her throat once more and put on her impermeable lawyer face. She'd been thinking about him in his barn again, fucking his fist because of her, and she liked it. "Being unbreakable is quite a claim. I suggest you prove it."

He snatched her around the waist and took a few faltering steps toward the doorway. There were two possible ways to go, and maybe he didn't know the floor plan. He chose the left way, though, and dropped her onto all fours onto the sofa.

Instinct had her spreading her knees wider against the cool leather and pressing her cheek against the cushion. She awaited the searing press of too much cock.

It didn't come. She looked back to see why.

He seemed to be straining with indecision.

"I can touch you?" he asked.

"Yes, of course you can touch me! I'll tell you if I change my mind. Fuck, don't keep me waiting, Dillon."

He hadn't assumed anything, and given their past, he couldn't. He needed a firm yes.

Grunting with satisfaction, he spread her pussy with his thumbs.

She couldn't make out the words he mumbled against her flesh, but soon, the broad swath of his tongue met her.

He licked her in rough circles at first, and that picture he'd painted of her riding his tongue embossed in her mind. He used the tip to probe her tingling clit. He dipped it into the entrance of her sex and flicked and swirled.

"Dillon!" she shouted as he stuffed a finger into her, then another.

Three or four, maybe, she couldn't be sure.

She was on fire and ready to consume him whole, whether he got his cock into her or not.

"I'm wet. Fuck me."

She was wetter than she'd ever been, anyway, and she wanted the friction and the delicious pain that unlocked pleasure.

Pulling her ass up to meet his press, he notched his cock head into her opening, and she bellowed with frustration.

"All of it, Dillon. The whole thing! Don't you want to?"

"I want to do it right. That way I get to do it again." He gave her an inch more and tucked his fingertips deeper into her haunches. "Fuck, you feel so good." Another inch. That one came with a little figure-eight swirl that opened her up even more for him.

It made her eyes cross and legs turn into jelly. "Oh, God, Dillon. Yes! More. *Please.*"

"I dream of it." Another torturous inch. Another hitch bringing her ass up to meet him. "Going home every day. Letting you do what you want to me. Just like this."

Letting her do what she wanted didn't seem to be what they were doing. Faith had thought she was the one in control, but he was the one withholding the pleasure. He was the one with the vise-like grip, holding her body exactly where he needed it to be. He was giving her one drop of pleasure at a time, and she was whimpering.

"Would you like that?" The end of him ignited electric sparks in her midsection as it pressed against her G-spot. "You like knowing that's why I can't talk to you? It's like trying to talk to a fucking fantasy."

His fantasy, apparently, just like he'd been briefly hers a year ago.

Her toes curled violently, and her jaw dropped open. She was trying to take air into her throat, but he'd pushed that button and turned off the supply.

She slapped the sofa with her palm, begging for mercy.

"Tell me you want it, Ms. James. You can have every bit of it."

And he gave her every bit of him—or at least as much as he could fit into her. He plunged into her with force, and suddenly she could breathe.

Suddenly, she could hold on the sofa fabric and hook her legs around his powerful thighs.

"You want it, Ms. James?"

His rhythm was building speed. She found one, too, and squeezed him in her pussy. She tried to hold him deep inside of her every time his dick invaded, but he won every battle.

"Do you *see* what you do to me?" His voice was laced with frustration, and she was a lawyer. She knew that sound.

It was the voice of a man who didn't think she believed him.

"I . . . I *believe* you," she panted. "I believe you, Dillon."

He expelled a growl of satisfaction and finally let her down onto her belly. He got an arm beneath her and raised her up just enough to make the angle easy.

Then he fucked her hard.

The sound of their skin meeting and slapping drove her wild with hunger. Pressed beneath his weight, she couldn't move much, but she tried to grind her ass against him, anyway. The rough fabric of the sofa against her nipples triggered spasms low down in her.

She squeezed his cock tighter and tighter, ready to combust, but welcoming the rapture.

When he shoved his hand beneath her and pressed his fingers against her clit, her pleasure exploded.

The orgasm ripped through her like lightning surging outward, making her whole body tremor.

With a shout, he shoved himself into her one more time before his crest made him crumble beside her.

There wasn't much room on the sofa.

He was on the very edge of it and breathing raggedly.

She took up most of the space, laying on her belly, trying to remember where her bones were.

She could lay like that all day, blissed-out, euphoric, and so satisfied.

But the transaction, or . . . *whatever* it was, wasn't quite over.

She rolled onto her side, pressing her spine to the sofa back.

He didn't shift over to claim the space she'd made. He just looked at her.

His face burned with the red of exertion. Or perhaps of processing what had transpired and the things that were said in the heat of moments that had gone out of control.

She'd meant what she said.

She believed him. And she could be his Mrs. Shaw for another week.

After that, they could see what happened.

"It's . . . just the two of us way out here, Dillon."

She danced her fingertips across his softly furred chest until his breathing slowed.

"Tell me all about why I'd want to be married to a man like you, and then . . ." She wrapped a hand around his semi-erect dick and milked a hiss out of him. Then she laid a soft kiss on his parted lips and whispered, "And then we'll both get nice, long tastes. How's that sound?"

"That's a deal I'll happily make, Ms. James."

"Faith. Call me Faith."

HOT POCKETS

Angelina M. Lopez

Rosemarie took a final tired look around the baby's room and was about to turn off the light when she noticed smudges on the switch. Chocolate? She rubbed the switch clean with the bottom of her nightshirt, then turned it off. She leaned over to scoop up the kids' dirty sheets and groaned when she straightened. That groan was becoming more common.

She tossed the sheets to the bottom of the stairs and then looked through her bedroom doorway.

The last room to tackle.

The midmorning sunlight warming the room and the halcyon call of the rumpled bed made tackling it the last thing she wanted to do. Right now, their little chaotic house was calm and quiet and almost clean.

Five minutes, Rosemarie told herself as she dropped the bucket of cleaning supplies and collapsed facedown on Jacob's side, her bear-claw-slippered feet on the ground and her blue-satin-undied ass poking out. If she crawled all the way onto the bed, she'd be out. Just like this, halfway on and halfway off, for five minutes, with the sun on her face, her eyelashes still tacky with the mascara she hadn't gotten around to removing after work and Friday night pizza and a Disney movie.

The squished-up sheets gave off the clean-skin scent of her husband, who always smelled like fresh-cut grass, even when he'd been camping in the Blue Ridge Mountains for four days.

She kind of resented how good he always smelled.

She was so grateful Jacob had started taking charge of Saturday morning sports and birthday parties, leaving her to get to the housecleaning. She was grateful their therapist had recommended it. When she was young and envisioned growing old with Jacob, she imagined they would only fight over impossible stuff: the billionaire who wanted to steal Rosemarie away, the movie star who Jacob would ultimately resist.

She never imagined getting into scary hissing matches—hissing because they wanted to scream but didn't want to wake the babies—over the dishes. She never imagined Jacob storming out because of a disagreement over a closet rack. She'd thrown a dried flower arrangement at him when Naomi needed to be picked up in the middle of the night—again—because she didn't want to stay at the sleepover she'd begged to attend.

The cut under Jacob's eye from the distressed wooden flower box had been Rosemarie's last straw. They needed help.

It wasn't that one of them hadn't been doing enough. They were both doing too much: work, kids, house, parents. Jacob's dad moving in had been necessary but awful in the beginning. And there'd been no clear delineation of duties, so they both felt they were half-assing and doubling up and overseeing and being analyzed on everything.

It was embarrassing to be in your early thirties and need a chore chart.

That chore chart had saved them, giving Rosemarie her husband back. But in some ways, it took him further away. Because now, as a hardworking, double-booked mom of three kids, she never got to see the hardworking, double-booked father of her three children.

Much less fuck him.

"Date nights" the therapist said. Rosemarie and Jacob looked at each other and thought about his father's slow slide into dementia and their bank balance and their therapist bills. And they laughed.

"Patience," the therapist then advised. "This is just a period in your lives."

"Find pockets of time."

Well, their pockets had been coming up empty. And they'd promised forever.

Rosemarie curled her husband's sweet-smelling sheets around her face and gave herself two more minutes.

She blinked awake when she heard a groan. She hadn't slept long, but she'd slept hard, and waking up was like swimming through tub water. She heard quick steps and then a thump directly behind her, in the direction of her exposed blue-satin bottom and oversized slippers.

"Jacob?" she mumbled groggily, hoping the kids weren't standing in the room with him, but too cozy to fuss much or even bother to open her eyes all the way.

"Shhhhh," he hushed her, an urgent note in the sound. Then she felt her Snoopy nightshirt sliding up, and lips, warm lips, giving soft, wet touches to the small of her back.

Bursts of heat, like those fast-motion images of flowers opening, bloomed where his lips kissed. "Jacob, what . . ."

He straightened, and her husband—her mild-mannered, assistant coach, moving company manager husband—grabbed two hard handfuls of her satin-covered ass.

"Gotta . . ." His tongue licked at the base of her spine and liquid heat shot down her thighs. "Forgot the juice boxes. Libby's watching Dad and the kids. Just let me . . ." Then his mouth—his lips and his tongue and even his teeth—followed his fingers as they dragged her panties down, abandoning them at the bend of her knees.

Rosemarie wondered if she was still dreaming when he ran his tongue back up between her thighs, anchored both hands at the small of her back, then licked, stroked, swirled, and burrowed his tongue into her.

Her arms were buried beneath her and her head felt heavy with shock and sleep and she was making helpless *uh-uh-uh-uh-uh* sounds into the mattress.

Her husband was making her fuck his face; she'd never felt so bonelessly out of control.

"God, Rosie, your taste. Forgot how creamy you are." There was the soft clink and clang of belt and zipper before his strong, baby-catching hands bit into her hips. "Let me, Rosie, you gotta let me . . ."

She slid her trembling thighs as wide as her panties would let her. "Please," she begged, feeling needy and bountiful at the same time.

Jacob pushed into her slow and hard until he hit deep. He held himself motionless and she heard his heavy breaths.

"It feels so good in here."

Rosemarie couldn't be bothered to move her warm arms from underneath her or even lift her face from its nest in the sheets. But she arched her spine, letting her muscles grab at him. He gasped low.

The mattress shifted as he dug his fists into it. He started to move, pushing his hips into her, and although he'd screwed up his back helping with the neighbor's roof, he still could do that thing, that rolling thing that hit that spot, that spot that made her shriek the first time he'd touched it when she was nineteen and made him look at her with shocked pride. She moaned into the sheets as her body gobbled him up, gripped every inch of him, rippling and flowing around him. His panting breath sounded like it was coming through his teeth. She could smell the clean sweat of his morning in the sun, and it had her straightening her legs around him, pointing the stuffed claws of her slippers into the wood floor and using her thighs and ass to squeeze him harder, love him deeper. She was melting over him.

He moaned helplessly, "Ah . . . don't . . . I don't want to . . . God, you've got me . . . please . . ." His words—pleading words from a man who owned her everything—sent the orgasm rolling over her like a drowning wave. She squeezed him mercilessly and he grabbed her shoulders, shoving hard inside her and yelling. It shocked her, that primal sound in their sweet house, and she jolted and it squeezed him and he groaned and the cock that she'd never had a disagreement with kicked and she gasped and shuddered and he yelped and she laughed then he laughed and then . . . oh God, they were going to suffocate and die like this.

They'd be found dead cold with his cock in her cunt and crazy grins on their faces. And her in her bear slippers.

She giggled so hard she shook him where he'd slumped on top of her, also laughing. His dick trembled out.

"Get off," she gasped. "I can't breathe."

He slid to the side with an *oof.*

She finally lifted her face from the sheet and the air was cool and smelled of sex and Pine-Sol. She turned to look at him.

He was staring up at the ceiling with a goofy grin and awed-wide eyes. "I'm gonna stop declaring my hatred of Saturday mornings."

She frowned. "Do you hate Saturday morning?"

She thought he liked the T-ball practices and stalking the Target toy aisles with the kids for sales so that the birthday party gifts didn't bankrupt them.

He turned to look at her. His lashes were so thick, they felt like kitten fur when she rubbed her thumbs over them. "No," he said softly. "But remember what Saturday mornings used to be like?"

Long mornings in bed that often blended into early afternoons. Some Saturdays all they'd accomplish was ordering a supreme pan pizza. They hadn't had a TV in their room, but hadn't lacked for entertainment. Their twin bed meant that only one person could lay on their back at a time. They'd slotted together like a peg and board.

"They'll be like that again," she whispered.

"This is just a period in our life," he said.

"We'll find pockets of time."

"This was one hell of a pocket."

She felt almost dizzy with possibility.

"How hard was it to get away?"

The next weekend, Jacob found her in the living room, finishing the vacuuming. He told Libby he'd forgotten the snack crackers this time.

As he was squeezing her nipple through her nightshirt and backing her toward the ottoman, he murmured, "God, I love these little cotton nightgowns."

She pulled her mouth from his earlobe with a wet suck. "You do?"

His big hands smoothed down the plain yellow nightshirt with white buttons, over a waist that wasn't so small anymore and hips that weren't as sleek. "Yeah. Why wouldn't I?"

"Just . . ." He pushed her down on the ottoman and kinda

loomed over her, and her voice went weird and breathy. "I thought you'd like sexy pushup bras or crotchless panties or . . ."

He smiled right into her face. She suddenly felt like a little lamb about to be eaten, like she didn't have fifteen years of bossing him around at her disposal.

"Rosie, I don't need anything fancy."

But then he showed her fancy when he twisted her on the ottoman, flipped her head where her hips used to be like she was an arrow in a spinner game, and buried his head between her legs, getting her panties nice and soaked with teasing before he ripped them down her legs and really went to work.

Rosemarie helplessly thumped at his jeans with her hands before he was nice enough to unzip and get his cock out, put his knees up on the ottoman, and carefully and gentlemanly fuck her throat.

She came with a wail and Jacob had to shower and Rosemarie had to find the fabric cleaner for the ottoman.

Libby was not too happy with him when he showed up. Without crackers.

For the next six days, Rosemarie felt seventeen again.

Her husband flirted with her. He gave her long, lusty looks from under his kitten-soft lashes. She put on lipstick for him and left kiss prints on his side of the mirror and on his lunchbox Tupperware and centered on the crotch of the boxers at the top of his underwear drawer. They sat too close on the couch, and his dad privately warned him that if he knocked up the Thompson girl, there'd be no college for him. Jacob gently reminded him that he'd already knocked her up. Three times.

Each kid individually asked in their own unique way for them to stop acting so weird.

They didn't have sex during the week for the same reasons they normally didn't have sex—too busy and too tired. But whether she was crashing into sleep or tossing and turning with her standard worries, there was a low hum in their bed that grew as every day passed. When her husband gave her an exhausted smile right before he turned off his bedside lamp, she knew he was thinking the same thing she was.

Six more days 'til Saturday.

Five more days 'til Saturday.

Four more days . . .

Three more days . . .

Two . . .

One . . .

But when Saturday came, Rosemarie was taking forever to put the cleaning supplies back under the sink and thinking that, really, she should have changed out of her nightshirt and into real clothes already when she got the text from Jacob.

Rosie.

So sorry.

Libby didn't come to game.

At second birthday party.

We'll be home in an hour.

I love you.

Well, she had an hour.

Rosemarie sat on her kitchen floor in her nightshirt and cried for thirty minutes.

Then, as is the way of things, just when they thought they were geniuses who'd figured out what no one else could: A kid was sick and home the next weekend.

The other two caught it and were home the following week.

A spring thunderstorm soaked the ball fields the week after that.

And then, terrifyingly, Jacob's dad fell. It was only a broken wrist, but Rosemarie and Jacob had to have a serious conversation about whether they were providing the best care and whether they could afford anything else. The doctor reassured them that, yes, they were doing a good job. But, for two weeks, it felt evil to want anything for themselves.

The next weekend, when Rosemarie was helping load the fruit snacks and juice boxes into the minivan in her knit pajama pants, Jacob grabbed her pinkie with his through the driver-side window. "Maybe that just wasn't our pocket," he said, shaking her hand. "We'll keep searching."

She smiled but saw the same suck-it-up sorrow on his face. Because when? When would they have the time to look?

So it was one hell of a surprise the following weekend to hear everyone banging home just twenty minutes after they'd left, and the TV come on, and then to watch her wild-haired husband charge through the bedroom door to grab her and shove her back against it.

He kissed like he'd been slowly suffocating since he'd gotten in the van. He kissed her like it was the only way he could breathe.

"Jacob." She trembled against his mouth, tasting his breath and the familiar steam of his tongue.

He shoved her nightgown up to her shoulders. "Fuck pockets, Rosie," he growled against her nipple before sucking on it and sending her up on her toes. "Let's just rip a hole in the material if we have to."

She let out a sob that she hoped was drowned out by PAW Patrol's latest rescue.

She got her hands in his jeans just as he buried his hand in her panties and they could jack each other off as well as they could do themselves—they'd never lost those terrified, furtive arts they learned before they visited Planned Parenthood—but she wanted so much more than that. She was all but crawling up him and pushing down his pants with her bare feet when the door tried to come open at her back.

"Mommy, can we . . ."

Two fingers inside her, his callused thumb rubbing so good and sweet, Jacob shoved her back to keep the door closed. Her man had love handles and big, strong arms.

He paused as she took a gulping breath. "You need anything, baby?" she called.

"Can we open the doughnuts?"

Their eldest knew the doughnuts were for Sunday, and he had the kind of sweet tooth they were trying to put a kibosh on . . .

"I'll make sure to share with the girls and Papi only gets one."

Their eldest was the wiliest kid and the best big brother around.

"Yeah, baby. Thanks for asking."

Her husband looked her in the eyes, smiling, knowing, as he slowly worked those two fingers in her, swirling, testing, then pulled them out. He slid her a little up the door, put his cock to her pussy, and let her slip slowly down onto it.

She bit her lip and his eyes went heavy at the thick, liquid, tight, full, hot sensation, like they were both feeling the same thing. She arched up high on the ball of her foot while the other thigh gripped his hip. He squatted to push in deep. They weren't going to be able to do it like this for long.

They wouldn't need long.

Jacob was rocking into her, into her, and thank God for old houses and not being able to find a plumb line anywhere because the door stuck in the jam just enough to keep it from thumping.

Still, Rosemarie made a sound and Jacob groaned "Rosie," before pushing their mouths together as tight as the stuck door, and here, she suddenly realized, here they'd found their pocket.

Here, she could be as loud as she wanted. Here, he could be as filthy as he could dream up. Here, in the rips that they would tear, in five seconds here and five minutes there and twenty minutes when they got really spoiled, they could celebrate with their mouths and minds and the magic of their bodies what they had, and have, and would have for years to come.

She cried as she came, and Jacob kissed away her tears.

They swiped off with washcloths. Rosemarie pulled on the first thing she could find. Then they walked downstairs holding hands and took their family into the summer sun, letting the screen door close on the dirty house and the blinking phones and the birthday presents, and, instead, filled this little tear with only what they wanted to carry.

TULSA

Erin McLellan

We only fuck when we're in Tulsa.

Tonight, I need this. I *need* Tulsa.

The lights go down on the Cains Ballroom stage, and cheers rise up from the audience. The end of a set is usually a huge adrenaline release, but not now. My heart is hammering a country train beat in my chest. I try not to glance at her, but she grabs my hand and lifts it over our heads like we're boxers. This is how we end every show. Normally, I whoop and grin and wave. Normally, I say something to amp the fans up for the headliner, but the grasp of her calloused fingers rolls me. I can't do anything but stare.

We're in Tulsa, and I want her.

I always want her, but in Tulsa, I can admit it.

She gives my fingers an extra squeeze and leads me off stage. Roadies, stage crew, and our band bustle around us. Someone takes my fiddle. Someone else takes her guitar. She chugs a bottle of water. I take a shot of whiskey and grimace.

"Burns?" she asks.

There's sweat on her neck. I long to lick it off. "Yes. Good though."

"Yeah, you are."

We've been in a band for eight years. We've kissed twice. We've had sex seven times. She has never, ever flirted with me.

I drop my plastic cup. She grins.

"You going to the bar?" she asks.

I don't know the name of the bar. It's one of those dives that changes ownership so often that the name is different every time we come to town. It's close to Cains, though, and a cheap Uber ride back to a hotel or the tour bus.

"I suppose. If you are."

Five years ago, I went to that bar after a show and tried to write away my sorrows on a cocktail napkin. She found me, told me my ex-boyfriend was a dickhead, asked if I liked the lyrics I'd written, and offered to look over them in her hotel room.

I showed her a lot more than a cocktail napkin, and that song is our biggest hit.

Ten months later, we stopped in Tulsa for another overnighter. I went to the bar after our set, praying she would show. She did.

It's our little secret. Our little routine.

We don't talk about it.

I want to talk about it. I want to shake everything up.

Her gaze flickers down to my lips. I almost dive in right in front of everyone, but she takes a step back. I lose her in the crowded backstage.

Once my aftershow obligations are done, I head out. Our next show is in Dallas. We're staying the night here to give the bus driver a break. It's a happy accident—one I absolutely suggested to our tour manager when I saw the schedule.

When I make it to the bar, an old man is singing karaoke love songs. I'm the only other customer. I grab a cocktail napkin and scrawl down a few lines out of habit.

After the man finishes his fourth song, she finally walks in. She reaches me in a breath, and my skin flashes hot with need. I'm touch starved and hungry for her.

Without looking at it, she grabs the cocktail napkin and stuffs it in the breast pocket of her flannel shirt. We both changed after the show, but just like on stage, we're polar opposites. I'm in a summery romper. She's in loose flannel and baggy jeans.

She sits down and grips my calf where it's crossed over my other leg. I about fall off the barstool.

"Camilla," she says in my ear. I love how she says my name, like it's the whole chorus of her favorite song. "We have to leave."

"To a hotel?"

A tiny smile ticks up the corner of her mouth. "No. We have to leave for Dallas. I tried to call you."

I fumble out my cell phone to find a cacophony of missed texts and calls from everyone—her, our manager, other bandmates. "What's going on?"

"They're expecting bad storms throughout the state tomorrow. We can't get stuck here or sidelined. The whole tour is driving overnight to Dallas."

"But . . . we're in *Tulsa*." An embarrassing whine tinges my voice.

She slides her hand up my leg. "I know."

"It's been over a year." I'm skirting close to things we never say out loud, never acknowledge.

"I know," she repeats. She cups my cheek for a fleeting second. "Come on. The bus is waiting for us."

Eleven months ago, during a recording session, she stripped down to a tank top, showing off her strong, tattooed arms, and I lost the beat. A week later, she laughed at a joke during an interview, and I lost my head completely. It has been small things, this change in me. The smiles, the eye contact, the scent of her body wash. We're friends. We're bandmates. We're fuck buddies when we're in Tulsa.

Only in Tulsa.

But I've been writing songs about her in my head. I've been playing my body, pretending my fingers are her fingers.

To lose this, our one night together, hurts. She seems fine. Unbothered. She smiles at me from the backseat of an Uber and tells me good night when we make it to our bus.

Everyone is tucked away in their bunks, so I crawl into mine and pull the curtain closed. Within an hour, we're on the road. The sway of the bus usually puts me to sleep. I imagine the empty road ahead of us. The dark. The moonlight on fields of gold. I imagine that cocktail napkin she filched from me at the bar. The taste of her mouth.

It could be a year before we find ourselves in Tulsa again.

Or longer.

My curtain swishes open and before I can gasp, a hard hand presses over my mouth. It's pitch black, but I can tell it's her. Her fingers slide off my lips, and I whisper, "Lucy?"

"Quiet. Come with me."

I slip out of my bunk and follow her to the lounge at the back of bus. This is our music space. We write songs and jam with the band back here. She slides the door closed behind us.

She's still wearing her flannel shirt but with no pants. It reaches the top of her thighs. I'm in sweats and a sports bra. Within a breath, she's in my space, her body pressing mine into the sliding door.

I push her toward the couch, and she goes down willingly. It's dark back here, the glow of passing headlights the only illumination. Her flannel shirt scrunches up around her waist and her legs fall open. I land on my knees between them. She isn't wearing panties.

I don't know the rules yet, the rules of whatever this is, but I need two things: a kiss and her arousal on my lips. I'm tired of waiting. The entirety of our weird fuck buddies routine has hinged on her stepping up, on her making a move.

I go to the bar and wait.

She shows up.

She takes me back to a hotel room.

She puts me where she wants me in bed.

I follow along because I'm starved for her and for this.

But I'm ready to take what I want for once. I'm ready to shock us both. A kiss is scarier by far, so I dip my mouth to her cunt. Her bright, citrusy taste rings through me, and she gasps, the noise an arpeggio of pleasure that I wish she didn't have to stifle.

"Cami," she says. "Camilla. Fuck."

I suck hard on her clit and run a thumb between her folds, reveling in the heat there. She squirms against my lips.

I lift my head. "What do you need?"

"This."

I roll the hard nub of her clit with my tongue. "And?" We've only been together seven times, but I know what she likes. It's branded in my memory.

A laugh rolls through her. "You know what."

I unbutton her shirt, revealing her small breasts to my eyes and my hands.

For long minutes, I strum her nipples with my thumbs and drive her crazy with my mouth. She clamps her thighs around my shoulders and arches her back. She's close. I can feel it, but she yanks my head away from the hot place between her legs before tipping over the edge.

"What?" I ask, panting. My chin is wet.

"I brought you something . . . us something."

"What is it?"

She reaches under the cushion behind her head and pulls out a black bundle. With a flick of her wrist, she unrolls the bundle and uncovers a cadre of sex toys—everything from plugs and vibrators to dildos and nipple clamps—slotted into little pockets.

A jolt reverberates through my stomach. We've never used toys together. Toys indicate at least a minor degree of pre-planning, and I've always pretended that sex in Tulsa was just something that happened, even though we obviously premeditate it. *An oopsie-daisy, sorry I fell face first into your tits, my bad, let's never talk about this, thank you.*

"What's off limits?" I ask.

A timbre of vulnerability passes through her eyes. We're vulnerable with each other all the time. When we write together. When we're on our tenth show in as many days and can hardly think straight. When one of us flubs a note or an interview. The one time we're usually not vulnerable with each other is in bed, so it amazes me that she's letting me see it now.

"Nothing. For you, nothing," she whispers.

"Close your eyes, then."

I pull out the nipple clamps. They're black with a delicate gold chain. I also grab a butt plug. When I grip its base, my thumb nudges a button and the toy jumps to life.

She smiles, eyes still closed. "There's lube in there too."

I press a laugh into her leg and run my fingers over the toy. It's not vibrating exactly but has tiny rotating beads at the neck under the silicone.

I start with the nipple clamps. She makes a low noise when I snap the first one into place. Her eyes fly open.

"Okay?" I ask.

She nods, so I clip the other one on. Her chest heaves as she adjusts to the pain.

"You good?"

"Yes."

"Close your eyes and keep them shut this time."

Her eyelids flutter on a sigh, and she threads her strong fingers into my hair as I kiss down her stomach.

"I like this version of you," she whispers. "Very take charge. It's nice."

I spread her pussy open with my thumbs. So fucking pretty. "I'm done holding back, Lucy."

She's soaked, her arousal slicking the insides of her thighs. I lube up the plug, press the button to turn it on, and tease the rim of her ass with it.

"Do you want this?"

She's shaking now, her body reacting in a way I've never seen, her muscles strung tight like a bow.

"Please, Camilla."

I work the plug into her slowly, incrementally, loosening her up bit by bit. Once it's seated, she groans.

"Shhh, baby."

A beat of silence, then another. I've never called her baby before. It sits heavy between us, full of possibility.

Finally, she says, "It feels like being rimmed."

I take her in. The sweat beading along her breasts. The clamps on her nipples. The tattoos on her heaving ribs. Her glistening pussy and the base of a plug peeking out between her cheeks. She's frankly the hottest person I've ever seen.

"Do you wanna come?" I ask, knowing she's dying for my mouth. I want her to fly. I want her to love this so much that she keeps coming back for it. I want her to need this so badly that she can't wait until the next time we're in Tulsa.

"You fucking know I do."

I fall back into her. Face first. I lick her until her legs are trembling at my ears. Her hips lift off the couch toward my mouth, so

I pin her with one arm across her stomach. My fingers snag in the chain of the nipple clamps and inadvertently pull on it.

She starts to come. I press the fingers of my free hand into her cunt. She muffles a cry with her own forearm and convulses against my mouth. As the tremors slow, she yanks the chain between the clamps until they pop off. Her inner walls pulse hard around my fingers.

"Ow, fuck." Her hands fly to her tits, cupping them. "God, I love that. Thank you."

I nudge one of her hands out of the way and cover her breast with my palm. It's warm and perfect.

"Want me to take out the plug?" I ask. She nods.

It feels more intimate to take care of her than to eat her out. She normally doesn't let me take care of her. The first time we had sex, all those years ago, she finger-banged me until I couldn't think or walk. Then she left before I managed to roll out of bed. At the time, I was worried we were fucking up our careers, our band. We ignored it. The next time, I left before she woke up.

This time, I can't leave and she can't leave and I don't want to. I hope she doesn't either.

She flips me onto my back without another word.

I'm about to explode. I could sneak a hand to my pussy and come in a second flat. I'm a hair trigger when it comes to her.

She tears my sweats and underwear down in one go, and I pull my sports bra over my head.

"Did anything in my bag of tricks catch your eye?" she asks. "Everything is clean and sterilized."

"God, I don't know, but please hurry."

"I've got what you need."

She tugs a thick vibrating dildo out of the fabric bag. It has a cute little arm that flares off the middle. I assume that nub is for my clit.

She straddles my ribs and lifts the dildo to my mouth. "Suck it."

The toy slips over my bottom lip and onto my tongue, the flared head skimming the roof of my mouth. I moan. Her eyes flame, barely visible in the dark. This is out of our comfort zone, but in a good way. An exciting way.

She rearranges herself beside me and pulls the dildo out of my mouth. Her gaze never leaves my face. Her body melts into me, and her lips come closer and closer.

"Kiss me," I whisper. She does.

It's hot and slow and *everything*. Right as I lose my breath, she pushes the dildo into me and turns it on. A hot, sticky wave of desire washes through me as vibration hits my clit and G-spot. I kiss her harder as she moves the toy in miniscule thrusts.

Tension grows in me, an ache blooming from the base of my spine and rising in intensity, but I'm lost in her lips and the slow roll of her tongue against mine. My body clenches around the toy. She pulls back to watch me.

"Camilla." Her voice is rough and ragged.

I raise my hand to her cheek and hold on. My eyes can't stay open. I'm too close. She snags my thumb with her teeth and sucks it into her mouth.

Pleasure crescendos in me, and I come apart completely. My body's an amp turned up to eleven, blowing out the speakers. She doesn't try to soften my cry. She lets me belt.

When she kisses me again, it's like the verse of a song. The lifeblood that links the high points. The lyrics that tell the actual story. I wrap my arms around her and kiss her until my lips hurt.

Soul-deep contentment settles in me as we cuddle. It will end soon. We'll go back to our bunks and pretend this never happened. My heart will feel like it's breaking every day she's not mine, and I'll hold out hope for Tulsa.

She opens the curtains on the window beside us. Headlights momentarily illuminate her face as she gazes out at the dark. I let her look, happy to have this time in her arms.

"We just passed the exit for Atoka," she says.

"What's in Atoka?"

Her eyes meet mine. "I don't know. But it's not Tulsa."

"Oh." I prop myself up on an elbow. "We're not in Tulsa."

"No. We're not."

She brushes her fingers through the hair at my temples. I need this to mean so much more than it probably does.

"I'm glad," I say. "I want . . ."

"Yeah, Cami. I want too." She lifts her lips to mine. "With you."

We kiss, and it's gentle and tender and not at all like any of the other times we've kissed. She flops back onto the cushions and pulls my cocktail napkin out of the breast pocket of her flannel. Heat blazes up my cheeks, even though I can barely read the words.

On it, I've written:

We only fuck when we're in Tulsa
Soaked in spotlights and alcohol

In her spiky handwriting underneath my lyrics, she has scribbled:

But not anymore.

GRAVITY

Gwendolyn J. Bean

One day the earth tipped, suddenly a jolt, and everything was different. After that day things were never quite right. I wasn't prepared. None of us were, I guess. Who would be? It was a surprise to all of us. The earth tipped and, at first, gravity intensified and we were flattened to the ground. A slight shift the other way, gravity eased up, and we were floating. It took a few years for the nausea to subside.

When I woke up today, the world had changed. There'd been several days of heaviness before gravity finally gave in and lightened up. Everyone was exhausted from days of being weighed down. You could feel it crawling down the streets, a heaviness of the heart. And then suddenly the world tipped the other way and everything changed. I bound out of bed. On the streets now it feels buoyant, people bouncing down the roads like the earth's a trampoline, somersaulting through the air, calling to each other like old friends. The energy is contagious and my mood lifts for the first time in a while. The pressure, the literal weight on my lungs, is gone and I can breathe again.

When I get to work, Jolene and Mac are running around setting things up. It'll be a total changeover from yesterday, a heavy day. Total game changer. Light days are my favorite. I love the feeling, like I'm in the circus on that swing in the air, swinging between partners, tangled in each other as we fly.

We're not the only gravity-play brothel in town. A bunch of 'em have sprung up over the years since it first happened. Lots of demand. What else d'ya do when you suddenly find yourself on a planet with changing gravity, never knowing whether you'll be bouncing through the streets or dragging yourself like a worm? It's stress relief in a way, a chance to play with it, have fun, and get off on it. A break from all the troubles with gravity outside.

Inside, it's a game, a sexy game. Finding all the new ways to fuck when gravity changes. Wrestling is a big thing on the light days, popular with a lot of the old guys. I think it brings 'em back to all those homoerotic moments they had when they were young adults grappling with their friends. Only this time, it's naked wrestling with a girl and she's a sure thing to fuck you after. You were picturing those little wrestling outfits, I know. But naked wrestling is more our thing.

I walk by the ring on my way in and I see Ivana, the owner, leaping 'round the room with an old client. They look like some sort of cross between sumo wrestlers and grasshoppers. I step in to watch for a few minutes. That's the other thing about wrestling—most people like an audience. I take a seat on the bench along the side just as Ivana slams the man to the mat. He thrusts up and wiggles out from under her, scrambling to his feet and moving into position. He's wearing nothing but a Mexican wrestling mask. This is a Lucha Libre fantasy, which works so well when gravity is light 'cause you can do all the pro moves. Ivana and the man are locked together in an embrace and bouncing around the room, periodically hitting the mats and grappling before flying through the air again. Ivana pounds the guy into the ground, and I hear him moan as she wriggles her naked, sweaty body over him. I watch for a few minutes but then get called for a client.

When I get to my room, I see my toolbox has been filled with all the regular light day implements. I first take out four long silk handkerchiefs that float into the air as I pull them out of the box. I tie the client to the bed, first one arm and then the other. I bounce down to the other end of the bed and tie each leg so he is spread-eagle and naked, hovering slightly over the bed. I slowly, deliberately walk around the bed to give each scarf a tug, making sure they'll hold, as he watches me. I contemplate the toolbox for a moment and decide to start with a feather. Kneeling beside him, I draw the feather over his body, and he shivers. I dance and tease my way along his most sensitive bits, up and down his whole body. With my other hand, I rake my nails over his stomach and down the insides of his thighs, and follow with the feather, stopping to dance over his growing erection.

As it glides over him, soft and barely touching his skin, he arches up to push into the feather, but only succeeds in bending the downy hairs. I swirl slowly down and then up his body again, teasing him. He wants a firmer touch, to feel a body pushed against him, but I don't give in to him. He's a regular and I know exactly how to keep him wanting. I keep running the feather over him ever so lightly until he groans in frustration.

I climb over him, straddling his legs, with my feet hooked under to keep from floating away. I slide my body up ever so lightly over his skin, stopping when his hardness brushes against my pussy. He lifts his hips up to press against me harder, but I pull back just barely out of reach. I lower myself and slide up the length of his erection, just enough so that he can feel my wetness, lightly, teasing without any pressure. I'm feeling particularly feisty today and I'm not ready to give him what he wants. I run my hands up his chest and back down, almost brushing his cock, lingering on the insides of his thighs. I keep doing this, feeling myself get more and more aroused each time I am close to him without touching, each time his cock jumps as my fingers hit a sensitive spot. I run my hands down his legs until I reach the tops of my thighs, then brush a thumb along my labia as he watches, opening myself slightly.

My pussy aches, but instead of going further I untie each of the scarves. We spring into the air, floating and rolling, then returning down to the ground. Clinging to each other as we float and tumble, I can feel every ripple of his muscle against my skin as he wrenches his body this way and that, maneuvering through the air. Now that he's free, he's taken the lead.

"Aerial sex?" he asks. No more waiting. I smile and nod. When we return to the ground, I grab the bed corner to hold myself steady. He reaches down and positions himself just right. I can feel him press against my opening.

"Ready. Go!"

I let go just as he pushes up inside me. I feel him penetrate me as we fly, propelled up by his thrust. The trick with aerial sex is figuring out how to push against air. Takes a while for two people to discover how to work together, but Nikolai and I have been practicing for over a year now and have a pretty good rhythm down. He thrusts into me on our way up, hard, and I counter by pushing back, just enough to hold me against him. We fly like this, up and down, thrusting together, tumbling and fucking at the same time. I'm building, getting closer, each thrust deeper and more insistent. I can feel his adrenaline and I push back just as hard, our bodies crashing together as we fly. He's straining against me now, holding me to him, until suddenly his body tightens and explodes in a powerful orgasm that ripples through me.

The next thrust I don't counter; we somersault on the way

down, attached at the hips, landing sprawled on the bed. I feel dizzy and spent. I'll be honest—this type of fucking is my favorite. It's more about the exhilaration than a sensual experience. It's always fast and hard, and when it works, when the adrenaline is high and he hits just the right spot inside me as I'm flying up through the air, I can have the most intense orgasm.

Nikolai looks over at me, sprawled beside him, out of breath and smiling. "Well, that was fun. Remember when gravity was just regular?"

We only have a few light days, then the world shifts and it's heavy again. Some of the others at work like it heavy, keeps 'em more in control; they say it feels sexier. Jolene will be happy. She never did get accustomed to the lightness, the sense of freedom, of flying on the light days. I prefer the light days, makes my work easier. But this morning is heavy.

Ugh, I need to find my groove or today's gonna be long. Time slows down on heavy days, everything is sluggish and weighted, dragging along. The others think I'm crazy. Maybe they're right, I dunno. Lying here, I feel gravity pull down on my skin, tugging it away from my bones. I roll outta bed and land flat on the floor. Dang it. I strain hard to lift myself to all fours and heave each arm and each leg up off the ground like I'm stuck in glue that's almost set. I make my way to the closet. I wish I could stay home in bed today. I put on whatever is closest and on the floor, so I don't have to reach up, and head out the door to work.

The sidewalks are crowded with people crawling, dragging themselves along, some lying flat on the pavement, resting, worn out from the effort, others crawling over 'em, not wanting to stop, to lose the small amount of momentum they have going. It's a slow, exhausting trek. What we took for granted when gravity was always the same, always moderate . . .

Eventually, I make it to work and haul myself through the automatic door. Inside, folks are busy, and despite being heavy, there's energy. Heavy days can be tough, but folks at the brothel really go all in, creative and such. No trampolines and rope swings today, no need for the scarves. Heavy days are for extra soft pillow beds that you sink into when you lie down, and candles, incense. The whole feel of the place is different. You can't light a candle on a light day or you'll burn the place down, but also it doesn't feel right, not the right mood. Light days are playful and lively. Heavy days are sensual and slow.

This time, Ivana is behind the desk lying down with a sleeping mask over her eyes, moaning quietly. Heavy days make her horny, but also busy and she needs to prepare mentally. Her husband Bear is kneeling at her side, massaging first one arm, then the other. It's hard to see it on these heavy days, but Ivana is the driving force behind this place. Developed it from scratch, created the theme rooms, everything, from her own fantasies. Everything came out of her head, her vision. Mac stands beside them checking the computer inventory.

"Are the weighted blankets set up in my room?" I ask on my way by.

"Sure are, hon," says Ivana, lifting her mask to look me over, then returning to semiconsciousness.

Mac smiles at me, but Bear shoots me a look for interrupting. He doesn't really mean it, he's just protective, so I flash him a cheeky grin as I drag myself at a snail's pace across the lobby to my room. It'll be busy today.

My first customers are a middle-aged couple. I guess them to be mid-forties. She's curvy with a bit of grey hair, dressed in a modest skirt and a tight top that squishes her breasts just nicely. He's thinner, with glasses and a receding hairline, wearing jeans and a button-down shirt. Casual date night attire. But underneath, they both look tired. We get lots of couples on heavy days.

They need to get the spark going on those days when the world's dragging them down and they don't even have energy to crawl up into bed, never mind fool around with their partner.

The couple's nervous, not sure where to begin. I lead them, all of us crawling, into my room. We talk for a minute about what they'd like and then I tell 'em there's a weighted blanket on the bed if they'd like. Couples normally like to start covered up, and weighted blankets are the best for heavy days. Imagine the softest blanket, microfibers or something, luxurious. On days like this, it's pressed into you, but with only the softest pressure. Then when you pull it across them, it teases its way down their bodies with the firmest, smoothest of touches. The couple haul themselves up onto the bed, clearly still uncertain. I tell 'em, "Take a few minutes, get comfortable, lie down if you want and just ring the bell when you're ready to start."

When I'm called in, the two are lying together under the blanket, side by side on the bed, eyes closed. I ask the man to put a blindfold on the woman as I crawl over to my toolbox. I decide to start with the rolling pin. Oftentimes I don't get any further, it's that good. The feeling of the rolling pin on the fluffy bed is kinda like being firmly massaged into a pile of feathers, kinda like stretching and sinking at the same time, but in a good way. Gravity doesn't feel so heavy when you keep sinking. If you've never felt the constant bombardment of extra gravity crushing every fiber of your being that may not make sense to you, how you can get off on a rolling pin, the absolute agony and delight of rolling out all the pressure that builds up inside you. But I tell you, it's my most requested tool.

I start rolling the woman, over the blanket at first, up her calves, up and down, first one then the other, then thighs. When the woman sighs, the man opens his eyes to watch. Sometimes couples feel weird about watching each other, but once they get into it, watching their partner writhe around in ecstasy is a huge part of the thrill, part of coming together. People, when I tell 'em about it, always picture couple sessions as a big group cuddle fuck, but it's really a lotta taking turns that is some of the most erotic stuff, being able to relax and focus on your partner's pleasure. Then with a tug, the blanket glides over them and falls to the floor. They both sigh. I keep rolling, but on her bare skin now. He's watching as I roll higher and higher, and I can see him getting as turned on as she is. I take my time on the thighs. When I feel her lift slightly, pushing her ass up to meet the rolling pin, I roll all the way down to her calves and start over. She deflates, disappointed, as I roll again over her calves and thighs, calves and then thighs. This time, I stay on the thighs, nudging the bottom of her ass cheeks. She spreads her legs ever so slightly and I can see how turned on she is. This time I firmly roll up over the curves of her ass, pushing her down into the bed. I take my time, massaging out the day's tension from each glorious cheek. She pushes her crotch into the bed to get more of a release, more pleasure, but it's too soft to push back in the right places.

The man has a full erection now as he watches. I take his arm, pulling him onto his side, and with my hand on top of his, I rest his palm halfway up the back of her thigh. I push his hand higher, his fingers dragging up her tender skin. I can feel the heat from her pussy as I bring his hand close enough to just barely touch. She spreads her legs further, giving him access. I guide his hand under her, between her legs, fingers pressing and pushing their way up her wet mound until they rest on her clit, his whole hand cupping her. She moans.

I return to the roller, pushing her ass down onto his hand. She grinds herself on his fingers, moaning and bearing down. With gravity being so heavy, she doesn't have to strain much to feel the pressure of his fingers, slight movements bring her closer. I keep going with the rolling pin, pushing her clit down hard against his fingers in a rhythm. She starts to go faster, tensing, pushing and straining against us both, against gravity. Suddenly, her whole body tenses, quivers, and then explodes in a juicy spasm, before relaxing. She collapses onto the pillow of feathers that envelops her and lifts the blindfold to look at her partner. She smiles at him and then up at me, all of her nervousness and tension gone.

I reach over to the man and touch his stomach. His erection lies flattened, weighted down. With a spot of lube on the palm of my hand, I firmly push my way up his erection, slowly nearing the tip. He relaxes back and closes his eyes. I slide my way up again and again. Slowly, the woman reaches over hesitantly and puts her hand on top of mine, increasing the weight as we both push up the length of him. He moans. I wrap her fingers around him now, and she continues pushing her hand up and then pulling her way down.

I stop for more lube and then slide my hand down to the spot below his balls, while the woman continues sliding up and down his erection. I press deep, until I can feel the base of his shaft under the skin and then I massage up and down, a deep tissue hand job to release all the built-up pressure. He's moaning and arching his hips up to meet our hands. Up and down, and again. He reaches out to squeeze the woman's tit, moaning and twisting his body. I can feel him swell.

"I'm gonna come," he says, straining against our hands. His body tenses, and then releases, and his hips buck as he comes. The woman, his partner, leans in to kiss him and rests her head on his chest. They are both smiling, relaxed and together. After some time, the woman says softly, sadly, "Do you remember when gravity was just regular?"

At break time I look to find Mac. I'm super turned on from my session but also more than a little sad, and I need a release. He's not at the front desk, but I find him in one of the rooms, rolling across the broom floor. Doesn't sound fun, I know. None of this does if you have regular gravity. But trust me, on a heavy day, it's the best. The floor's not actually made of brooms—it's just a carpet floor that feels like the ends of one of those soft but stiff, industrial kinda brooms, hence the name. It's not so nice to walk on when gravity is heavy, but if you spread your weight over the bristles, it touches you in all the right ways.

So I find Mac rolling around moaning, all naked on the floor by himself. Sometimes I think Mac doesn't need anybody else.

"Can I join you?" I ask anyway.

He opens his eyes and smiles up at me.

"Sure, come lie with me."

I take off all my clothes and throw them in a heap at the door. Then I crawl over, naked, and lie down beside him, feeling the heat from his body.

"Ready?"

"Ready."

With that, we roll together from one side of the room to the other, moaning and then laughing ridiculously as gravity pushes us into the bristles of the broom floor. On our way back, I slow down and Mac crashes into me, still laughing. After a minute, he lifts his arm over me, struggling to roll onto his side. He examines me for a minute.

"What's wrong?" he asks.

I shrug, but he doesn't let it go.

"Is it the heaviness?"

I look over at him, and just seeing Mac and the way he's looking at me, tears well up. Suddenly I don't want to talk about it.

"My last session . . ." I start. "I don't know, it was fine. But then, at the end, the woman, she just looked so sad, so damn sad. And she says to both of us, or maybe to no one really, she says,

'Remember when gravity was just regular?'"

I look at Mac, but I can see he doesn't get it. He's trying, but he just doesn't feel the weight of the heavy days like I do.

"It's stupid, I know," I say, trying to shrug it off. "Just bugged me, that's all."

"I know," he says sympathetically, as he drags his nails down my tits and over my belly, already sensitive from all the rolling around on the broom floor. He keeps doing this, hard, drawing crisscrossing patterns of red welts all over my body, sending waves of pleasure through me even as tears roll down my cheeks.

When I'm fully raw and on fire, he runs his hand over my skin as lightly as he can with so much gravity. I can't take it; I'm writhing around on the bristly broom floor, every sensation mixed up into one. I'm not sure whether to moan or sob, so it comes out as a strangled mix of both. It's a weird feeling, the heaviness of a light touch, but totally erotic, and it drives me crazy. His fingers trail down my belly to my most sensitive bits. I groan and raise my hips up against his hand, pushing his fingers hard against my clit, pressing against the pressure of his hand.

I pull Mac onto me. His naked skin, weighed down by gravity, seems to soften into me, pliable compared to the bristly floor, molding to the shape of my body. When he pushes his lips against mine, the weight is almost unbearable. We stay pressed together like this, deep into each other, feeling our bodies melt together. Everything is slow when gravity is heavy.

Just as I'm thinking I'm not sure I can go on, Mac begins to move, lightly pressing his erection into my opening. I rise up to meet him and he pushes all the way in. I feel pulled apart by the intensity of the sadness holding me down and the sudden waves of pleasure. He pushes harder now as I rock my hips. As the heat spreads, I know I'm getting closer. Another strangled sob finds its way out, as I cling to him.

I push against Mac more urgently now, grinding myself into him. It doesn't take long before I hear him moan. He's thrusting over and over, driving into me. I keep going, rocking rhythmically against him. I'm so close, the waves stronger. "I'm gonna come . . . I'm gonna . . ." He pushes harder and faster now. I strain against him. And then he hits the exact spot I need to push myself over. My whole body explodes in a heaving, sobbing orgasm. A second later, as I'm still feeling the aftershocks, Mac tenses against me, pressed so tight to me I can feel him swell inside me as he comes. We pull apart and fall back onto the broom floor, sweaty and out of breath. Mac looks over at me.

"Fuck," is all I can say, eyeing him gratefully.

"You look awful," he says, laughing. He pulls me in for a hug and I curl into the warmth of his body, feeling the full weight of gravity.

BITCH

Inga Gardner

Jessica smelled tomatoes the moment she stepped into the house. Also garlic, olive oil, and basil. From the kitchen came the sounds of cooking, and there was soft jazz playing. Jessica stood in the front hallway and blew out a breath, fighting the urge to turn and walk right back out the door.

This is not what I want, she thought as she dropped her bag.

What she wanted was to fill her largest wineglass to the brim with cheap Shiraz and grab the package of Oreos stashed behind the paper towels in the hall closet. She wanted to take it all up to her bedroom and strip off her work clothes, which were both unsexy and uncomfortable (as office appropriate attire for women often seemed to be). She wanted to slide under the covers wearing only her fuzzy bathrobe and watch garbage reality shows while drinking wine and eating Oreos—crumbs be damned—until she was numbed enough to fall asleep.

And she wanted to do it *alone*.

But, of course, homemade red sauce meant that wasn't going to happen.

Motherfucker.

"That you, babe?" Chris called from the kitchen.

Jessica barely contained an irritated groan. But Chris didn't deserve to bear the brunt of her . . . call it a mood. So she cleared her throat, pasted on a neutral smile, and said, "Yeah, it's me." She kicked off her shoes. Then, reminding herself to keep that rictus smile in place, she went into the kitchen.

Chris, her husband of almost eighteen years, was standing with his back to her, checking the contents of a pot from which steam billowed. He was wearing a pair of blue sweatpants and a gray T-shirt, the outfit he often changed into after he got home from work. He'd showered, too, judging by the damp ends of his dark hair. If she were in a better mood, she might've said he looked good, all broad shoulders, long legs, and a high, tight ass.

Alas, she was not in a better mood.

"Where are the kids?" she asked.

Chris replaced the cover on the pot and turned around. There was an open bottle of wine sitting on the counter with two glasses; he smiled at her as he picked up the bottle and one of the glasses. "Sleepovers. All three of them." He winked at her as he began to pour. "Looks like it's just me and you tonight." He handed her the glass.

She knew she should smile, say something flirty back, but all she wanted was to throw her glass against the wall and scream. She opted for taking a healthy swallow of wine instead.

"Dinner's ready," he said after checking the food one more time. "Why don't you have a seat?" He nodded toward the kitchen table.

Jessica pulled out a chair and sat stiffly while he started putting food on plates. She stared at the table in front of her, at the wine-glass.

God, she hated this, the way it seemed like she was always

just a pressure cooker of bad feelings these days. She hated being unable to enjoy good things, like the husband she adored planning a romantic evening. But there was all this guilt—that she wasn't a good enough mother, wife, daughter, employee. There was frustration that she could never seem to get ahead of . . . anything. There was sorrow and exhaustion and sometimes shame.

And always underneath it all, threatening to consume her and everything else, there was this inexplicable, simmering rage.

Jessica raised her glass to her lips and took two more long swallows.

No, actually, the rage wasn't inexplicable at all. Her fury was, she thought, perfectly rational. It came from pretending that she didn't know her direct reports sometimes referred to her as "that bitch." It came from smiling placidly while her boss dumped ever more of his own assignments on her. It came from the way her brother saw nothing wrong with expecting her to take care of their parents as they aged. It came from dealing with customers every day who seemed determined to test the boundaries of "the customer is always right" and Jessica's sanity. It came from the million little wounds and jabs to Jessica's self-esteem and mental health that she was evidently supposed to just endure with a smile and unending good humor.

The irrational thing was that she had to pretend it was so inexplicable, and that pissed her off, too.

She stared down at the pasta Chris slid in front of her. She was forty-one years old. Was this what life was? Just swallowing shit sandwich after shit sandwich and never being able to say how angry you were about it? Never being able to fight back? She spent so much energy pasting stupid, bland smiles on her face because if she let that mad out—even a little—then she was a bitch. Maybe a cunt. And every woman knew that wasn't okay.

Did no one else feel furious about that?

"Parmesan?" Chris said suddenly, thrusting the plastic container of grated cheese in front of her.

And just like that, the seething bitch inside of Jessica slipped her leash and Jessica lost her control.

"No, I fucking don't," she snapped as she backhanded—literally *backhanded*—the container out of Chris's grasp.

Shame washed over her immediately. "I—Chris, I'm sorry. I don't—" she started but then looked up at him and stopped. She'd expected to see him staring at her with shock and horror, but he wasn't. He wasn't watching her at all. Instead, his dark head was bowed slightly, his gaze downcast, his hands clasped loosely in front of him.

"What *would* you like?" he asked. His voice was softer and yet deeper than usual. Something about the odd timbre made her shiver.

She opened her mouth, but nothing came out, so she closed it again. It occurred to her that he wasn't cowering from her, regardless of her uncalled-for violence. In fact, despite the loose grip of his hands and his lowered eyes, there was a tension to the line of his shoulders, and the way he was holding his arms, and perhaps the muscles of his belly and . . . she expelled a breath when her gaze reached the front of his sweatpants and she realized that his dick was half hard.

What the fuck was happening?

Whatever it was, it was . . . thrilling.

She must have stayed silent too long because suddenly he sighed and his body relaxed. His expression turned rueful, and he chuckled softly. "Nevermind," he muttered; she wasn't sure if he was saying it to her or to himself. "Let's just—"

"Wait!" she blurted. And then, entirely on instinct, she said, "Don't fucking move."

He didn't fucking move. In fact, she was pretty sure he was holding his breath.

Heart pounding, she said experimentally, "Get on your knees."

Slowly, slowly he dropped to his knees in front of her. Then he bowed his head and rested his hands to his thighs.

Oh, she thought, and it was suddenly a little hard to breathe.

"Take your shirt off," she snapped.

Faster than anyone in this house had ever done anything the first time she asked, Chris reached back and pulled his T-shirt over his head, tossing it to the side before he lowered his gaze again, looking somewhere at the floor between her feet. The muscles of his shoulders rippled. His chest heaved. Jessica's mouth went dry. She swallowed thickly.

"What are we doing?" she finally whispered.

"Whatever you want . . . *ma'am*," he said, his voice silky and submissive, full of promise. If you'd asked her this morning whether that was something that turned her on, she'd have said no. In fact, she'd have said that she preferred the opposite. And yet, the way he said that word—*ma'am*—made her pussy throb once unexpectedly.

Still, she didn't know this game, didn't know the rules, and that wasn't entirely a comfortable feeling. "So," she said slowly, "you want me to . . . yell at you?"

His cheeks colored above his beard. "I guess I kind of want you to . . . use me?" He looked up at her. "You know, be kinda mean, tell me I have to do whatever you want, tell me I'm not allowed to come. Be a . . ." He trailed off.

"Bitch?" she suggested.

He nodded.

Jessica blew out a breath. Here was her big, handsome husband, kneeling in front of her as though he was about to service her. And he *wanted* her to be mean to him. That . . . that she could definitely do.

One thing was certain: the next time she touched herself, she would be thinking about a man on his knees.

"Okay," she said.

He grinned, surprised and delighted. "Really?"

"Yeah," she said. "We probably need a safe word?"

His gaze slid around the room before coming to rest on her. The corner of his mouth kicked up. "How about *marinara?*"

"Okay." Jessica had about a thousand questions—How long had he been into this? What exactly *was* this? Why hadn't he ever said anything?—but they could all wait. Because the bitch inside of her was restless, pacing, hungry for release.

And tonight, she wasn't going to be denied.

Jessica let her body go loose until she was sitting in a splay-legged, almost masculine pose. A power pose. She tipped her head back and let her lips curl up into a half-sneer, the kind of expression she realized she spent most of her life suppressing. It felt good. It felt *right.*

"Stand up. Take off your pants."

Chris stood a little unsteadily and his hands trembled as he slipped his thumbs under the waistband of his sweatpants and slowly lowered them down. He stepped out of them, and then he was standing in front of her completely naked. He kept his arms at his sides and his eyes downcast, but his breath was shallow. His cock was fully erect, straining toward his navel.

She let the silence stretch.

It was fascinating the way that the tension in his body seemed to grow as the seconds ticked past. Chris was not generally a fidgeter, but as time went by there were subtle movements. His bicep flexed. His fingers twitched. He bit his lip. He shifted his weight.

"Should I—" he started.

"No."

His dick, rising out of its nest of coarse, curly hair, jumped.

The head flushed redder. A giddy kind of joy bubbled up in Jessica, but she hid it.

She rolled her shoulders and then her neck, feeling like she'd dropped a giant weight at some point in the last few minutes. She folded her arms and pressed her lips into a hard line. "Go upstairs and lay on the bed. On your back."

He shivered. "Yes, ma'am."

"And don't fucking touch yourself," she said over her shoulder as he walked by her.

She listened to his footsteps move quickly across the kitchen floor, then the stairs of the old house groaned as he went up. She heard the bedroom door squeak on its hinges followed by the subtle rustle of the sheets being pulled back. The bed creaked and then the sounds stopped.

Jessica took her time getting undressed. She carefully, deliberately undid the buttons of her blouse and thought about making him lick her nipples until she was slick down her thighs. She undid her pants and stripped them off, thinking about grinding her clit against his hairy leg, making him lie there while she ignored him and his dick. She removed her bra and underwear and her sheer knee-high socks, leaving everything on the kitchen chair, before strolling down the hall and up the stairs.

When she got to the bedroom, he was lying motionless on the bed, his head on the pillow. His hands were fisted at his sides. His eyes were closed and his expression under his dark beard was drawn tight, his full lips pressed into a hard line. He was still so sexy after all these years. Other women flirted with him, probably envied her, likely wondered how someone who looked like a middle-aged mom had snagged this tall, fit man. She let her gaze drift down his body. Would they envy her now, with that muscular body laid out on the bed, patiently waiting for her to use it however she wanted?

If they wouldn't, they were idiots.

She pushed off from where she'd been leaning against door-frame, and he opened his eyes. He watched her, his gaze sleepy with arousal, as she strolled across the room. "You are so beautiful," he said, his tone low and dark.

Funny—normally when he said that to her, it made her feel awkward. She never knew whether to believe he meant it, and she never knew how to respond. Tonight, that wasn't a problem. "Stop talking," she said.

His mouth snapped shut.

"So," she said, putting a knee on the bed, "you want to be used?"

His only answer was to suck his lower lip into his mouth.

"All right, then." She moved forward on her knees.

His Adam's apple bobbed as he swallowed hard.

Grabbing the headboard, she planted one knee next to his ear. "*Yes*," he growled as she brought her other leg across him so that her vulva—throbbing and hot and slick—was directly over his face.

"Shut. Up," she said, and then without waiting for any response or permission, she pressed her pussy to his mouth.

Oh fuck yes. She ground down, felt him struggle to catch up. He opened his mouth, his tongue slipping out to split her sex, find her clit, and press hard against it. Of all the possible ways to have sex—and in the decades they'd been together, she and Chris had tried them all—sitting on his face had always been her favorite. Normally, though, she felt like she really ought to wait for an invitation, at least ask permission. Screw that, though—let him use his safe word if he didn't want this. She dropped her head back with a groan and swirled her hips in a tiny circle, the pressure exactly what she needed.

When she did it again, a little harder this time, Chris moaned, and his hands came up to grip her bottom the way he knew she liked. His tongue swirled when she leaned back to grind the opening of her vagina on his hairy chin. His hands urged her on, but she didn't need the encouragement. She was rolling her hips faster and faster as the pressure built. She could hear him growling and groaning each time she ground down on him, his hands squeezing, pulling the cheeks of her ass apart and pressing them back together. She was nearly mindless with pleasure, though, wave after wave of it breaking over her as she closed in on climax. She dropped one hand to Chris's head, and he moaned as she held him in place with a firm grip on his hair.

She was close. She was *so* close. Her hips were moving on their own, tiny little motions that brushed the shaft of her clit against his upper lip, against his teeth, exactly where she needed it. There was no subtly guiding him where she wanted him to go, no hoping that he'd manage to stroke her the way she wanted, no trying to find the right way to say what she needed. She was just *taking* what she wanted, and it was glorious. She rocked harder and he squeezed her hips, and still the climax built and built. Her pussy was clenching, her legs trembling, and she had to hold onto both the headboard and his head for support.

When it finally did crest, Jessica felt as though she might actually explode. Her body curled in on itself, her legs snapping together against his head. He probably couldn't breathe, but she was too busy riding a wave of outrageous pleasure to care. She kept her clit pressed against him, kept him trapped there beneath her, while her pussy clenched on itself and she screamed.

When she finally flopped off him onto the bed, they were both breathing heavily. He lifted one hand to wipe his mouth, and she could see his beard glistening with wetness.

Chris rolled his head to the side, giving her his usual easy smile.

"Fuck, I thought you were going to kill me for a second there," he said with a chuckle.

Jess narrowed her eyes, arranged her features into a sneer again and said, in her tightest, bitchiest tone, "Did I say you could start talking again?"

Chris's breath hitched and he dropped his gaze. It was fascinating that he could manage to look both aroused and chastened at the same time. At some point in the future, she'd have to examine why she liked that so much. "No, ma'am," he said.

"Good." She threw her leg over him so that she was straddling his hips, her sex hovering just above his cock. "Grab the headboard."

His arms immediately flew up, his hands gripping the slats of their bed, making his thick biceps bunch. She imagined handcuffing him to those slats and had to suppress a groan.

She brushed her labia against the underside of his dick where it was lying against his belly and he flinched. The wood of the bed groaned as he gripped it tighter.

She did it again, and then again, enjoying his response each time, the way his biceps and chest flexed, the way his stomach twitched. It was dizzying, being given this kind of freedom to torment a person. She kept her expression a bitchy mask, but inside she was grinning.

Pretty soon, though, the brushing sensation wasn't enough. She needed more. And because this was her game, she got to take it. She ground down on the thick, hard erection beneath her, letting it split her open again. She sat herself firmly on his dick, and then slid forward so the whole length of him rubbed against her clit and her opening.

"Fuck, Jess," he said as she did it again.

She slipped a hand between his belly and his cock, holding it in place as she began to slide forward and back, harder now, coating it in her silky moisture. With every slide, the veins and head of his penis stroked her clitoris. She used her hand to give herself a little more leverage.

"*Christ*," he ground out, his eyes closed, his head thrown back.

"Don't come," she said as she rolled her hips. Another dizzying wave of pleasure crashed over her, while his shaft hit several wonderful places at once.

He shook his head emphatically, groaning as she brought her hips forward and circled them at the head, letting the flared edge rub around the edge of her clit.

She had just enough conscious brain space left, however, to know that regardless of how firmly he shook his head, regardless of how much she could tell he was trying to hold his own orgasm off, he wasn't going to last. From the way his hips were rocking in tiny, unconscious thrusts, and the way his dick was swelling even harder in her hand, she knew he would come if they kept going like this.

Fuck that.

With one last sweep of her pussy up his cock and over the head, she lifted up. "No!" he bellowed as she climbed off him.

She leaned forward so her lips were right next to his ear. "You were going to come," she hissed.

He shook his head. "No, I wasn't. I won't." His knuckles had turned white he was gripping the headboard so hard.

"Don't lie to me. You know you were. Fucking unbelievable," she spat. She had to turn her head away to hide her smile. This was the most fun she'd had in a long time.

"I won't. Jess, I won't. Please," he begged.

She flopped over onto her back and sighed with princessy petulance. "Make it up to me," she said, letting her legs drop wide.

He was on her in a flash, his mouth back to licking and sucking. Without opening her eyes, she reached into the drawer in her nightstand and felt around until she found the smooth length of her vibrator. She tossed it to him. "Use this," she said. "Your mouth, too."

He grunted against her, but he did as he was told. So Jessica lay there as he penetrated her with the buzzing vibrator and continued stroking her with the flat of his tongue. Her body clenched against the silicone toy, the relief of being able to grip something profound. Sweat broke out along her hairline and between her breasts as all of her awareness narrowed down to the tiny muscles and nerves of her sex. She came again, this time soaking herself and Chris and the bed as she did.

When she peeled her eyelids open, she found Chris kneeling between her splayed legs, his breathing still labored, his gaze lowered submissively. He remained silent. *Learned his lesson*, she thought with bizarre and savage satisfaction. And his dick—that was still on high alert, flushed almost purple, bigger and harder than she'd seen it in . . . ever. The sight of it, the knowledge of how much this turned him on, had her post-orgasmic languor evaporating, and she was ready for more.

She rolled over and got onto her hands and knees, her back to him. Shooting him a sharp glance over her shoulder, she said, "Fuck me like this and make me feel good. Then you can come."

He shuffled forward, positioning himself at her entrance.

"What're you waiting for?" she snapped. "I'm tired. Let's get moving."

His eyes flared with humiliation and arousal just before he thrust forward. She was so slick that even with his already size-able cock swelled even larger than usual, he slid right in. He pulled back and then slid forward again. "Fuck," she breathed as the ridge of his cockhead hit all sorts of nerve endings inside of her.

As he labored behind her, grunting and cursing under his

breath, she thought how strange it was that she felt so powerful, so free. This was a position she'd always thought of as submissive, but she felt completely in control. "Harder," she said, and now he was slamming into her so hard that their flesh meeting sounded like a slap. It was raw, animalistic. It was perfect. "Fuck, yes, just like that," she said. Something dripped onto her back and she was pretty sure it was sweat from his brow. Everything inside of her was so swollen and aroused she wasn't sure she was going to be able to come again. It felt so good, though, she wasn't sure she cared.

"I should tie you to a chair," she said. "You could struggle. Try to fight it." It was just stream of consciousness rambling, but it was making her pussy clench hard, and he groaned something that sounded like *yes* behind her. "But I'd just ride you like my own personal fuck toy. Because that's what you are, right? My own personal fuck toy."

"God, yes," he grunted behind her.

"Just for me to use however I fucking want."

"However you want," he echoed, his rhythm starting to become uneven. He was close.

Two more thrusts and, astonishingly, she was there, too, passing the point of no return and barreling toward yet another climax. "Come," she gritted out, the sound broken and barely intelligible. "Come inside me."

He thrust deep and roared her name. His orgasm seemed to go on and on forever, the pulsing of his cock inside her triggering her own spasms. She was soaring, almost out of her mind with pleasure.

She was so light, she could have been a feather.

As she collapsed onto the bed, Chris on top of her, his penis still buried deep inside of her, she felt cleaned out. Her rage, the normal simmering fury, was just . . . gone. She knew all the irritations of life were still there, would be just waiting to piss her off again, but the boiling cauldron of frustration and anger that usually lived in her gut had vanished, like steam after a release valve opens.

Eventually Chris rolled off of her, sighing contentedly. She rolled onto her back, trying to get her heart rate under control. She opened her eyes and their gazes met.

They both burst into hysterical giggles.

"So," she said when they finally got themselves under control, "bitchiness, huh?"

He chuckled.

She cleared her throat. "Is it . . . is it because I've been such an epic bitch lately?"

He blinked a couple of times and then snorted. "No. Were you worried about that?"

A little.

She shrugged.

He slipped an arm around her and pulled her closer to him, a maneuver they'd done approximately a million times in the course of their life together, and it was almost overwhelmingly comforting. "Nah," he said, giving her a small squeeze. "It's just, I don't know. Everybody likes being treated like a piece of meat sometimes, right? To be the instrument of someone else's pleasure? And maybe it's kind of hot if they sort of resent you for how much they want it." He shrugged.

She supposed that made sense.

"Did you . . . did you have fun?"

Her turn to chuckle. "Oh my God, yes."

"Good," he said. "We should probably take a shower."

"And strip this bed." She moved her leg off the frankly impressive wet spot she'd made.

"Dinner is still downstairs," he said.

She hummed. "It smelled great, but I'm not sure I'm up for a full pasta dinner."

"Wine for dinner?" he asked with a grin.

"Sure. I might know where there's a package of Oreos in this house, too."

He cocked an eyebrow at her. "Well, aren't you just full of surprises."

Jessica just smiled.

DRIPPING

Adriana Herrera

"We need to be ready to go by four a.m. tomorrow," my friend
and fellow fashion model bemoaned as we made our way out of
the elevator in our hotel after an extremely long day of shoots.

I sighed, my eyes fixed on the screen of my phone looking
through our very busy schedule once again. "I can't believe they're
able to pack so much into one day." We were on location in Paris
for a job with Maison Dauphiné, the world-class jeweler who for
the last year had contracted me, Julissa Mora the first fat—not
to mention Afro-Dominican—model to ever wear their creations.
It had been the opportunity of a lifetime and an amazing experience, but they made us do two weeks' worth of work over a
weekend whenever we had shoots.

"They make it worth our while though," Sarita said sugges-
tively, bumping my elbow. I looked up and saw *her* waiting for me
by the door of my room. Immediately I felt my body tensing and
melting in all the right places.

I turned to Sarita, giving her a disapproving look as I intentionally slowed my steps, making myself wait a little longer before

getting to her. "Last time I tell you my secrets." I chastised her in hushed tones. "You know this is not for public consumption. At least not until I'm out of contract with Dauphiné."

"Ay, niña. You know I'm just playing with you. You two have been up to no good going on a year, and nobody's heard a word from me. Besides this is our last shoot with them."

I made a noncommittal noise in response, already too caught up on what was waiting for me. But it was true. Sarita hadn't betrayed my secret. She'd known for months that since our first job with Dauphiné, their head of security and I had been . . . getting to know each other. Intimately. And she was right that after this weekend I'd be done, and hopefully, maybe, it would be the beginning of something else.

Freya Lund's job was making sure the jewels that adorned us on every shoot were securely stowed away once we were done modeling them. She didn't usually do that herself, of course; she had staff. But with me she paid special attention. It was a little game we played; I'd scurry away before she got a chance to get them from me on the set, and I'd find her waiting outside my bedroom. Then she'd take them off herself . . . along with every-thing else I was wearing.

Even in my four-inch red-bottoms, she topped me by a few inches. She was tall and imposing, and beautiful. Her powerful body, ramrod straight. Gray eyes tracking my every step. Like ice. Until we were behind closed doors.

I could feel the wetness at the vee of my thighs already. My clit throbbed as I glanced at her mouth, knowing the things those sinful lips could do to me. She was wearing one of her bespoke suits. All black today. From the graphite wingtip suede Oxfords on her feet to the onyx diamond studs on her ears. My mouth watered thinking of sucking on her earlobe while her fingers stroked me.

"Oooh, girl. You got it *bad*," Sarita teased, startling me out of my very not-safe-for-coworkers thoughts. "Get it, ma. I'll see you *before* the crack of dawn. Don't be late."

"See you." I distractedly lifted a hand to Sarita when she stopped in front of her door and kept walking to my own room, which was only a few doors down.

"Miss Lund," I said hoarsely making sure I kept myself a few feet away. Anyone who walked by us would think this was a cordial exchange. Two people obligated to go through the motions. Professional acquaintances.

Freya looked at me, assessing, shoulders propped on the wall by my door. Her wide mouth in a secret smirk that I knew meant she was in a particularly wicked mood. A smirk that promised dark deeds and moans of pleasure as soon as we were alone. My core throbbed and it was all I could do not to slide my hand down and press my palm to where I ached.

"Miss Mora. You ran off on me again," she rebuked, then proceeded to bite her bottom lip as she looked me over like I was the most tempting morsel she'd ever seen.

She took in the blood-red satin dress I was wearing. It was a long, decadent affair that clung to every one of my curves. The skirt was tight, with a tail that dragged two feet behind me. But the top slouched off the shoulder, plunging down to reveal my fan-fucking-tastic cleavage in all its glory. I felt like a goddess in this dress. I knew I looked it too, especially with a few hundred thousand dollars in marquise-cut diamonds dripping from my wrists and neck.

"Those need to come off," she practically snarled as I tapped on the necklace with a pointy black nail.

"Oh, I'm aware, Miss Lund. Here . . . " I turned around, knowing that the back off my dress did as much for my ass as the front did for my boobs. I grinned at the grunt of appreciation

I heard when I swept my mass of dark brown curls over my shoulder to reveal the clasp at the nape of my neck. "Take it."

"For fuck's sake, Juli," she whispered, voice shaking. My nipples tightened at the want I heard there. It was always like this, even after almost a year together. The lust, the all-consuming desire. "I can tell you're wet for me."

I gasped at her words, at the heat of her as she came closer. Her body was like a furnace and she always burned me up in the best way possible. I felt the pad of one finger trace the line of my spine all the way down to the spot right between the dimples at the top of my ass—the dimples she loved to explore with her tongue until I melted into a puddle. I shivered under her touch. Desperate to get my hands and mouth on her, but I knew how much better it would be if we waited. "Tell me, Julissa," she insisted, still waiting for my confession.

I looked at her over my shoulder, my eyes focused on the hard line of her mouth. "Not wet . . . I'm *dripping* for you."

She sucked her teeth, palm pressed to my lower back. "Get the door before I do something reckless in this hallway." I laughed at the urgency in her voice. My woman needy and desperate, for me.

"Okay, babe. I'm coming." I loved a pun with innuendo and she could never let one slide.

"You're going to be coming soon enough," Freya said in a humor-laced whisper. "Get that luscious ass in there. Do we have all night?"

I sighed at the reminder, feeling some of the weariness of the day edging into the excitement of getting alone time with Freya. "Yes." If the six hours between now and the time I had to be ready could be considered an entire night. "But I have to be ready to go by four," I murmured, pushing the door open.

"We'll put the time to good use," Freya asserted with a nod and extended a hand for me to go first.

She loved watching me walk in and out of rooms. Said that the way my hips moved was like watching music. So I gave her a show. Swayed my ass and worked those hips until I was standing in the middle of the room, my back still to her. I could feel the heat of her stare, those icy gray eyes taking in every inch of me.

"Did you get what I sent you?"

"Yes." I pointed to the two black boxes sitting on the dresser by the wall. She hadn't made a move to come to me yet, and my hands itched to touch her. But she liked making me wait. Revving me up from a shadowed corner of the room while she told me all the dirty things she'd do to me.

And she loved surprises.

She'd send fancy little boxes to my room whenever we were on these trips. It could be anything: chocolate, a pair of silk panties, a bracelet . . . nipple clamps. Whatever struck her fancy. The deal was that I wasn't allowed to open them alone. She had to be here with me. Usually there was only one box, but this time there were two, and I'd been dying to know what treats were in store for me.

"There are two today. I'm excited." Before Freya, I'd hated surprises, never knowing how to react to them. Always feeling a little underwhelmed by gifts that weren't quite what I'd expected or even wanted. From people that didn't totally see me or get me. Not with Freya. My lover never disappointed me.

My back straightened with alertness as I heard the scuff of her shoes on the carpet coming closer to me. My body pulsed with need just from having her near. When she reached me she pressed her front to my back, arms coming around to cup my breasts. Mouth by my ear, her teeth grazed the skin there and my knees buckled.

"One surprise you get now." She ran a short nail over each nipple as she talked. The scratchiness of the lace covering them, making the sensation more pronounced. "The other one is for after." She used the tip of her tongue to trace the outer shell of my ear as I leaned on her, letting her touch me.

"I want your mouth on me baby," I begged, unashamed. "I'm aching, mi amor."

She sucked in a breath at the endearment. "I'm going to address every ache, sweetheart. But first, this needs to come off." She gently set about taking off my dress, careful not to tear or damage the expensive garment. Once I was bare to my waist she peppered kisses on the skin of my shoulders and neck. Hands tracing the edge of my bra, then dipping to the lace triangle covering my mons. She turned so we were face to face, still fully dressed in her black suit, looking like every butch fantasy I'd ever had. "Finish taking it off for me, but leave on the shoes. Keep the hardware on too. I want to fuck you in all those diamonds."

Her smile was that of a shark and I laughed, carefully sliding the dress down until I could step out of it. Without a word, she picked up the pile of red satin and placed it on a hanger in the closet. I stood there waiting, trying to still my mind and tune into the anticipation vibrating under my skin. The fevered need for her. I swayed with my feet firmly planted on the ground, waiting. I heard a rustle of fabric and assumed she'd taken her suit jacket off. But I didn't turn. I wanted to be surprised.

When she came back her shoes, tie, and jacket were off, her shirt unbuttoned so I could see the black bralette covering her breasts. She was more sports bras and boy shorts, while I was lace and thongs. Her, tall and lean, hard planes and angles. I was all curves and softness, but when we came together it was like we were built for each other. I reached for her, no longer able to wait.

"Ven aca, mi amor," I coaxed, running a hand down my belly until my fingers grazed the edge of the fabric covering me. "Or should I start without you, baby?"

Her eyes on me were hot, hungry. Like she was trying to decide where to touch first. "Hands off. That pussy's mine."

We were only a few feet apart now, and I was sure she could smell my arousal, but I was in a bratty mood tonight. I lowered my hand again just a bit more, so the tips of my fingers were now under the edge of my panties. "This pussy?" I asked innocently.

Her nostrils flared, skin flushed red. "Julissa." The one word made my toes curl. It promised so much deliciousness.

"What?" I asked, feigning confusion.

She finally came closer and grabbed my wrist, smiling. "You're a brat. But that greedy little cunt is going to have to wait. I've got plans for this ass first." She said it with both hands kneading my bottom, then dipped in for a kiss. In the heels, I was tall enough to just need to tip my head up to kiss her; when our mouths came together and she pulled me in tight, I swooned.

Freya kissed like she fucked, with single-minded focus and unapologetic hunger. I never had to doubt how much this woman wanted me. She devoured me. Our tongues tangled together for a moment, then she sucked on my bottom lip. And I tasted her, ate at her mouth, got what I'd been wanting all day.

"Your kisses are going to be my perdition," I huffed out, as she kissed my neck. "Play with my ass, baby," I begged and she dipped a finger in the cleft, grazing the pucker there with the pad of her finger.

"Mmm, I love that. I want more," I said, backing into her touch as I licked at her mouth, arms circled around her neck, clinging to her as she gave me what I craved.

After a few more fevered kisses she stepped back. Her eyes were stormy now, a darker gray, and her mouth was stained with the red of my lipstick. She looked debauched and this was only the beginning. By the time we were done, we'd both be wrecked.

"Hands on the desk, Julissa," Freya snapped, already walking to the dresser. My heart raced, knowing the really filthy part of the evening was about to get underway. "Push that ass up, legs spread. And I hope you don't care about those panties, because I'm about to tear them off you."

I literally stumbled, whimpering with need at her words, and bratty or not, I made sure I waited for her just like she'd asked. But because I also liked to get a rise out of her, I turned as she was walking over to me and said, "You bought me these, so . . ."

"You're asking for it," she warned, smacking my ass for good measure.

"You love it," I teased and she nodded with a helpless expression on her face.

"I love you and your bratty ways." My heart still skittered every time I heard her say that, my chest feeling too small for all the feeling there.

"I love *you*," I said in a breathless little whisper as she came down to kiss me. One quick taste. Tongue sliding in and out, and then it was back to business.

"Spread your legs wider, baby." I complied immediately. I knew which orders were in my best interest to obey.

I looked over my shoulders, an eyebrow raised in question, waiting for the unveiling of my surprise. She stood behind me and opened the box, pulling out a small red satin pouch.

"I'm gonna plug this ass, so I can play with it when I eat you out." My clit pulsed and my mouth went dry when I saw the black silicone anal beads she pulled out. She tossed the box and the pouch on the floor and pulled a little tube of my favorite lube out of her pocket. My ass clenched in anticipation.

"You're the perfect woman," I said reverently, not even bothering to ask where she got the lube. My woman was always prepared.

Freya shook her head as she used one finger to tug at the thong that was getting in her way. "That would be you, my love. Perfection," she practically purred, running a finger down one butt cheek then bending to bite it gently, licking where her teeth had been. "And all for me."

"All for you," I agreed. I bent over the desk, head resting on my forearms as she worked. I heard the snick of the lube and soon silky warm fingers were nudging at my hole while her thumb stroked my clit. "Fuck that's good. I'm gonna come so fast."

"And you'll keep coming," she assured me. "Once I've plugged you, we're moving to the bed. Going to sit you right at the edge and take my time with that hungry cunt of yours." Between the filthy things she was saying, her fingers in my ass and on my clit, the sensations were almost too much, but I sank into it. Braced my legs and let her work. I could trust that she'd give me exactly what I needed.

"What else are you going to do?" I asked, as I felt the first bead pressing at my hole. I relaxed my ass, loosening to the invasion as the first one slid in easily. The second was not too far behind; I hissed at the stretch. "Damn. I love this."

"It's gonna get better," my lover promised, confident in what she knew she could make me feel. "I'm planning to slap your clit until you're screaming. Then tongue you so good while I fuck you with these." She said it as she pushed the rest of the beads in, until I could feel her knuckles tracing my rim.

My skin felt tight from all the stimulation. Electric. "Ah, mi amor. I'm so full. Touch me."

She bent down so she was covering my back, and brought a hand under me to pinch my nipples. "We have to take these out, sweetheart. I think I'll play with them first. I wouldn't want to neglect them. Tend to them a little, before I put my mouth on you." Even as she said it, her hands were already busy cupping my tits. Fingers tweaking and teasing over the lace of my bra. I gasped, while I felt more wetness gathering between my legs. I wiggled my ass, knowing the friction would be right on her crotch.

"That's right, work that ass, honey. Let me feel you. I bet you're soaked already."

I moaned as she bit the skin behind my ear and twisted my nipples exactly how I loved it, the stimulation setting my skin on fire. "Harder, baby. I could come like this."

"I'm gonna take my time with that kitty, so I'm gonna leave her for last. Then maybe I'll let you lick me until I come on your tongue."

My knees gave then, but Freya was ready for me. She helped me slide out of my stilettos and as she kissed and nipped, we worked on getting the rest of our clothes off. Soon we were naked and pressed together, her smaller breasts right at mouth level for me. I went in for a taste. I could take one almost fully in my mouth. They were pert and tight, and I licked at the nipple while she gasped. Always touching.

"Just a taste, sweetheart. I haven't gotten enough of you." I nodded, busy biting a nipple while I moved my hand down to the trimmed patch of hair between her legs, and then she was the one gasping.

"Here's my gatita," I teased, raising up for a kiss, feeling her grin against my mouth. "I've missed her. Can't wait to go down for a visit later. Oooh she's ready for me," I said, dipping a finger into her warmth. She responded by tugging on the plug, making me shiver. I pushed my ass back as she moved it in and out a few times while I fingered her. I could've come just like that, still standing in the middle of the room, the bed untouched, but I knew she had plans for me. As if she read my mind, she tapped the end of the plug one last time and pulled back.

"Bed. You're coming with my tongue on you."

"Yes, please." I hurried over and planted my ass on the edge of the bed like she'd asked. I spread my legs wide so she could get a clear view of my bare pussy. My lips were a darker brown than my own skin, the inner ones almost black. My clit was a ruddy pink and when I was like this it stood out like a beacon. I could feel the cold air on it as I looked at Freya who stood only a few feet away, her short blonde crew cut already mussed from my hands, her flat belly moving up and down as her breaths came faster.

But her attention was on that little pink button between my legs. Her eyes heated as she licked her lips. When she lifted her gaze to meet mine she was back to the evening's program. "Wider, and tip your hips up so I can see the plug." I obeyed, so turned on I could barely breathe. I brought a hand up to play with my nipples, needing some stimulation.

"That's good," she encouraged as I touched myself. "Play with your tits. Show me how you want me to touch them."

I teased one and then the other, using my thumb and index finger on them, hard. "Come here, Freya," I begged, but she stood there just a few feet away still looking. She ran a hand over her own breasts, flicking a rosy nipple with a nail, teasing too.

"Spread your legs for me, mi amor," I beckoned. "Use your fingers. Let me see my gatita." She smiled, almost shy, but did what I asked. She widened her stance and used two fingers to show me her clit. Her heat was all shades of pink and purple, and my mouth watered with the need to taste her.

"That's so pretty." And I meant it. Everything about Freya was irresistible to me.

Without a word, she finally came to me. She bent down for a kiss, taking my lips hard, mouth hungry on mine, delivering drugging kisses as she covered the hand on my breast with her own. She trailed her lips down my neck, grazing the diamonds I was still wearing and making her way to my breasts, which she laved with her tongue, flicking one, then the other.

She brushed my belly with her lips, biting on the soft flesh there. Pressing her nose to my skin. Inhaling me. "I love you," she breathed out as she pressed kisses to the spot right above my mons, her mouth so close to where I desperately needed her. Finally she was there, lips right at my own. She looked up at me, tongue coming out for a lick.

"Kiss it, baby," I pleaded, then held my breath for the delectable sensation I knew was coming.

That first wet stroke always rocked me, and soon I was lost in the feeling. Freya ate pussy like she was born for it. Mouth, fingers, and tongue engaged in a full attack on my senses. It felt so hedonistic to be like this, splayed open, my girlfriend between my legs with diamonds plastered to my chest. It was what being with Freya was always like. Decadent and so dizzyingly satisfying.

I groaned as she circled the hard tip of her tongue on my clit and worked the beads in and out of my ass. "I love your tongue," I moaned, head lolling back as she pressed the flat of it to my heat and worked two fingers inside. The pressure on my ass combined with just the right assault on every nerve ending in my pussy was like a wave crashing over me.

"Ungh, Freya." I did scream for her when she slapped my clit— twice, then a third time—in-between swirls of her tongue and soon I felt my legs start to tremble with an incoming orgasm. I hummed at the sensation, breathing through the pulsing pleasure. "Ah . . . I'm right there."

She redoubled her efforts, using her lips to suck on the engorged nub, sending another wave of tremors through me. "Umm yeah, suck on that," I bit off as Freya worked me until I was wrung out. She took her mouth off my pussy and pressed soft kisses to the insides of my thighs before gently pulling the beads out.

I took a moment to get my breath back, but still found myself wanting more. Wanting *her*. She was caressing me as I lay on the bed with my eyes closed. Pads of fingers pressing, nails grazing. Loving me in that way she did. I felt worshipped in Freya's hands. It was addictive. It was what I deserved.

We moved and shifted around quietly as Freya got on the bed. She laid her long body over mine, and planted a kiss to the base of my neck, murmuring sweet words against my skin. "Te amo, Julissa. Mi reina." Her queen. I smiled lazily at her attempt at Spanish. She'd practiced those words for weeks before she'd said them to me. As with everything she did, it was intentional, deliberate. The same way in which she loved me. Like I loved her.

When she finally came up for a kiss, I was ready for her, my hand drifting to search for her heat. "I'm starving, Freya," I growled in warning, smiling into the kiss she pressed to my lips. Our tongues slid together as I touched her. Thumb flicking over her hard nub, pulling out a shiver and a lusty moan. "You're dripping for me too, baby. You gonna bring this up here? Sit on my face, so I can love you? Make you scream for me."

She was panting now, stern Freya replaced by the one that only appeared for me. Needy, desperate, and demanding. Soon she was scrambling up my body as I shoved pillows under my head to prop me up. I ran my nails over the tight skin of her thighs.

She looked down at me, flushed. "What are you waiting for?" This side of her was devastating to me. Cheeky and horny. Happy.

"I love it when you boss me around." I kept my eyes on her as I touched her. Pads of two fingers circling her clit. The palm of one hand on her ass, bringing her forward, closer to my mouth. Once I had her where I wanted her, I blew just a little bit right at her core, bringing out a hiss.

"Lick me," she begged with a gasp, as she rocked her hips toward me. I complied, tasting her, lapping at her with long licks, filling my senses with Freya. I used my fingers to spread her, revealing that little knot of nerve endings that turned my composed, starched-up lover into a mewling kitten.

"Umm, there it is," I crowed, mouth pressed to her warmth. "So sweet, baby." I ran the pads of my fingers over her folds as I flicked her clit with the hard tip of my tongue.

"I feel you everywhere," she gasped, making my own core throb. I scissored my legs as I worked my mouth and fingers on her.

I pressed two digits inside her, and kept the pressure she loved, then alternated between hard sucks and swirling my tongue on her nub. I felt the muscles of her legs tighten and heard the shaky exhale which usually came right before she fell apart. I groaned in encouragement, sucking harder. Moving my fingers in and out of her as her body rocked through an orgasm. I lapped and touched until she was too sensitive and then let her slide back down to me.

She put her hands on my face, kissing me sweetly for a long moment. When she pulled back, her smile was radiant. "That was worth chasing your gorgeous ass after the shoot." I laughed at that, remembering what the weights on my chest and wrists were.

I ran a hand over the jewels and pushed up to kiss her again. "Might be a good time to take these off." She made quick work of it and placed them carefully on the side table where I noticed she'd put my other surprise.

I raised an eyebrow as she grabbed it and put it in the spot between us on the bed. My heart raced as I looked at it. A small red and gold box. Like the ones Maison Dauphiné used to display their pieces. It was not the first time Freya had presented me with one, but the way her eyes softened and her cheeks flushed with pink, kicked up the flutter in my chest.

"What is it?" I asked, breathless again.

She leaned in to kiss me, and I came to her. Her hands roaming, already looking for that spot between my legs that was aching for her once more. But after a moment she pulled back. "Open it," she encouraged. My hands shook as I picked it up. There was a knock on the door just as I lifted the lid that revealed a small ring box. "Did you call up for anything?" My lover grinned as she got up from the bed and grabbed a robe that was on a chair. She winked as she slid it on and just as I flipped the top open she said, "Champagne."

I bit my lip and watched her stride to the door, my hands holding a diamond I never planned to take off.

SEALING THE TREATY

Ann Castle

Erica squeezed her thighs together and moaned into the mattress, loudly enough that the entire planetary capitol could have heard her.

"No," her fiancé, Harrule, whispered from behind her. He rubbed her back with a hand far warmer than human body temperature.

Obediently, she spread her legs apart again, missing the tiny bit of pleasure and relief the pressure had given her. "I can't do this," she said plaintively.

"We can't back out now."

"That's easy for you to say. You're not the one who has to suffer."

Harrule grinned. "It'll be worth it. You'll see stars."

"I was a starship pilot. I've seen half the fucking galaxy." She took a deep breath and tried to push the arousal away. Harrule had started edging her the evening before, fucking her until he was satisfied. Sagonites apparently had more stamina than humans. He'd brought her to the brink three times before they retired for the night. He'd slept deeply. Erica had had only fitful rest. Once she'd woken with her hand between her legs, and jerked it away, panicked.

Too much was at stake. She had to make it through one more night, somehow, for Harrule, for the peace between their solar systems.

Harrule's hands raised her hips and she obediently pushed back toward him as he penetrated her. She exulted in the sensation, so good, so full, so . . . incomplete. A shameful whimper escaped her mouth. She'd lost count of the number of times she'd nearly come that day.

"Shhh . . ." he said, snickering.

"You're enjoying this."

"Fucking my beautiful fiancée again and again while she squirms, unsatisfied? Of course I am. Maybe I should thank Lorrat for the idea."

Erica shuddered, partly at the feeling of Harrule sliding in deep and slow, partly at the mention of Lorrat Jenkar. Her current predicament was all his fault.

The negotiations had started out like any other. But the Sagonites, despite being a star-faring civilization with technology more advanced than Earth's, were old-fashioned and insisted the peace treaty between Earth and Sagon be sealed with a wedding. They'd chosen Erica and Harrule as the lucky couple.

Erica didn't want to give up piloting starships, or the feeling of power, control, and focus that it took to guide a ship through treacherous slipspace, but Sagon technology made her obsolete. Besides, she'd already fallen for Harrule, one of their top stardrive engineers and, conveniently, the heir to the Sagon throne.

Most importantly, she'd been a pilot during the war. She'd seen too much, lost too many friends. She would fight for peace with every bone in her body—and with the softer parts.

She strained back under Harrule's smooth hands, trying to urge him in deeper, as if that would grant her release. She felt full as he plunged in and pulled out again, each stroke sending waves of pleasure through her.

All she needed was a brief touch on her clit. She could slide her hand back . . .

"No," Harrule said firmly, leaning into her and grabbing the hand she hadn't even realized she was moving.

"Please," Erica moaned.

"Tomorrow," he said. "At our wedding, you'll come. All the guests will see how much you desire me. The alliance will be sealed."

"I'll come tomorrow even if you let me come now. Jenkar won't know."

He slapped her ass. "That's not how it works. Ancient rules, but we have to follow them."

Erica scowled into the mattress. "If you insist." She hadn't realized how deep the Sagonites's traditions went, even after Harrule warned her about the Jenkar family and their designs on the throne. Lorrat Jenkar wanted the negotiations to fail, and had dredged up an archaic marriage law to ensure that they would.

Harrule came with a quiet sigh, and Erica quivered beneath him. She was desperate for her own release, but she'd never felt anything like this before. It wasn't just physical. There was something wonderful about turning her pleasure over to his control, making sex something she did for him, for their planets, rather than for herself. It was the most unselfish thing she'd ever done, and she'd piloted the *Talon* through the last-ditch Final Attack.

He pulled out slowly and she whimpered at the loss even as she prided herself on her self-control, finely honed in the pilot's chair. Sagon stardrives might have made her training and experience irrelevant, but Jenkar's attempt to derail the treaty had given them purpose again.

"Roll over," Harrule whispered.

Erica obeyed, lying on her back. Harrule's bedchamber in the imperial residence sparkled with bright lights reflecting off glass and chrome. His hands, pale green against her human brown, spread her legs wide. She felt so exposed, and she loved the appreciative look in his dark eyes as he admired her. Other than his heat and color, he could have been human, though he was better in bed than any human man she'd ever had. She admired the darker green spots that dotted his chest before his head dipped down between her legs. She moaned in anticipation, then gasped when his tongue met her clit. Her back arched as her body detached itself from her brain. Harrule laughed softly, the vibration tingling against her.

Erica panted. Her breaths came faster, faster, in time with his throbbing tongue. She mumbled nonsense syllables like *please* and *yes*. Words no longer held meaning. Harrule would do what he liked.

What he liked was to stop. Erica groaned when he pulled away.

"Tomorrow," he promised.

"I won't make it. I'll get myself off in my dreams."

Harrule ran his warm hands up and down her thighs. She lifted her hips toward him, straining for a touch.

"You can do it," he said again. "Sweet dreams—but not too sweet."

Erica whimpered. There was no way she was going to sleep.

She must have drifted off. She opened her eyes from a dream of being fucked by a dozen men, one after the other, while she begged to come, to find Harrule smiling at her and rubbing her legs. Sunlight streamed in through the room's round windows. Several stories below, a few clouds drifted by.

"Only a few more hours," he said.

Erica spread her legs for him. All she wanted was to be fucked.

He slid in and took her quickly, laughing when he was done. "Sorry I couldn't make that last longer. I've been listening to you moan in your sleep for an hour."

"Do you expect me to be sympathetic?" She left her legs open, hoping he'd take her again, with his fingers or a toy.

"I suppose not. Not much longer to go, love."

"I can't wait." In the afternoon they'd be wed, Harrule would fuck her before all the assembled officials and guests, and she'd come harder than she'd ever had in her life, and the treaty would be sealed.

These past few days of pleasant agony would be worth it. A tiny part of her wasn't sure she wanted it to end, but she shoved that thought away. She couldn't do this for much longer.

Someone knocked at the door. Erica grabbed the sheet to cover herself, but Harrule shook his head no. "They'll all see you in a few hours," he said. "Don't move."

Erica flushed beet red as the door opened. *Don't move* meant *don't turn your head*, too, so she couldn't see who it was. But she heard his gasp.

"Yes?" Harrule's voice was full of humor.

"Uh . . ." Their visitor sounded young.

Erica couldn't resist peeking. It was a messenger, face flushing dark green, his eyes locked on Harrule's bare chest.

"Don't mind her," Harrule said. "She's almost ready for the wedding. She can't stop thinking about how good it's going to feel."

Erica hissed. The messenger took a shaky breath, which only deepened her arousal. Her pleasure gave her power over men in a way she'd never had it before, even when piloting. She shivered and clenched her fingers against the sheets so she wouldn't reach for her aching clit.

"Well . . ." the messenger said.

"What?" Harrule sounded impatient.

"The wedding's delayed until tomorrow. The ambassador from Parethon arrived early so there's a state dinner tonight instead. You're both expected to attend."

"Oh god," Erica said. She barely noticed Harrule dismiss the messenger until he sat on the bed and pulled her up into an embrace. His chest was hot against her breasts.

"A dinner? I'll be jumping the silverware." She thought of sliding the silver handle of a fork inside herself and squirmed in Harrule's arms.

"This is Jenkar's doing, I'm sure," he said. "We won't let him win. We'll get through this."

Erica took a deep breath, grateful for the long hours in the pilot's chair that had taught her to focus on things more important than the sensations in her body. "I was a starship pilot," she said. "I've faced worse trials." She felt like she was trying to convince herself.

Harrule kissed her, beaming. "You're an amazing woman," he said.

"Will you make it easy on me?" She hated asking, hated showing weakness. But she knew Harrule loved it.

His throaty laugh made her nipples tighten. "One of us has to be satisfied enough to behave," he said. "So no."

He pushed her down against the bed on her stomach. She let her nipples drag against the sheets as she lifted herself to her knees. Her breasts swung as he slid inside. "I could do this all day," he whispered.

"I'd like to see you try." She clenched around him, gripping him tightly. He moaned and she grinned, looking out the window at the purple Sagon sky. Sex, even submission, gave her power. Power over Harrule, over Jenkar, over Sagon's solar system and

Earth's. Suffering at Harrule's hands—or at his cock—gave her the power to solidify a fragile peace.

For that she could deal with anything Jenkar might throw at her. Even a state dinner.

That was easier said than done, she realized when they entered the wood-paneled banquet hall hours later.

Despite a perfumed bath, the musky scent of sex clung to her. Harrule had taken her mouth in a small antechamber, and she still tasted his bitterness, overpowering the scent of the night-blooming lilies planted around the hall.

Her nipples strained against the tight front of her silk dress, rubbing against the smooth fabric with agonizing pleasure, clearly visible to the servant who escorted them, his eyes glued to her chest.

Two-dozen heads turned when they were announced. She knew they were all speculating about how desperate she was. What exactly Harrule had been doing to her. What they would see tomorrow when he fucked her at their wedding.

She held her head high. Let them stare at her sharp nipples. Let them wonder what she wore under the gown, whether humans had spots like the Sagonites did, and whether the thin silk that aroused her nipples had also hardened her clit. Let them see the sash wrapped around her waist and the laser pistol secured there and keep their mouths shut.

She made sure she knew where her hands were at all times, lest she accidentally start masturbating at the table. She gripped the silver handle of her fork tightly, resisting the urge to stroke it, to bring it to her mouth and lick along its length, to lower it beneath the table and slide it up under her dress.

Erica put the fork down and put her hand flat on top of it, breathing hard. She glanced to the side, at Harrule. He smirked.

Knowing that he understood her predicament only made her hotter.

As the first course was served, Harrule's hand slipped beneath the table onto her thigh. It wriggled underneath the skirt of her dress, sliding up her leg. Obediently, she spread her thighs, so that her knees hung off opposite sides of the chair, giving Harrule full access to her sex as he ate his salad.

His fingers rested lightly on her labia. Erica shivered, resisting the urge to wriggle closer to him, to shift until he was touching her clit. She ached for him to touch her. At the same time she knew that if he did she wouldn't be able to control herself. She was so inflamed that she'd forget the formal dinner, wrap her arms around him and beg him to take her on the table before all the guests.

Not until tomorrow, she told herself. Tomorrow she'd get what she longed for. For now, she'd focus on her salad as if she'd never been so fascinated by anything in her life.

Erica ate her bitter lettuce, let the sweet, fruity dressing coat her tongue and wash away the taste of Harrule. She kept as still as possible. Without movement, Harrule's fingers lost their stimulating quality. The slight pressure on her labia became just part of the background, like the pressure of the chair against her back or the chill of the air on her bare arms.

She made it through the salad course without incident. Knowing that Lorrat Jenkar was only a few seats down the table, watching her every move, made it easier. She'd piloted the *Talon* through the worst days of the war, through the desperate Final Attack and the resulting shamble of a retreat. She could pilot herself through one more evening, one more night. The concentration required wasn't all that different. Erica smiled at Jenkar and spread her legs wider for Harrule's fingers.

She barely tasted the main course, a Sagon delicacy. Dessert was rich chocolate, imported from Earth at great expense. Normally she'd claim chocolate was better than sex, but *better than sex* was no longer a concept she understood. Through it all Harrule touched her, sometimes stroking a finger along her upper thigh, sometimes sliding one inside her while he made small talk with some ambassador or minister.

Lorrat Jenkar accosted them on the way out, a gaggle of curious onlookers surrounding them at the top of the grand staircase. Erica stood proud and straight, close to Harrule, whose hand rested protectively on the small of her back. Her own hand rested aggressively on the grip of her laser pistol.

Jenkar either didn't notice or didn't care. He was far too traditional to imagine a bride armed, far too removed from the front lines of the war to imagine any diplomatic function being disrupted by violence.

"Enjoyed your dinner, I imagine?" he asked in his oily voice.

"Oh, quite," Harrule said, with a degree of politeness that only Erica could tell was entirely fake.

"And you?" Jenkar's eyes, a shade lighter and colder than Harrule's, traversed her body.

"I can't say I noticed the food," she breathed, making herself avoid any threats. "I've been a bit distracted."

Jenkar smirked. His eyes slid to Harrule. "You'd better be careful. It doesn't seem like she's going to make it."

With a note of pride, Harrule said, "She was a starship pilot. She can handle this."

Jenkar's brows narrowed in puzzlement. He had no idea of the concentration it took to guide a ship through slipspace, to focus only on the warp and weft of the universe, not the discomfort and exhaustion in her body from working the controls for hours. Not the cries of joy, terror, or anguish from her crewmates and friends who relied on her to pilot them safely on routes where the slightest moment of distraction might embed them in a planet or vaporize them in a sun.

Part of her thrilled to the challenge Jenkar had set her. It was the most difficult thing she'd encountered in a life made easy by the end of the war and Sagon stardrive technology. She hadn't realized how much she'd been missing since the war ended.

She dropped her hand from her weapon and grinned at him. "Thank you for suggesting this," she said, pitching her voice so it would carry across the hall as if she were giving commands on the bridge of a starship. "I've enjoyed the challenge."

Harrule laughed and bent to kiss her cheek. Jenkar looked even more confused. Even those who'd served in the war didn't really understand. None of them had been pilots.

As she and Harrule left the hall, as he whispered the erotic things he was going to do to her into her ear, Erica smiled. Being teased by Harrule made her feel whole again.

Feeling whole didn't mean she was comfortable enough to sleep, even though Harrule took pity on her and didn't tease her much as he fucked her after the dinner.

But she was too excited to feel tired. Today was finally the day of the ceremony, the day Harrule would take her before everyone, the day she'd be allowed to come and show that she belonged with Harrule according to the stupid law Jenkar had dragged up.

More importantly, today was the day the treaty would be sealed and peace between Earth and Sagon guaranteed. And she, Erica, had done it. No longer an obsolete starship pilot, she was a peacemaker.

She took Harrule in her mouth and sucked him until he hardened. Then he pushed her back on the bed and slid into her. Her desperation was clear from her wordless grunts. He fucked her agonizingly slowly, while she tried to focus on her breathing rather than her pleasure.

When he finished he rolled her over and brought her to shoulders and knees. She spread her legs as wide as she could for him. He fingered her gently, then licked her. Erica gasped.

"You like that?" he asked.

"Of course," she snapped. "But I can't take much more."

"Soon," he promised. He stood and helped her off the bed.

Her legs shook with desire. "I hope there's not another delay. I think Jenkar did that on purpose."

"I'm sure he did." Harrule handed her a white cloud of fabric, her wedding gown, and helped her fasten the sheer dress down her back.

It was not as tight as the gown she'd worn to dinner the previous night, but see-through, and she was naked beneath it.

"It doesn't cover much," she said. "Why bother?"

Harrule laughed. "You can't be naked at your wedding. That would be inappropriate."

"*That's* what's inappropriate about this wedding?" Erica spun before the mirror. The little the dress did to conceal her made it more erotic than being naked would have been. Her hard nipples rubbed against the fabric, dark areolae clearly visible. The cleft between her legs was only a shadow, but left little to the imagination.

Harrule put his hands on her shoulders and kissed her hard, leaving her breathless. He pulled the fabric tight between her legs and tugged. Erica moaned and tried to rub herself against the dress.

Harrule chuckled and dropped the fabric, leaving her untouched once more. "I was worried that you weren't aroused enough," he murmured.

"You have nothing to worry about," she said.

"I don't know about that. You can still talk, after all." He pinched her nipple gently and pulled her by it toward the door.

She stumbled after him. He kept rubbing her nipple as they walked, rolling it between his fingers.

"I'm afraid I'll trip," she panted.

"You've got good balance," Harrule said innocently. "I want to make sure you're really ready for the ceremony."

"I'm ready, I'm ready."

Harrule stopped at the elevator and kissed her hard, tongue sliding against her pliant lips. "I need you desperate. I need you on the edge. I need you to come screaming as soon as I enter you and not to stop until I'm done."

Erica shivered. "I don't remember that requirement being in the contract."

"It wasn't. I simply think it will be fun."

Erica's heart pounded. It would be amazing. She gasped as Harrule released her breast, then again when he pinched the other nipple. She had no doubt Harrule would get what he wanted, she thought as he pushed the button.

In the elevator, he said, "Lift your skirt." When she obeyed, breath hitching, he dropped to his knees and took her in his mouth. She whimpered and sagged against the wall, hips bucking. He pulled away. "Soon," he whispered.

Erica shivered.

By the time the elevator doors opened on the top floor, revealing a glass-enclosed rooftop garden, Erica could barely hold herself upright. All her senses were concentrated on Harrule and how good it would feel to finally achieve release.

The announcement of their entrance was an unintelligible sound, the cheering crowd a blur of green skin and colored fabric. Jenkar's smug face jumped out at her, and Erica focused long enough to smile at him, to register his disappointment at her clear success. There was no way everyone in attendance wouldn't notice how aroused she was, how desperate, and know what it meant.

Harrule whispered, "Nice try."

Jenkar shrugged and said, "She won't make it through the ceremony. She's too weak."

The insult lifted Erica's fog of arousal. "You have no idea what strength is," she said, and punched Jenkar in the mouth. The crowd gasped.

He staggered back, hand to his face. Green blood dripped down his chin.

"I love you," Harrule said.

Erica grinned. "I know. Now let's get this over with so you can fuck me."

She squared her shoulders with pride at what she'd done for her planet, for Harrule, and for herself. It felt like everything she'd done in her life had pointed her toward this moment. She wasn't an obsolete starship pilot or a third-rate ambassador; she was a powerful woman—and everyone there knew it.

She'd been bored through the multiple rehearsals but now she was grateful that she knew where to stand, which gestures to make, what to say, because her brain could only think about Harrule's cock and how much she wanted it inside her.

The vows and applause were followed by a ridiculously chaste kiss and laughter when she collapsed against Harrule. He pushed her away, holding her up with firm hands on her shoulders.

"Almost," he whispered with a smile.

"One last thing will seal the bond between you," the official said.

Erica still had enough brainpower to murmur *and the treaty* and to be pleased at Harrule's grin.

"It's time for the consummation," the official finished.

Lewd shouts and whistles filled the hall. Erica's knees shook. Harrule's eyes darkened with lust.

Erica would have been happy to do it on the tile floor, but Harrule led her to a raised bed in the center of the garden, surrounded by flowers that Erica was too aroused to care about. She sat on the edge of the bed, the audience and official fading from her perception. The only sounds were her panting breaths echoing in her ears and the quiet moans coming from her own throat. All she saw was Harrule stripping slowly. She took in his muscular arms and smooth, spotted chest and breathed faster.

When he freed his cock, already hard, she leaned forward.

"Suck," he commanded, stepping closer to the bed.

She took him in her mouth and swirled her tongue around him, making him gasp. Even as focused on her own body as she was, the power she had over him thrilled her.

When he pulled away, she whimpered in disappointment. "Patience, darling," he said.

He pushed her flat on the bed, grinning when she spread her legs. "Not yet." Instead he brought his mouth to her breast, sucking her through the thin fabric.

Erica's back arched off the bed and she groaned. She ached to have him inside her. At this rate she thought she really would come as soon as he filled her. "Please, now," she demanded.

Harrule chuckled. He rolled them over so she was on top. The skirt of her gown billowed onto the mattress like a curtain, but hid nothing. "Are you sure you want this?" he said with a grin.

Erica rubbed herself along his shaft. "What do you think?"

He grabbed her hips and raised her over him. "Remember what I told you."

How could she forget? She could already feel pleasure building inside her. Erica slid down over his cock, feeling it fill her. He rubbed a finger across her clit. Her eyes closed and her head arched back at the sensation. She screamed, her whole body shaking. She would have collapsed if Harrule hadn't been holding her up, his hands at her waist, his legs bent so she leaned back against his thighs.

Everything in the hall, in her life, faded, other than Harrule's cock filling her and waves of pleasure rushing through her body. She'd never done anything but ride Harrule, never would do anything again. She screamed out all her air and gasped for more, lungs burning, then screamed again. All the while Harrule pumped in and out of her, stroking her clit with his fingers. All the sensations blended together into a burst of pleasure.

The world darkened. Beneath her, Harrule tensed with his own orgasm. Then everything went black.

When she woke, Harrule held her tightly on the platform in the garden. A blanket was draped over them, smelling of roses.

"I fainted?" she asked. Her whole body felt heavy, and for the first time in days she wasn't desperate for sex.

"Yes," Harrule said. "You should have seen Lorrat's face."

"I wasn't thinking about *Jenkar*," she murmured. "I was thinking about *you*. About the treaty, about the peace you and I will build between Earth and Sagon."

"I have to admit, the treaty wasn't at the top of my mind just now," Harrule said. "But we've done it. The war is over, for real."

Erica closed her eyes, remembering lost crewmates, friends, the feel of guiding a ship through slipspace, of racing Sagon ships to the next battle. No more of that. "Life will be different."

"Different, but good," he agreed. "I wouldn't change a thing."

"Just one thing," Erica said.

Harrule looked at her, surprise and worry etched across his face.

She grinned at him and laid a hand across his chest. "What we just did, the edging. We should do that again."

Harrule laughed and kissed her. "We will, I promise. Without Lorrat Jenkar having anything to do with it."

"Perfect," she said.

SYMMETRY

Angela Kempf

I walked into the movie theater, hand in hand with my boyfriend, Sam, and his best friend, James. That's the way dating in college had always worked for me: what I thought was a date was just another event where Sam had invited one of his friends to tag along. I was in a little black dress, far too sexy for what was turning out to be a friendly hangout.

It was a sunny midwestern Saturday afternoon, and watching a Korean horror movie seemed as good a way as any to fritter away the weekend. Usually, Sam would have had a problem with me holding his best friend's hand. Despite our long-term, open relationship, he had a slight jealous streak that was, for the most part, kept under wraps. But every once in a while, the knife edge of his insecurity came out of nowhere and would only retreat after lots of sex and reassurance. Though my boyfriend's possessiveness annoyed my friends, it reassured me; I had knives of my own, ready for battle and in need of restraint. We had similar issues; we were comparably armed. In college, this meant we made sense together. Beyond college, well, that's another story.

Today, though, his insecurity wouldn't rear its needy head. He wanted to put an end to the silly game that had started at a party the night before. More than that, he wanted to live up to his infamous advice.

Imitation is the sincerest form of flattery, or so they say, but someone who copies you is also generally accepted as kind of a pain in the ass. This didn't stop my boyfriend's friends from engaging in a beyond-juvenile game of copycat after a few drinks the night before. When drinking in a room chockablock with philosophy majors, mimesis happens. At least, they call it mimesis. I call it a throwback to third grade when the boy sitting at your lunch table would try to make what you just said sound stupid by saying it back to you. But, for philosophy majors, the process is called mimesis. At a college party full of self-identified intellectuals, you're supposed to walk this very fine line between scholarly banter and beer pong. Sam did not walk this line.

Sam said something pseudo-smart, and then mimesis happened, as in, everyone repeated it but in a dumber way. Sam was riffing too eloquently for a drunken, crowded, loud party where the penetrating smell of weed and a bass line from a familiar but unrecognizable song made it indistinguishable from any other party. Everyone in his audience, or, rather, earshot, was too drunk to either confirm or deny his proposition, so they parroted it in a caricature. *Why talk philosophy here?* My question went unanswered, for I was a lowly poli sci major who understood naught of the needs of the philosophical.

As I wondered why every Friday night included Kant, I noticed everyone at the party. Perhaps I noticed them more than usual, or perhaps the overwhelming smell of weed had taken effect, as it does in all those urban legends. Or maybe I had just been to too many of these parties.

Sam and his best friend James resembled each other, I thought, as James repeated Sam's words over and over. I had seen them together a zillion times, but that night was the first time I realized they looked similar. They looked like they were each standing on opposite sides of a circus mirror. Where Sam was tall and lanky, James was shorter and muscular, but they had the same overall mien. Their look, if you can call it that, could be summed up as what you would get if you went to a drive-through stylist and ordered the "philosophy major"—a guy with a slightly untrimmed beard, glasses, nose ring, an all black head-to-toe getup, and a Kerouac tattoo somewhere underneath those black clothes. Depth, within this sect of philosophy majors, was a religion. Individualism, a luxury.

Sam had said this at the party: "The uncontroversial life is hardly worth living," and he punctuated it with a long drag on his Nat Sherman, removing it from his mouth with a flourish befitting Truman Capote. It's not that he was overconfident. He was precisely as confident as he should have been, by my extensive, though flattering, calculations. He was smart, charming, and funny, and honestly, it got a little old. It was nice to bask in the sarcasm of his friends who were, as I was, a bit tired of the pontificating.

A pretty woman next to me at the party took a long drag on an imaginary cigarette and said in a needlessly British accent, "The uncontroversial life is hardly worth living." It was a silly, pompous thing to say at a party, and now, it was a joke, an experiment, a demonstration, a revolution. The joke passed around the party like a game of drunken telephone until I saw a jock jump on a table and yell, "I have hardly lived un-controversially," to great response from the remaining partygoers. And yes, eventually James got in on it, too, so intoxicating was the draw of making fun of perfect Sam. Sam gave him a look that slurred, *Et tu, Brute?*

Unfortunately for Sam, the imitation game was still going long into the next day. In the summer sun and humidity of the movie theater parking lot, Sam shot me a gaze full of existential despair and hunger for overpriced Milk Duds. He said, "Did you bring snacks to sneak in?" Again, I thought this was a date, and I was wrong. I shook my head no. "Damnit," he said.

James got out of the car and said, "Damnit." And, as Sam grabbed my hand to guide me into the matinee, so did James. He decided to take the imitation game to new, infuriating heights.

James's hand was a similar size to Sam's, which struck me as strange since their bodies were so incongruent. James was a very affectionate hand-holder, clutching my fingers and rubbing the skin between my thumb and pointer. Sam's hand-holding reflected our years-long sexual engagement: lovely, but predictable. Clutching each other like we were already facing the monster starring in the movie, we made our way inside. All three of us were avid horror movie fans, the cheesy lines keeping us coming back.

"You're, like, really good at holding hands." This was something I said without considering the aftershocks. James grinned and kissed my knuckles as we waited in line at the ticketholder booth.

"Oh, for fuck's sake," said Sam.

"Oh, for fuck's sake," said James.

We paid. Well, I paid. Sam forgot his wallet, which was his signature move, and James said he forgot his wallet, precisely as Sam had. Whether it was true or just part of the mimesis, I will never know. But we made it—hand in hand, ticket in pocket, giant bucket of popcorn underneath Sam's arm, Milk Duds zippered into James's jacket—into the theater where we hoped to find horror and subtitles in equal measure.

The lights dimmed, and I sat in between James and Sam,

holding the bucket of popcorn like a truce for a fight that hadn't happened yet. Sam playfully fed me a kernel of popped corn, like maybe I wasn't such an idiot for thinking this was a date. Sam leaned over and whispered in my ear, though it was louder than he had intended, "Sorry James is being such a dipshit. Just ignore him."

James leaned over, his voice entirely inside my ear: "Sorry James is being such a dipshit. Just ignore him." Then he fed me a piece as well, leaving his forefinger in my mouth slightly longer than Sam had. I laughed.

"James, you're going to get your ass kicked," I joked.

James smiled, tossed his head from side to side as if to signal *maybe*. He leaned over again and said, "I don't care if you don't care."

I leaned over to say that I, too, did not care, but James turned toward me, and we kissed. It happened so fast that it took me a moment to realize how long I'd imagined it, without naming it: that kiss from James. It was zealous, considerate, and kind of perfect. It was an antidote to dating someone for so long that they forgot to take you on dates.

"If you're not into this—" James started to say, but I interrupted with a kiss. It wasn't quite as perfect as the first, but it was a decent contender.

"Hi!" Sam said in my ear as the beginning credits came to an end, and the movie came to a beginning. We had been in an open relationship for a long time. That's how we made the long, maddening distance between us work. This time his energy didn't seem like jealousy—it seemed like tradition.

I turned toward Sam. "You know how you've been asking about a threesome?" Sam sat back in the theater chair, visibly considering my indecent proposal.

For a moment, we all turned our gazes to the screen, where

the giant lizard whose face bloomed like a rose promised to eat humans and also to momentarily relieve us from the awkward subject at hand. The monster leapt from vehicle to vehicle, taking what he wanted, which seemed to be humans for snacks, and I was jealous of his assurance. I meekly asked for what I wanted and sat there waiting in the dark for rejection.

As my nerves mounted, I felt James grab my hand. I looked around the theater and saw that it was mostly empty save for an old man, potentially already asleep, in the very front row. That boded well.

Sam leaned across me to address James. "Are you seriously going to fuck my girlfriend with me?"

James leaned over, casually, and said, "Sure, yeah, if you're amenable to the idea."

"I swear in front of God, that lizard monster, and all the children he just ate, if she leaves me for you, we're going to have a problem." James winked at Sam.

Sam leaned back, popped in a piece of popcorn, and then bent across me to whisper again, "You know, the more I think about it, I am interested in the idea."

James leaned over to respond. "It's like I always say: the uncontroversial life is hardly worth living."

"Shut the fuck up," Sam said with a smile.

I was surprised—delighted even—that Sam had said yes. It was these two sometimes insufferable dudes who I was fated to fuck, much as the people running and screaming away from the lizard monster were fated to be lunch. I smiled and whispered, "No more talking."

I took a piece of popcorn and placed it between James's lips, then pushed it inside with my forefinger lingering, much as his had. He ate the popcorn, and then deliberately freed the Milk Duds from his warm, secluded pocket. Giving me as much eye contact as I could handle, he put a half-melted Milk Dud in between his lips, waiting for me to share it. I was ready for the Milk Dud. And I was ready for a threesome.

I placed my mouth on James's and stole the Milk Dud from him. I ate it hungrily, greedily, like the monster that seemed to thrive on some never-ending feeding schedule. There was no sleeping or conversing with other lizard monsters, there was only ceaseless human-eating. I decided to take inspiration from that monster and focus on precisely what I wanted from this not-a-date turned date.

I knew what I lusted after, but I only had an imprecise idea of the technique. Two people having sex is intuitive if you get the right pairing. But now that everyone had agreed, I felt a bit frozen. The lizard monster ate one unassuming human while he kicked away a man climbing up his leg with a gun. *Okay,* I thought. *If that monster can take on two people at once, so can I.*

I hadn't had anything to drink since the party last night, and yet, I was suddenly at ease. The green light from the monster lit up the otherwise dark theater, and James's eyes glowed with anticipation. I don't know why I had never noticed him like this before. He always seemed happy to stay in Sam's shadow. He deserved more attention than I had given him.

I kissed James again, and I guided him onto the floor in front of me. He rested his face on my knee. I would just have to summarize the plot for him later.

Sam's fingers traced mine. Seconds later, I felt James's fingers tracing my thighs, same speed, similar pattern. James was watching us intently, and he persisted in copying Sam. Now, with the confidence of eleven lizard monsters, I knew what I would do. I hiked up my dress just a bit and slid down in my seat to give James an easier vantage point.

James had never seen me naked before, and we'd never had the essential "here's how to go down on me" conversation. I figured I could use Sam's mouth to my advantage since James seemed content to continue our game of copycat.

I told Sam, "Kiss me everywhere but my mouth."

Sam complied, kissing all over my hair and neck, and James got the point, too. He lingered over my thighs, he nuzzled underneath my navel, and he drifted around my hips. His lips brushed my knees. I breathed deeply and shut my eyes to take it all in.

"Kiss my face everywhere but my mouth," I whispered again to Sam, this time a bit raggedly.

Sam kissed my eyelids, ears, cheeks, and chin with deliberate attention—first-date type of attention. He led his hand under my dress, another first-date move. James zeroed in a bit more, too, pulling my underwear down around my ankles. He kissed my outer lips and bit gently where my thighs met. I almost forgot we were in a theater, but screams from the screen reminded me. I stifled as much noise as I could and peeked once more around the theater to ensure we were not being spotted. The old man in the front was still the only one I could see.

"Now you may kiss me," I whispered unintelligibly. Sam knew what I meant, and he kissed me deeply. James followed suit. James licked gently around the top of my clitoris, circling his tongue slowly, just as Sam was. It seemed impossible that he could see what Sam was doing, but they had that strange best-friend connection sometimes. I felt my muscles starting to clench already, my toes curling in my boots. But it was too soon. I sat straight up.

"Stop," I said. "Just for a minute."

I saw someone running from the lizard monster in futility. They dropped their weapon. They tripped. They screamed. Their bodily fluids splattered against the screen. I knew that was almost my fate a few seconds ago. I had very narrowly avoided peaking too soon, underestimating the force of my opponents.

I took a few deep breaths. I guided Sam onto the floor next to James. I gestured with my toes, tugging at their pants. With some contortion, they were now only in boxers, pants around their shoes, erections pointing at each other accusingly. Without my prompting, they each took each other's cock in their hand, shrugging. It was this don't-knock-it-until-you-try-it nature that drew me to philosophy majors, I supposed. It certainly wasn't their persistent use of "ipso facto" at keggers. They massaged each other up and down with uncertainty, and I enjoyed being the instigator of the newfound sexual side of their friendship.

When Sam once again got his bearings, he leaned in to go down on me. He knew precisely what I wanted, and his mouth on me felt like my vagina was slipping into my favorite sweater. What he did was ignore my clit until I begged him to stop. He licked up and down but avoided the very places that most desired his tongue. When he knew I was getting desperate, he stopped to come up for air.

"Your turn," he said to James, then kissed him with a very wet face.

James had seen how Sam had tortured me so thoughtfully and did the same. After a few minutes of waiting, I nearly grabbed James to force him where I wanted him to go. But before my hand moved, James stopped and kissed Sam. James came suddenly and silently, just as the lizard monster ate the comic relief. Surprised, Sam came, too, only moments later. James blushed a little, and then returned to his post.

I was far too close to stop myself anymore. I knew the slightest pressure would be the end of me. I worried about the noise I would make; I worried about getting kicked out of the only theater in town.

Reading my mind, Sam whispered to me, "No one can hear you scream." I held back until I saw a bloodbath waiting to happen—

the lizard monster emerged in a busy shopping mall. Everyone began screaming, including me. I was pushed over the edge by James's tongue, by Sam's earnest look of enjoyment watching me. I moaned louder than was strictly necessary. No one batted an eye. The edging had elongated my orgasm. My body clenched up and pulsed, overwhelmed by James's licking. I was caught in the grasp of my own pleasure for the full length of time it took the lizard monster to trample everyone at the mall. I breathed deeply once I finished, and both Sam and James leaned in to kiss me. They tasted the same.

We quietly dressed, tuning in to the movie with our full attention for the first time since we sat down. Sam grabbed my hand and said, "This movie was nothing like I expected. Let's see this again next weekend."

James grabbed my hand, too. "Let's see this again next weekend."

YOUR NAME ON MY LIPS

Joanna Shaw

Her leg bounces like a jackhammer, the swish of her pants rubbing together at the thighs sounding nonstop. Lila can't stop it any more than she can stop the way her teeth grind together as she stares at the screen waiting to be called. She'd be fiddling with her hair if they hadn't shaved it in preparation. This is the culmination of years of her life. Years of waiting for the surgery to be perfected, for spaces on the waiting list to open up, for her insurance to green-light the procedure—all of it led to this moment at this hospital. Now that she's so close to what she wants, every second before it is agony.

Andrew puts a gentle hand on her knee, easing the frantic energy coursing through it, if only for a moment.

She smiles, close-lipped.

"It's okay," he insists. The tops of his cheeks round as he grins. "I'm excited, too." He leans in for a kiss, which they both know will soften the anxiety that snapped her jaw shut.

This time, her expression is much more genuine. She doesn't say anything in response, but she doesn't have to. She can't. Andrew's learned to understand her without the explicit words or even the signs when she's too tired or upset to bother. They'd been together for nearly a year before she lost her voice, and his patient understanding is one of the few things that never fails to get her through the hardest days. He joined her lessons on sign language and uses it regularly. He was there every time she applied for the operation. He sat by the phone with her when she was rejected time and time again.

Lila drops her head onto his shoulder and grips the hand still on her knee. He shivers lightly at the prickle of her short hair against his neck. Their relationship as it stands now was forged in those first few months after her accident, but she knows without a doubt that the first thing she'll see when she comes to will be his face. This will just be a new chapter in their lives together.

A nurse calls her name from across the room.

Rocketing to her feet, Lila makes her way over to him, Andrew in tow. She read all of the instructions the day she got them; she knew that until they were actually wheeling her into the operating room, her husband could stay with her. They diligently followed the nurse down the hall. The room they were brought to was less a room and more a deep alcove with a curtain. Closing the barrier for privacy, the nurse gives them the room alone. She doesn't hesitate to strip down in front of Andrew.

He folds her clothes up and slips them into a patient bag while she pulls on a gown, not bothering to tie the back. "We're done," he calls out once Lila is in the bed.

The nurse pulls the curtain open a few feet. "I'll set you up, and then the surgeon will be along shortly." Seemingly sensing the tension his patient carries, he makes quick work of his checklist, asking his questions in as few words as possible and inserting her IV with an expert hand. It's all standard procedure. Is there any chance she could be pregnant? No. Has she consumed any alcohol within the last day? No.

Andrew quietly brings a chair over to her bedside. He finds her hand again and envelops it in his own, a silent comfort while she's otherwise preoccupied. When the nurse finally leaves, he keeps it there. "It won't be long," he promises.

Turning her head his way, she rolls her eyes in an exaggerated fashion.

He snickers. "I know, but they can't be running too late. We've been here for almost two hours already." Still, despite his words, he fishes a deck of cards out from her purse and challenges her to a game of war. He shuffles them with a few jerky movements. One of the slick cards bends at the corner from the rough treatment, and he frowns as he tries to smooth out the crease.

Lila touches his arm to stop him. Taking the deck from him, she finishes the job with quick movements. She reaches over and tugs him into a quick kiss. It's obvious that Andrew's nervous, too, even if he tries not to be for her sake, and she loves him for the attempt.

He rests his forehead against hers, the cards forgotten between them.

By the time the surgeon comes by, they're deep into their fifth game, which Andrew swiftly clears once it becomes obvious the doctor isn't there to check in. This is where she leaves him. Two staff members disconnect the bed from the wall and push her out of the alcove without pause.

Andrew squeezes her hand once more before they're forced to part.

From the bed, Lila tucks her ring finger down and crosses her middle and index, sticking her pinkie and thumb out. She holds the sign up high as she's wheeled down the hall.

I really love you.

The surgeon talks about what she can expect from the anesthesia on the way. They went over this a month prior, but the refresher isn't unappreciated. He reminds her that the actual surgery will be done laparoscopically. Using what is in essence a robot, he'll make a small incision and locate the areas of the brain where language is processed. That's where the first device needs to be implanted, and also why they needed to shave her head. The second part won't be implanted at all but given to her afterward, and it will be her responsibility to have it on her whenever she needs it. Once she learns how to use it, it'll give voice to the thoughts trapped in her head and hands. He's just responsible for the operation, of course. A speech therapist will work with her on the rest.

Lila listens with one ear. She read so many articles, so many patient blogs, and did so much research into the actual methods that none of this is wholly news to her. Instead, she bites her lip and wonders how she'll sound. As part of the process, Andrew and her parents helped her compile all of the audio and video recordings of her they could find dating back the last few years before her accident. The collection was sent off to the company that made the two devices. According to all of the pamphlets and websites, their experts went through every piece to create her new voice. She should only need to direct her thoughts in the right way, and the words will be put together using her own sounds. She'll speak the way she used to.

In theory, at least. Lila wraps an arm around herself. There's no guarantee she'll ever sound like herself again.

One of the nurses pushes a button on the wall to open the doors to the operating room. There are several more medical staff preparing inside.

"This is our robot," the surgeon says, pointing to a white piece of machinery a few feet away from the wall. He smiles and glances over at her to see her reaction.

Lila swallows at the sight of it. It's clean, sterile, impersonal. There are flashes of silver here and there from the joints, but otherwise, it's as bland as the sheets covering the bed beneath her. Soon enough, that'll be rooting around in her brain. This was one of the things from the blogs she's had the hardest time conceptualizing.

Two nurses carefully shift her over to the operating chair. They strap her limbs down for safety. A third nurse approaches with the anesthesia. She pats Lila's arm as if to comfort her.

Lila blinks, clumsily licks her lips, and sinks under.

Her eyes roll slow as sludge. She can hear the nurses talking above her. One of them's gushing about her wife and something she did. Maybe for their anniversary? Her lips part to ask, but then she remembers.

She doesn't have a voice.

"Looks like she's waking up," a different nurse says.

Lila looks at her through lidded eyes. She wants to know if the surgery was a success. She wants to know when she'll get her second device. Mostly, however, she wants to know where Andrew is. He promised to be there when she woke up.

"We're just taking you to your room," the same nurse reassures her.

They take her around the corner and down another hall before slowing down and wheeling her bed into a small room. By the time they finish getting her settled in, there's a knock at the door.

Andrew carefully walks past them, Lila's purse slung over his shoulder, and sits in one of the chairs against the wall. He smiles when she looks over blearily.

It's the last thing she sees before succumbing to the exhaustion.

"You need to want to speak," the speech therapist explains. "The device isn't designed to pick up and project all of your aimless thoughts. Unless you put intent behind them, nothing will come out."

Lila grits her teeth in an attempt to keep the sneer off of her face. Of course she wants to speak. She didn't go through all that she had to get her device and not use it. The firm squeeze of Andrew's hand around hers helps a small amount but is nowhere near enough to ease her jaw.

The therapist sighs. "Why don't we try again?"

Fuck off, Lila thinks and hopes there was enough intent there this time. The second device hangs heavy around her neck.

Nothing happens.

"It might take time." As the therapist speaks, she packs her notes and slips on her coat. "Some people take to the device faster than others. Practice three times a day for a few minutes at a time until our next appointment, and we can evaluate your progress then."

Andrew idly strokes her palm with his thumb.

Turning to him, Lila huffs. She tries again. *I'm tired.*

He squeezes her hand. "Don't fry your brain. It's only been a few days."

Four days, to be exact. Four days of having the secondary part of the device, of having all of the tools she theoretically needed to regain her words. Four days of failing to produce a single sound. She gently extracts her hand from the embrace and raises both arms to make the sign for tired instead. Her head aches from both trying too hard and the healing incision on her scalp, but, even more than that, she's emotionally exhausted. Maybe it was foolish to think she'd work it out right away. She can admit that it wasn't an assumption based on logic.

The problem is that it's very difficult to be logical about her situation. She has all of the pieces of the puzzle and the box art, too. It doesn't seem like it should be that hard to connect them after all of the research she's done, and yet she apparently can't put a single pair together.

So, rather than take her time, Lila finds herself working nonstop to examine each piece. She practices—with intent—while they watch TV. Her first thought in the morning and her last at night are meant to be voiced. Her books are silently narrated. The dog next door should get verbal praise in addition to the scritches through the gate. Whenever she looks at Andrew, she throws herself into projecting not to the world, but to him.

I love you. I love you. I love you, Andy.

He never hears the words. He always feels the intent, always turns to smile at her.

But it never works, and so she changes tactics out of desperation. Instead of thinking about how much she loves this man— and God, does she—Lila focuses on the why. She watches the way he immediately zeroes in on her hands as she signs. He's gentle when he inspects her incision to see if it's healing. On the days she's feeling particularly hopeless, he's there by her side with a can of whipped cream. Whipped cream that's softened both of them over the years, though in her opinion, the little pudge around his tummy is much more gropable than the leanness he used to work so hard for.

Andrew catches her staring again and sticks his tongue out before turning back around.

Her gaze drifts down. He always did have a great—

"Ass."

They both jolt. The sibilant curse is dragged out for far too long and choppy, too, with the slightest of pauses between the *a* and the *s*, but there's no denying it. It was Lila's voice.

Andrew blinks. "Were you calling me an ass or . . . ?"

Hysterical laughter bubbles up in her throat. Part of her was on the verge of giving up on the entire endeavor. Weeks of failure where so many other patients were thriving at her stage was painfully discouraging. She bites her lip as the corners of her mouth twitch upward and shakes her head. Then she tries again. *Ass.* The giggles dissipate when it fails. She just spoke. It shouldn't be that difficult to do it again.

"Maybe you've been trying too hard," he suggests, wincing as it comes out.

But Lila knows him too well to take much offense. She scrunches her nose at the sour taste it imparts and thinks it over. She certainly hasn't been putting in too little effort. It's never been in her personality to slack off, and the number of headaches from overexertion she's had since the surgery is proof enough of that.

He gives her a quick kiss. "We'll figure it out."

She yanks him close for a longer one instead and grins against his shocked lips. There's one foolproof way she can think of to relax. All of the things she's been trying to say are there, and, as her eyes slip shut, she reinforces them. Maybe it doesn't matter that it won't work. The way he responds to her lets her know that he hears her all the same. He always has.

Even when they part, they move in sync with the familiarity born of years together, years of communicating silently. Lila pops the button of her jeans in the middle of the living room. A nudge gets them to clear her hips, and then they're slipping down her legs. He loosens the tie of his sweatpants. Neither wants to take the time to go to the bedroom. Not when the soft carpet will do.

Andrew slides his hands under her shirt and skims her sides until he reaches her chest, the fabric bunching up around his wrists. He tugs the shirt over her head to reveal her bare chest. Her breasts are soft and dipped down without a bra to shape them. He cups them in his hands as she kisses him, and the pressure of his fingers makes dimples along the curve of her bosom.

She gasps as he thumbs her right nipple. The room is silent but for the rustling of jeans being kicked to the side. *Please*, she thinks, squeezing her legs together as another deep pang of arousal hits her core.

Andrew's shirt is the next to go. The way he reluctantly removes his hands from her breasts to do so pulls a huff of laughter out of her. When he returns and latches onto a nipple, it's cut off with another inhale. He may be more laid-back than she is, but he doesn't do things by half measures.

The tongue against the stiff bud is too much and not enough. Biting her lip, Lila holds his head in place until she can't stand it any longer. She pulls away, lays on her back on the floor, and lets her knees fall out to the sides. It's the perfect Andrew-shaped space. The second device slides down past her collarbone to rest beside her neck. Deep muscle memory has her legs wrapping around him as soon as he finds his place, dropping his forearms to frame her face. She smirks up at him, breathless.

"Love you," he murmurs into her lips. He grinds against her instinctually.

His cock feels hard even through the layers between them. The sensation is distracting and delightful and nearly makes her forget about trying to return the sentiment, her want for him eclipsing her persistent worries for a moment.

"Love," the device against her neck projects in a stilted fashion. It's somewhat muffled by the way it rests against her skin in this position. The word itself is flat and devoid of the intensity with which she feels it, but the sound and shape of it is undeniably her own.

Andrew's hips jolt against hers.

Her heels dig into his ass. She focuses and tries again to no result.

He kisses the frustrated crease of her brow. "You okay to continue?"

Instead of nodding, she presses him closer with her legs. She needs this. She needs the ease and release of simply being with him. They've had sex plenty of times without her voice, and they can do it again.

Andrew shifts his weight to his left arm. He trails his free hand down the soft skin of her stomach and under the printed cotton of her panties to where she's already wet and eager. His fingers slip along the slick rim of her hole and back up to her clit. He traces circles around the nub as her thighs quake with the effort of staying open. He dips into her wetness once more before withdrawing, using that hand to push the waistband of his boxers down underneath the weight of his balls. Her panties strain as they're clumsily pulled to the side to allow him in. The slide of his cock along her lips is smooth and easy. After one, two thrusts, the head catches, and he angles his hips to fill her.

Lila clutches at his shoulders, her lips parting. She hadn't realized just how long it had been. The thought of her operation distracted her, but now all she can think of is the familiar weight of him within her.

"G-god," the device stutters in unison with her mind. This time, it doesn't bother her. She doesn't register the sound, just Andrew's groan in response, the way he steels himself above her and begins to move.

The slick drag out is slow, teasing. The push in is satisfying. He fits his head into the curve of her shoulder and scrapes blunt teeth along the tanned skin there.

She leaves long red streaks along his back to match.

He fucks into her harder but not faster. With every swivel of his hips, he bottoms out, cock grazing her G-spot whenever she clenches down.

The device pipes up again. "Andy," it says sweetly. There are no stutters this time. There's no need for it to piece together the syllables or make due with less heartfelt recordings, because she'd said his name so many times in videos and messages long before she ever grew to love him.

"Fuck, Lila," he moans and slips a hand between them again to find her clit. Her panties are soaked where they're held aside by his cock. Her nub, swollen and shielded ever so slightly by her lips, is slippery with her desire. He rubs a thumb around it. When her breath hitches, the circles widen until it evens out again.

"Andy." It's the same exact inflection and intonation as last time.

Her legs tremble, her heels likely bruising his ass where they dig in.

The effect is no less strong. Andrew screws his eyes shut, and his thrusts quicken. His teasing thumb becomes sloppier and more desperate, swiping across her clit regularly now.

"Please," the device projects plainly. "I'm close."

He doubles down, grunting with effort.

Lila's head thumps back against the carpet. Her mouth drops open in a silent wail. She squeezes him tight with both her legs and her pussy.

"God. Andy."

Crushing their lips together, Andrew fucks her through the sweet clenching of her muscles. His pace stutters along with her words, and he bottoms out as his orgasm rips through him, too. He lets his head drop to her shoulder.

She wraps tired arms around the slump of his back.

In the quiet of the living room, they hand each other their clothes. Lila puts a flat palm up to her mouth and dips it towards him in thanks.

The device stays stubbornly quiet.

Andrew catches her hand, kissing the tips of her fingers. "We'll figure it out together."

PHOSPHOROUS

Kim Kuzuri

Stranger sights had stumbled down the stairs of the Silver Dollar Hotel and Saloon than a drunkard wearing the petticoats of a woman he'd paid time for. As heads turned and a bit of murmuring started up, Billy kept her eyes on her cards. The whispers made their way to her like the rustle of wind through tall grass as her partner-in-crime and sometimes lover made his way through the scatter of tables. At this hour, with the lamps glowing warm overhead and the barroom half-full, the hush came and went with the haste of a summer shower, a quick change in the air and nothing more.

"Having fun?" Reaver asked. Dropping into the empty chair to Billy's left, his skirts caught the air, billowing like sheets on the line before they settled to outline the wide sprawl of his legs. The cotton was finely spun enough that she could read the soft, plump shape of his cock beneath it. The other fellows at the table hardly spared Reaver a glance now that he'd made his entrance.

"Passing the time," Billy replied. She flipped another coin onto the table's growing pile. Newer than the rest and freshly liberated from a lockbox, it gleamed in the lamplight. "What happened to your clothes?"

"Woman had claws like a wildcat, near tore 'em to shreds." Reaver tipped his hat back and his rag-doll slump deepened, chin tucking to his naked chest as his eyes fell to slits. He produced a quarter out of nowhere and rolled it across knuckles still scabbed and healing from the tussle some few towns over. Those fingers of his were on her mind more and more of late, whether they were deftly working the dial of a safe or rubbing thoughtfully across his lip. She pictured them falling to his lap and gathering up those skirts of his and a little flicker of heat caught between her thighs.

Billy spread a fan of black across the wood and collected a trio of dirty looks along with her winnings. "Seems like," she agreed, silently noting that Reaver's chest and back were unmarked, carrying only the usual old scars faded near to nothingness. If it were true, the bastard's pale skin would be striped red, but while Billy was quick enough to know that Rowland "Reaver" Kelley was daily held upright by booze and lies, she was also fool enough to let it be. She thought instead about the marks she liked to lay on him with her mouth—the kind of mottled bruises that sat plum-dark and lingered—and clenched, the heat building up in her cunt fit to start a trickle.

The cards whispered in Billy's hands as she shuffled them for another round. Beneath the rasping flutter she could hear an echo of the soft sounds Reaver made when they were sliding together with the same ease: the tremble of his breath when he moved inside her; the drift of his callused palm along her spine; the brush of his mouth against tender skin when his nose was buried against her clit and his clever tongue got put to better use than grifting.

"Tub's still full and hot if you want a soak," Reaver said, his chin lifting. He'd trimmed his beard into shape from the wild tangle the road had left it in and looked almost like a gentleman again. The ends of his hair were still damp, long strands plastered to his collarbones and trickling thin streams of water into the faint scatter of curls on his chest. A glance and Billy could see the pink of his nipples pebbled from the chill, and beneath her shirt and the snug fit of her waistcoat, her own went uncomfortably tight in response.

He rapped his knuckles against Billy's shoulder and pointed toward the stairs, as if Billy weren't sober as a stone right now and didn't know where he'd been. Since they'd started riding together, Billy had made it her priority to know where Reaver was off to. With a troublesome man like him, some days that meant making sure he didn't get his pockets turned out and some days it meant sussing out what was rattling around in his pretty head.

The cards in her hands murmured restlessly; the men at the table were narrow-eyed and mule-stubborn, determined to recoup their losses. She'd win big if she stayed. She and Reaver had enough of a reputation in these parts that no one would start a commotion if she took these idiots for everything. But the bump of Reaver's knee against hers was intentional, and the smell of his shaving soap was sweet and light.

Whatever his mood, the whoring hadn't satisfied it. His cock might be asleep between his legs right now, but a tug or two would see it rising proud and eager. Reaver was playing coy but he sought something from her. The man likely couldn't find the words, another puzzle to try and tease apart in whatever this was they had between them.

Billy left the cards and took the cash. Reaver's pale blue eyes were sharp as the Devil's as he claimed Billy's seat at the table and passed the deck to the next man to shuffle. "Last door on the left. Paid through to the end of the week for the room. Miss Elizabeth's only for the night," Reaver told her, scooting to perch his ass on the lip of the chair and propping a hand on his thigh. He grinned like a loon, looking for all the world like he had no idea he was sat naked to the waist in a woman's petticoats. By the keenness in his gaze, he wasn't swimming at the bottom of the bottle, but no one else seemed in on the joke.

Billy aimed to keep it that way. With a sharp look, Billy slapped a handful of coins back on the table for him to buy in, then headed straight for the bar, ordering herself a shot and informing the barman she'd pay extra in the morning if he watered down anything Reaver asked to be sent his way.

Upstairs, past the handful of rooms for let, she found the bath. It wasn't nearly so hot as promised. The only thing burning as Billy eased into the water was her gullet from that piss-poor shot of whisky and the spark of interest that fattened her clit. No sense in complaining though, Billy thought, as she sank into the tub and rinsed the grit from her close-cropped hair. She scrubbed herself to the bone, thinking wistfully all the while of the endless heat of a desert hot spring until the brush left her skin stinging and raw. She left the water cold and clouded by the time she stepped out, and with her desire for a good fuck building toward a steady glow, she wondered how long Reaver aimed to stay at the card table.

Figuring that unless folks were going around barefooted, she'd hear them in the hall, Billy didn't bother to put a stitch back on. Instead, she bundled up her clothes with her hat and boots and guns to let the air dry her off as she ducked across the hall.

In the room, plainly furnished but clean and well-kept like the rest of the Silver Dollar, Billy found the woman Reaver had paid for company cozied up in the bed. She'd near forgotten where Reaver had gotten the petticoats and he clearly hadn't seen fit to provide Miss Elizabeth with a word of warning. Eyes widening at the sight of Billy naked as the day she was born, the lady's startlement crackled like lightning, skittering across Billy's bare skin to fizzle out at her feet.

It wasn't that Billy tried hiding anything. Folk just made assumptions and Billy let 'em. Some got riled up like an over-turned wasp nest, some got squirrely. Most didn't give a damn so long as she did the work and pulled her share.

Miss Elizabeth went the way Reaver had when he'd wised up: the woman didn't stay confounded for more than the blink of an eye and smiled. She didn't treat Billy none the different as she drew Billy into the softness of the bed and cuddled close without a word. The woman didn't seem to mind in the least that half her clothes had walked off with Reaver, or that Billy wasn't in a rush to take liberties. She tucked herself up under Billy's arm when Billy simply lay there, staring at the rafters like they might tell her what her idiot man was up to.

"Your friend's a funny one. He the kind of fella who only likes to watch?" she asked, and Billy didn't answer.

Truth was, she didn't quite know what kind of man he was. Two going on three years now they'd been nigh inseparable and Reaver was still a mystery to her. Not even taking the man to bed gave her much of an idea of what aims he had beyond the next job or the next day's ride.

Eventually the woman touched Billy with intent, a feather-light question. Gauging Billy's stillness and the low cast of her eyes as permission, Miss Elizabeth rolled closer, her breasts pressing soft and plush against Billy's arm. Might as well, Billy thought, pulling the woman closer. Couldn't hurt to pass the time.

Miss Elizabeth was riding merrily atop her thigh when Reaver was done with his gambling and strolled in like a cat with its tail high.

When he pulled up a chair to the bedside, the woman leaned down to whisper, "Guess I was right about him preferring a show," in Billy's ear. Miss Elizabeth sat up straight, her tits twice the size of Billy's jiggling as she slipped her wet fingers along the creases of Billy's cunt and skewered Reaver with a knowing eye. Billy saw then why her partner had paid for the whore's time. Reaver, she'd found, preferred to deal with stupid men and sharp women, the first to fleece like plump sheep and the latter to give him a run for his money. With the way he usually got when he was feeling frisky, Billy just hadn't ever thought that extended to the bedroom.

"Prettier than me in that petticoat, don't you think?" Miss Elizabeth asked Billy.

The subtle curve of Reaver's smile hid pure wickedness. That faint slant to Reaver's sweet mouth made Billy want to kiss him and smack it clear off his face at the same time. It lit something up in her the way the fingers between her legs didn't.

"The lady never got a chance to see it on you, my dear," he said.

"You," Billy said sharply, giving Miss Elizabeth a light slap on the thigh, "git." As soon as the woman rolled off her, Billy scooted out of the bed. Her lip peeled back from her teeth and she rounded an accusatory finger at Reaver. "And you, Rowland Kelley, I might be a woman, but I ain't ever been a lady in my whole goddamn life."

"Didn't mean anything by it, Billy," Reaver insisted, a bit of pleading in his tone as she picked up her trousers off the floor. If she found herself appreciating how he looked out on the trail with the early morning sun soft on his face, the tender cast of his gaze here in the lateness of the hour hooked her like a fish. Threatened to gut her and leave all her tender insides exposed. Reaver was gentle in ways she'd never felt, and she didn't fight the tug when he caught her wrist and held it in the loose trap of his fingers.

"Wasn't planning on leaving," Billy said, shaking off Reaver's grip to dig a dollar of her winnings out of a pocket. She extended her arm to offer the bill to Miss Elizabeth. "For the petticoat. If you don't mind parting ways."

"Don't mind at all," she said, taking it and tucking it beneath the underside of one heavy breast. She swirled a shawl around her shoulders. "Especially considering your fella there already paid me for it."

Billy's mouth tugged toward a wry smile. "For warming me up, then," she said, and ordered Reaver to the bed with a nod. "And putting up with whatever nonsense this fool laid on you earlier."

"Only a fool on account of riding with a woman who'd just as soon blow up a bridge as cross it," Reaver crowed, not even bothering to tug off his boots before he tumbled into the middle of the bed with a merry laugh. He was back to seeming like a cat, sprawling and taking up more room than a man his size ought, his slender limbs askew and his cock already stiff as a flagpole beneath the skirt.

"Lord, you're that Billy," Miss Elizabeth gasped, voice gone breathy, pitched somewhere between reverence and terror. "You're Dynamite Billy Bowles."

"I am indeed, and I think you've worn out your welcome," Billy said, ignoring the woman to crawl back into the bed and put a hand to Reaver's chin. His pulse fluttered under her touch and his cock leapt, bobbing wildly before she caught it in her other hand.

He tipped his head back, lashes going heavy over those pretty eyes of his. Weren't much different than when they'd met, when it'd been a Peacemaker tucked up under his jaw and his balls in her grip.

But whatever this was, it was new. Thrilling. It was like lighting a fuse and watching the flame sputter and spark.

Lust hit her with a ruthlessness that snatched the air from her lungs. Billy had never disliked sex, and maybe it was not wanting a baby in her belly that kept it out of mind most days, or maybe it was just she didn't get randy in the same way as other folks. She'd generally had an agreeable time with anyone she sought to bed, and Reaver was a cut above the rest—he'd never left her finishing herself off after unless that's what she wanted. He'd also never asked her for anything in the way he was now, his mouth gone slack and a moan spilling out of him when her grip turned unforgiving.

The skirts, she thought, didn't have anything to do with how he saw himself no more than her own pile of clothes on the floor there did. It was a lace-trimmed invitation custom for her. Maybe she hadn't been the only one putting an ear to the ground trying to understand the rumblings passed between them. She thumbed the head of his cock through the cotton, the edge of her nail making him swell in the cage of her fingers.

For all his faults, Reaver wasn't a man that she'd ever thought of as *weak*—never on a job and never after, when he was keyed up and hauling down her britches to fuck into her with hard, slapping thrusts—but here he was making himself into something soft for her. He melted into the mattress when she shoved his head back and pushed fingers into his warm mouth, and his trailing touch raised gooseflesh as he caressed her flank with the same gentleness of his curling tongue.

Billy was wetter than she'd ever been when she pulled her fingers out of Reaver's mouth and wiped them across his fat bottom lip. A slap to the cheek stretched his face into a broad grin, and pins and needles crept up her limbs as she inched up the petticoat to bare Reaver's cock. The shape of it was as pretty as the rest of him. A drop of eagerness pearled at the slit. She threw a leg over his narrow hips to set herself down on him and his grin faded—lost like water spilled to sand—as she took him inside her.

Above the line of his beard a stain had risen on his skin from the slap and she couldn't help but admire it. He pinkened further under the attention and the line of his teeth closed on his lip as their bodies slotted together. Reaver always fitted so nicely in her cunt, yet it was the flutter of his lashes, she found, that made her ache beautifully at the peak of her thighs.

She leaned forward, driving the heels of her hands into his shoulders, and the way he arched under her broke her usual silence and tore a groan out of her throat. He fought her hold briefly, not to get away but to get her pushing harder. She reared back and struck like a coyote taking out a rattler, quick and fast—shoved him down and pinned him while she panted for breath. Dizzied, Billy showed teeth, the whole of her straining at the seams.

Beneath her, Reaver took to looking at Billy like she was something truly wondrous to behold, and maybe she ought to have seen this coming. She should've caught the significance of those fleeting moments before the sun came over the range, when they were saddling up, breath hanging in the air, and making conversation with only glances as the coyotes cried to one another.

That wordless exchange between them was different now she was finally listening. Reaver's silent begging was a river rushing into her. It filled her to overflowing, drove her to curl her fingers to claws in the meat of his shoulders and rock atop him, knees and cunt clenching.

If his need was a river, hers was the leading edge of a brushfire. Her thighs quivered as it crept across her skin, consuming her inch by inch until she was raging with it. She ground the tender fullness of her clit against the flat of his belly until her world narrowed down, filtering out the sound of carousing coming up through the floorboards, ignoring the lick of a breeze seeping in through the open window, forgetting everything beyond the space of where her body met Reaver's.

Their skin grew slick with sweat, the smell of sex rising thick between them. Billy hardly noticed. All she cared about was where

Reaver stayed pliant beneath the hard press of her hands and the needy throb she fucked against him.

Her hips moved with a rhythm more suited to a quick rut in an alley than a night in a room with a comfortable bed bought and paid for, but she couldn't slow down. Never had been able to once she got going. Reaver was better at thinking things through, but Billy was just like her namesake, and sometimes the fuse was shorter than it ought to be.

"Billy—"

She clapped a hand over his mouth, smothered the warning that he was going to spill inside her, and flattened the whole of her body atop his. The heat of his breath seeped between her fingers, words lost to a needful groan as she fucked harder against him. Her tits dragged over the little patches of hair on his chest and she could feel his nipples small and tight, straining like hers. His hands were wide on her bottom, fingers cradling her. She was so damn close . . .

Gasping and desperate, Billy fit her hand beneath Reaver's jaw again, forced his head to the side to seal her mouth to his throat and raise a mark near where his pulse ran jackrabbit fast. He bucked, shuddering and plaintive, when she reached down between them with her other hand, pushed past the press of their bellies to where there was no friction to be found. Where she was taut and tingling and the mix of her slickness and his seed spread from the juicy, well-fucked heat of her cunt.

A little flicker was all she needed, the match alight and sizzling. Her body seized up as she scraped her teeth down the slope of Reaver's neck, triumphant. The pleasure seared white-hot. Phosphorous. Burned and flared out quicker than it rightfully should— as it always did—left her breathless and shaky as she fell into the space beside him, all too aware of the mess and the sweat on her skin.

For Reaver, the glow lingered, as glassy-eyed as if he'd downed a bottle of bourbon when he turned and lipped at her shoulder. "I think I'm in love with you, Billy Bowles," he murmured dreamily. He dropped kisses on a wandering path down her body, stopping here and there to glance up at her and gauge her interest. "Have been for months now."

"You fall in love at the drop of a hat, you scoundrel," she muttered. Still, she gathered up a handful of his hair and moved him to where he clearly aimed to go. He made himself newly comfortable between her legs and began to lick her clean with wide laps of his tongue. Wasn't the first time she'd found that he didn't mind the taste of himself—the opposite maybe—as he pushed his tongue as deep into her as he could. He licked into her until she was restless again, then fucked her to trembling a second time with the curve of his fingers hard inside her and his lips sealed and sucking at her clit.

When she was done with him, he wiped his face and pillowed his head on her thigh. "Some truths aren't mutually exclusive," he pointed out.

It took Billy a moment to recall what he'd been on about.

"I ain't the marrying type," she reminded him. Tenderly, she picked out the tangles she'd left in his hair.

He twisted to look at her. After a moment, he moved to lay beside her again and pull her into his arms. "No, you ain't. Neither of us are."

Downstairs at the card table, she'd been certain she'd win big if she stayed. But what about this thing she and Reaver had? The quiet understanding that went beyond pulling a job to moments like this. When he wasn't boozing and she wasn't spitting angry. *As soon as blow up a bridge as cross it,* he'd said of her, and she'd certainly done plenty of that when it came to getting close to folk.

"Might tear you to shreds we go on like this," she said. Her nails were bit down nearly to the beds, but she could still raise rows across his chest. She did it now, lines of white blossoming to a fiery red as she watched.

"Surely might," he agreed, breath sucked in through his teeth. He only held her tighter.

PUZZLE

Gabrielle Johnson

If Kerri's phone didn't implode before her brain, the evening could be considered a success.

Two bridesmaids were already late and they were giving her shit excuses about it. Her sister's fiancé kept texting to ask if his bride-to-be was having a good time at her bachelorette party.

And her study group chat was blowing up. Kerri had assumed that getting in a group with uptight Melissa and nerdy Mark would result in excellent notes. If she was going to be the only Black girl in her law school cohort, she could at least have the benefit of someone else's obsessive need to succeed. At least they would have that in common.

She hadn't banked on Melissa's wanting to be in constant contact, or her insistence on a Friday night study group. Yeah, if Kerri could have chosen when to schedule her sister's bachelorette party, it would not have been the weekend before one of her biggest exams. Candace was just this side of becoming a bridezilla and there was *no* changing the date of the party. This was unsatisfactory to Melissa. She wanted to know why neither she or Mark could make the emergency study session that night.

On the one hand, Kerri kind of understood that: Mark's socials were full of him doing puzzles, binging documentaries, and making delicious-looking Thai food from his grandmother's recipes. Kerri also liked puzzles, documentaries, and Thai food. But, those things, plus his quiet demeanor, didn't really make him seem like a contender for wild and busy Friday nights.

The thought of him made her take another sip of wine. Some divine entity sure had gotten its wires crossed about Mark though: tall and broad with dark hair and a gem-cutting jawline. He should have been a model, not a dorky soon-to-be-lawyer who whipped out words like *preposterous* and *multitudinous* in everyday conversation. And in a deep voice that made her middle tighten when she thought about it too long.

They'd gotten along right away. She'd found any other people of color as fast as she could, and he had immediately put her at ease. His quick, brief smiles and serious approach to his work made them fast friends. *Only* friends. Her eyes certainly shouldn't have been wandering toward him during class. She definitely never ruminated on the way his forearms looked when he rolled up his sleeves. She really wasn't going to let herself think about how he never failed to make her laugh, with that dry humor of his.

He was as silent in the group chat as she was, leading to a string of increasingly demanding texts from Melissa. Being in party planning mode meant her phone was attached to her palm. It did not mean she had to listen to her classmates all night.

Besides, she needed the break from being herself. From being the good middle sister with the color-coded grocery lists and sensible shoes. She'd poured her extremely generous curves into a short dress, donned a pair of sky-high heels, and committed to having *fun*.

As she poured another glass of wine, her younger sister, Dinah, danced into the room to pour a round of shots.

"Are you going to come back to the party?" Dinah asked.

"I'm trying," Kerri said. "I was texting Harmony and—"

Before she could finish, she heard a loud pounding on the door, followed by *commotion*. She frowned as Dinah grinned. Music straight out of a 1970s porno blared over her curated playlist.

"Strippers?" Kerri screeched. She turned to her sister, who was twerking with unbridled excitement. "We said no strippers."

Dinah paused, ass in the air. "Girl, *you* said no strippers."

Fury on four-inch heels, Kerri strode into the living room, and the next few seconds seemed to take eons to pass.

There were two men in the midst of their women-only soiree.

One of them was a tall Black man who had no right to be so muscled or have a smile so bright. The other had his back to her, as he shook his pelvis in her sister's squealing face. That was a good back. Bronze and rippling with muscles in a way that made her suck her bottom lip into her mouth. He had dimples right above the waistband of his had-to-be-tearaway pants. The ass inside those pants filled them out like a dream. Sculptor's fantasy. It dropped low a couple of times before the man turned to yank those pants off.

It wasn't possible.

Mark.

Her Mark.

Mark of the study group and the puzzles and chess documentaries.

She skittered to a stop because *her Mark* was gyrating in her sister's living room.

Kerri yelped and clapped her hands to her face. Everyone, strippers included, turned to look at her. Kerri watched as half a dozen things slid across Mark's face. Surprise, worry, fear. Then, something else. Something almost sly.

Then, like it never happened, the moment passed and he

turned away from her. His hips kept moving, and most of the party resumed yelling and clapping. Kerri turned and ran smack into Dinah and a tray of neon pink shot glasses.

A quart of tequila promptly soaked through the front of her dress.

That was it. A bra full of tequila was finally, officially, too much. She had to get out of there. Right away. Kerri cast a glance back over her shoulder and saw Mark looking at her. He winced, so clearly sympathetic that her cheeks went red-hot. Oh, good. She'd never be able to look him in those beautiful brown eyes again.

Kerri spent the rest of the bachelorette party and the Saturday afterward trying desperately not to think about Mark. Or that look on his face. She spent the Sunday afterward with her vibrator and every memory she could recall. The way light bounced off of his oiled chest. The way his hips moved and dipped and reminded her of all the other ways rhythm could be useful. She just had to get it out of her system. After that, he could go back to the box in her mind that was adorably nerdy hobbies and ten-dollar words.

That Monday, she was back to normal. Back to her prim pencil skirts and yanking her tightly coiled curls into a bun instead of her wild weekend 'fro. She let work at the legal clinic distract her (almost) completely. By the time she decided to blow off her Legal Ethics lecture, she felt downright dignified. Obviously, avoiding him was the best choice. The responsible choice.

Even if it was, it was the first time she'd ever skipped class. Ever. And guilt tied her stomach into knots. To soothe herself, she dedicated the extra time to reading ahead for the next class. Twenty minutes after Legal Ethics would have ended, a knock sounded at the door.

With a sinking stomach, Kerri slid her shoes back on and moved to glance out the peephole. She found Mark leaning down to peer back at her.

"I know you're in there. I heard you walking around."

"Creepy," Kerri said, cracking the door an inch.

Mark stood on the other side, holding a giant iced coffee aloft. "Can I come in? Please?"

Taking a fortifying breath, she swung the door open wide, and let him step inside.

It was strange to know how perfect and delicious his body was underneath that button-up and those preppy boy khakis. He shoved the coffee into her hand and she took a long sip. Caramel.

"So," Mark said, hands in his pockets. "Let's talk."

Kerri found a coaster so she could put the coffee down. "Do we have to?"

Mark wheeled on her, flinty-eyed. "Okay, yes, Friday was weird. That doesn't matter. You're my friend. And more importantly, you're going to be a phenomenal lawyer one day, so you can't skip any more class. If it's really too strange, we don't have to hang out anymore."

Kerri blinked at him. "You think I'm going to be a phenomenal lawyer?"

His expression was solemn. "Tremendous. Remarkable. Superlative, even."

"Thanks. Mr. Thesaurus."

He gave her a little smirk. He was standing there, in his normal, everyday clothes, acting like his normal, everyday self. As though the world hadn't turned upside down.

"So, stripping, huh?" she said.

Mark held up a fist, lifting his fingers as he went. "It's good pay, it doesn't take too many hours, and I make rent every month." She opened her mouth, but he cut in. "I had no idea this was your sister's party before I took the gig. I probably wouldn't have if I'd had any clue."

"Probably?"

"Your sister and her friends are *generous*."

They both laughed. In the past seventy-two hours, she had been so tangled up, she'd almost forgotten how much she liked to joke with him.

"Plus," he said, "it helps me tap into a different part of myself. Sexy Mark."

Kerri rolled her eyes. "Please. You're always sexy Mark."

He gazed at her, eyebrow raised. "To you?"

Her heart went too fast, and she heard blood rushing in her ears. "Yeah, to me."

Mark took a step forward so, for some reason, she took a step back. That step was all it took. For the air between them to change. To get heavy and warm. "What makes you feel like sexy Kerri?"

She swallowed. He dared to ask her that question, in that molasses-slow baritone. His eyes so dark and lovely. It was so unfair. It compelled her toward the truth, even if she wanted to hold it in.

"The way you're looking at me right now."

He nodded, seriously. They did that dance once more: a step forward, a step back.

"What else?"

"That dress I had on Friday night."

Mark grinned. "That was a good dress. I didn't know you wore things like that. Or your hair like that. Or jewelry that big. You're full of surprises."

She snorted as they edged their way down the hall. "Me? You're the one with the sexy side hustle."

"You got something against the profession?"

"No," Kerri said, which was true. "It just caught me off guard."

They had finally backed their way to the doorway of her bedroom. Of course. She'd been a fool to think she could pack this away. This thing between them had been lingering, waiting. That night had only been the spark. The explosion was rushing toward her. It was in the heat of his eyes. The way his hands hovered near her, close enough to touch. The way his chest rose and fell, a mirror to her own quickening breath.

He lifted his hand, stroking a thumb over her cheek. The second she went to lean into his touch, he slid deft, teasing fingertips down the side of her neck. That touch burned her *everywhere*.

"If you want me to go, say the word," he said, quietly. "I won't treat you differently. But I want to stay, Kerri. Because your bed is right there and your lips are right here and I want to finally—"

She rushed in and kissed him, straining so high on her tiptoes that her heels lifted right out of her shoes. He yanked her to him with a graceless need that made her kiss him harder. Her hands fisted in his shirt, pulling it loose from the waistband of his pants. She only came away when the choices were to kiss him or breathe. Even then, they stayed so close that when she spoke, their lips brushed.

"Stay."

They stumbled together toward the bed, a flurry of kisses and wanting hands. Kerri was too desperate to bother with artful seduction. They fell to the bed together, Mark on his back and Kerri on top of him. She sat up, her skirt pulled taut over her thighs, as she spread her knees on either side of his hips.

Mark's palms felt like the best sort of burn as he eased his hands up the length of her thighs, bunching her skirt until he held two fistfuls of fabric. He used it to yank her down, bringing the hot, damp vee between her legs against the hard bulge in his pants.

"I haven't done this in years," he said, hissing as she took control and rode him through his pants.

"Sex?"

"Dry-humping."

He pushed her skirt up until it was a belt around her waist. He squeezed her bare ass in his hands. His gaze darted up to hers.

"Thongs? You've been wearing thongs underneath these skirts all this time?"

Kerri chuckled, even as his fingers brushed between the apex of her thighs, choking that sound right off. "Sometimes."

She whipped her shirt off without any fanfare, but his gaze lingered.

"Black lace," he croaked. "It matches your thong. You're a matchy-matchy kind of girl." Under his breath: "Of course you're a matchy-matchy kind of girl."

"Mark, two things?"

"Yeah?" he replied, clearly distracted as he reached around to undo her bra.

"Never say the words 'matchy-matchy' again, and please hurry up and get your dick out."

He sniggered, as her bra popped open and her tits spilled out of it. They both paused and then he hurriedly undid his pants. When that was done, she helped him out of his shirt and the T-shirt underneath.

She smoothed her hands over his chest, down his stomach. His muscles tensed under her fingers. "This is a little bit weird. The last time I saw you shirtless, you had your dick in my sister's face."

Mark tsked. "Yeah, but that was a work thing."

She snorted as he pulled a condom out of his pocket.

"Wow," Kerri said, "someone came prepared."

A faint red on his cheeks broke through the warm golden tones of his skin. His mouth was open, but whatever he planned to say died on his lips as she snatched the condom from his hands. She reached into his pants to stroke the aforementioned dick.

"Mark, oh my God, who *knew*?"

She pulled him free and rolled the condom on. He twitched in her hand with such fervent, undisguisable desire, a shiver ran through her.

Now.

Now.

It had to be now. Kerri unceremoniously tugged her thong to one side. Her first real relationship had taught her to let go of the qualms she had about being a plus-size girl and getting on top. She loved the way she could control the angle and set the pace. She loved the way she could watch Mark's lids go heavy and his eyes all dreamy when she sank down those first lovely, agonizing inches.

He palmed her breast in one hand, flesh spilling out around his fingers. He brushed a thumb over her nipple and Kerri jerked.

"They're sensitive," he said. She nodded and gave another roll of her hips, adjusting to the thickness inside her. "Good sensitive or bad sensitive?"

"Good," she said, and moved more insistently. "Really good."

He worried her nipple until it felt impossibly hard under his attention. Mark held her gaze with his own as he gave it a quick gentle pinch that had her moaning, taking him as deep as he could go. He pinched it again, with sharp, unmitigated pressure. The flush of pleasure through her was superfluous. She was already wet. She was already so wet. Even so, the bloom of pain twined with that building feeling behind her belly button and between her legs.

"*Mark.*"

"You like that," he said, and sounded more curious than smug.

She nodded and leaned forward, a wordless plea. He lifted his head until they met. His tongue swept out and lapped at her abraded nipple. He gave the other one a rough tug that scrambled any remaining thought she had. There was only the thrust of him inside her, the way she worked him deep. The way he sucked and laved and *bit* at her.

Mark lifted his head for a moment, but she pushed it back to her breast, and he laughed with her nipple in his mouth. It was that moment. That perfect blend of the man she knew and whatever mysterious man this was in her bed. She came. Hard. With sweat and clenched teeth and fingernails dug into his shoulders.

Trembling, she couldn't even put up a fight as he rolled them over and drove into her. Another fresh pulse of arousal blew through her as she watched his powerful body move above her. Hips in that rhythm she'd glimpsed at the bachelorette party.

She shifted and spread her legs to make more space for him. He made a rough, ragged noise as she grabbed his ass, pulling him deeper as he dipped his hips in a grind that bumped her clit with each pass. He dropped his hand between their bodies, to touch that sensitive place with practiced fingers.

His voice was barely above a whisper. "Let me feel you. Please, Ker."

Mark pinched her clit. Not with anywhere near his earlier roughness, but it was enough. She was so slick, that edge of pain exactly what she needed and she came, with a whimper she buried behind her hand.

Mark let out a swear and that was all the warning she got before he came too, folding over her, face pressed into the bend of her neck. Kerri held him close as her heartbeat calmed. Even as her rational mind came back to her, she found that she wouldn't have done anything differently. That both Friday night Kerri and Monday afternoon Kerri were equally pleased.

With a kiss to her shoulder, Mark left to find the bathroom and dispose of the condom. When he returned, he crawled into bed next to her. He smiled one of those blink-and-you'll-miss-it smiles before he slung an arm around her waist and let his eyes droop closed.

"We're not napping in the middle of the day kind of people," Kerri said, yawning, closing her eyes too.

"Today, we're napping in the middle of the day people."

They dozed, and had sex a second time. Slower, but needier still. After that, they napped more, until Kerri snatched awake, picking up her phone.

"Shit, we're going to be late for study group. Melissa will kill us both."

Or worse, stop sharing her notes. Exchanging glances, they leapt out of bed and began scrambling back into their clothes.

"I know this isn't the time," Mark said, hopping into his pants, "but I don't want this to be some amorphous . . . *thing* that's happened between us. You know I hate games. I'm into you. For more than sex. I'd like to take you on an actual date."

Kerri gave him an arch look as she started doing up her shirt. "What are you doing on Saturday?"

"Taking you out?"

"Well, I don't exactly have a date for Candace's wedding yet. And she's already pretty fond of you."

Oh, she really loved making him laugh. She picked up his wallet, where it had fallen open and out of his pants, after the second time. She glanced briefly at his license and her eyes went wide.

"You're licensed to ride a *motorcycle?*"

He gave her a sheepish nod. "We're going to be late. I'll tell you about it on the way."

Kerri shook her head, smiling in amusement. Clearly, there were many new discoveries about Mark to make.

She couldn't wait.

'OHANA

Lucy Eden

A warm, rough tongue passes over my palm. I open my eyes and squint in the moonlight that passes through our bedroom window. A huge lion stares back at me from the side of the bed.

I can tell it's Pete because his mane is shorter and darker and he doesn't have a scar over his eye like Jake. I also know it's Pete because he always greets me when he comes in for the night. I don't know if it's because he misses me while he does whatever he and Jake do as lions in the cover of darkness. Maybe, it's because he senses that I worry about them and he can't wait to let me know that they're safe. Whatever the reason, it's my favorite part of the day.

When I first met my lions, our connection was strong and instant but Jake was the only one who accepted it right away. Pete and I took some time to come around to the idea. He didn't like the idea of having a human for a mate and I didn't think I could handle living in Hawaii. Aside from the salty air and humidity wreaking havoc on my 3C hair, I was leaving my friends, family and my entire life behind in New York. But once we finally came together—pun intended—life with my two boys has been perfect. It's true when they say you can't escape fate and with fated mates like Jacob Palakiko and Peter Kahananui, I'll never want to. After years of running from love and almost giving up on my soulmates when they found me, I'm finally in the place where I belong, between my lions.

"Hey, handsome," I whisper and scoot closer to the edge of the mattress so I can run my hand over his muzzle and scratch behind his ear. "Did you have a good night? I can't wait to hear about it."

He rubs his warm wet nose into my palm and licks me again, which I take as a *yes* before he turns and moves toward our bathroom, swishing his tail contentedly. The shower is already running which means Jake is in there, fully returned to manhood, possibly washing off blood from a fresh kill. I wonder if it was a feral hog or a deer, but I suppose he'll tell me later.

Their deep voices carry out of the bathroom door, which they've left open as an invitation because I'm sure Pete has told Jake that I'm awake. Usually, I wouldn't pass up this opportunity but today my boys took me to The Big Island and we spent the day hiking mountain trails. The sights were so beautiful that I could weep but despite being a New York City girl who usually spent most of her day walking, I was completely unprepared for how sore hours of trekking up and down dormant volcanoes would make me. They took turns massaging my aching muscles on the plane ride back to Oʻahu. Once we were home, they took turns massaging me in other places until I drifted off to sleep.

I hug my pillow and listen to their muffled voices and laughter wearing a lazy smile. I imagine Jake using a giant sponge to massage Pete's back, pressing his brand of rough kisses on his shoulder. I imagine Pete threading his fingers through Jake's long dark hair, rubbing shampoo into his scalp while lovingly gazing into his dark brown eyes. The temptation to creep into the shower is becoming unbearable when I hear the water stop. My boys fill the doorway, with dark, golden brown glistening skin, all bulk and sinewy muscle covered with a light sheen from the water.

Pete has a towel wrapped around his waist, showing off the tattoo that covers his entire left arm and half of his chest. Jake is completely nude except for the towel wrapped around his head in a makeshift turban. He knows it makes me laugh and I giggle as they stalk towards me, Pete's muscles flexing and rippling; Jake's long, hard cock bobbing with every step that brought them closer to home, closer to me.

They crawl on either side of me, smelling like soap and mint. Four strong arms cage me in, locking me into an embrace you would think is reserved for lovers reuniting after a long journey, but this is the way they hold me every night after they come home from prowling the night as lions, my lions. My lovers, protectors, best friends, and fated mates.

"Hey, beautiful," Jake whispers and plants a kiss on my neck. "How are you feeling?"

"Tired." I punctuate the word with a small yawn. "And still sore from hiking."

"So, we'll let you get your rest." Pete presses a kiss to my shoulder. "Right, Jake?" He shoots a stern, pointed look at our mate, which Jake ignores.

"Is that what you want, Dawn?" Jake's brown eyes bore into mine with a mischievous glint. The muscles between my thighs tighten and my belly flutters.

Sleep is the last thing I want.

I shake my head. He kisses me and says, "I think Pete needs a little convincing."

It doesn't take much, because when I reach under the towel around Pete's waist I find a rod of velvety steel. I squeeze and stroke him as he finds my mouth with his and slides his tongue over mine in a soft, hungry kiss.

"You're such a greedy girl, aren't you?" Pete whispers when our lips separate and I nod. "You're lucky there are two of us. I don't think one of us would be enough for you." He shoots a look at Jake, who has pulled off his towel turban before pressing kisses and licks on my spine making me shiver.

"Definitely not," Jake whispers, "but there isn't anyone else I would want to share her with." He pushes me onto my back and slides a hand over my belly to lock hands with Pete as they move in unison down my naked body, teasing, tasting, and kissing. Two heads jockey for position between my legs as my thighs are spread and hoisted onto muscular shoulders. The hands interlocked on my belly hold me in place as I squirm, squeal, and dig my heels into the backs of my lovers. I'm overwhelmed with sensation and ecstasy as I'm being licked, kissed, and nibbled past the point of sanity. My hands shoot between my legs to palm Pete's bald head and tangle my fingers in Jake's damp and messy brown locks with highlighted golden strands kissed by a lifetime of living in the sun.

Two fingers find their way into my pulsing, clenching pussy and a probing digit replaces the tongue lavishing the tight pucker of my ass. Pete and Jake take breaks from kissing me to kiss each other in a sexy chorus of ravenous slurps, growls, and groans. I want to prop myself up on my elbows to watch but I can't coordinate my limbs to make the necessary movements.

Every single one of my senses is on high alert and inflamed, pushed past the point of reason. I can smell the scent of my arousal, mingled with sweat and the lingering floral smell of the shower. Every nerve ending in my body is ringing with sensation. The messy wet sloshing sound of Jake and Pete working between my legs is ringing in my ears, mingled with my own desperate whimpers and grunts. I can taste their lingering kisses, but I can't see them.

I need to see them.

After somehow summoning the focus and strength to pull my elbows underneath my body, I peek between my thighs.

The sight reminds me of a *National Geographic* documentary. Two lions working on devouring a freshly caught prey, and that's exactly what it is, but instead of an antelope, it's me. It's the sexiest fucking thing I've ever seen and I'll never get tired of it. I suck my bottom lip and bite down trying to stifle a loud moan. It doesn't work.

Jake notices me first. He pauses for a second, which is how I know it's his thick finger twisting and probing the tight bud of my asshole. He grins with his mustache and beard covered in the glistening evidence of my desire for them. Pete picks up his head next and they're both gazing at me, smiling.

"She's watching us," Pete whispers to Jake, loud enough for me to hear while never taking his eyes from mine.

"Do you think she likes what she sees?" He grins, also watching me like I was prey. I love it when they do this. They talk about me like I'm not a sentient being, I'm just a vessel for pleasure and my pleasure belongs only to them.

"Should we show her more?" Pete raises an eyebrow and glances at Jake.

"Yes," I breathe out in a desperate whisper. "Yes, you should." The fingers filling my cunt curl in response. A moan tears itself from my chest.

"So greedy." Jake shakes his head and clucks his tongue before lowering his mouth to my core, covering the sensitive fleshy pearl between my thighs with his lips and gently sucking. My hips buck against the strong hands holding me into place on the bed. My elbows fly out from under me and I flop backward onto the mattress, drowning in waves of ecstasy and endorphins as a giant orgasm hits me like a truck. Their fingers and hands vacate my body, making me feel empty and weightless. I feel like I can float but I don't. Instead I giggle as a heady rush of euphoria washes over me.

Jake and Pete rejoin me in the bed and are holding me again.

"Has our little flower had enough?" Pete asks, adjusting the knot in my headscarf so he can kiss my sweaty forehead.

"No," I shake my head. "Not even close." I roll over onto my stomach and crawl between my gentle giant's legs. I pull my knees underneath my body and raise my ass in the air as an invitation to Jake.

"Fuck, Dawn," Pete hisses as I grip his length and stroke up and down before running the tip of my tongue along the thick crown of his cock.

"Yes, little flower." Jake is smoothing a palm over one round globe of my ass as he watches Pete's dick disappear and reappear into my mouth. "I'm gonna fuck you while I watch you make our mate feel good. Would you like that?"

"Yes," I moan. "Please, fuck me. Please." The dripping slit of my cunt is hoisted in the air, pulsating, achingly empty and desperate to be filled.

Jake doesn't make me wait long before wrapping his huge hands around my waist and filling me with one smooth motion. I grunt in shock and pleasure, humming as my head bobs between Pete's legs.

"Yes, little flower," he moans. "Shit. Your mouth feels so good. So fucking good."

"You should feel her pussy, Pete." Jake's voice is husky with need as he fucks me slowly, feeling me stretch and tighten around his cock. "How does that feel, little flower?"

"Mmmm," I moan around Pete and I feel his muscles clench. It's too soon and I'm nowhere near to being done with him.

"No, not yet, baby," I pant when I pull away. "I need to feel you. I need to feel both of you."

I look over my shoulder at Jake who gives himself one more deep stroke in my pussy before he withdraws and leaves the bed.

I'm sleepy, sore, and sensitive but so far from sated. I crawl into Pete's lap and straddle him, wrapping my arms around his neck. I lean down and plant a kiss on the large black paw print tattooed over his heart and run my tongue along the four raised claw marks etched into his skin, Jake's mark.

"Hi," I whisper when I pick up my head and brush my lips over his.

"Hi," he answers before sucking my bottom lip between his teeth and biting down. I make a mewling noise like a cat and roll my hips back and forth, sliding his erection between the swollen lips of my pussy, desperate for the pressure and friction against my clit as we wait for our third to complete us.

"I love you, Dawn," he whispers.

"I love you too, Dawn." The mattress dips as Jake walks over to us on his knees and settles behind me on the bed.

"And I love you. Both of you. More than I ever thought was possible." I feel tears stinging my eyes before Pete leans forward to kiss them away.

"Finding you was the best thing that ever happened to us." He sighs and traces his long-healed bite mark on my shoulder with his tongue and lips.

"I'm glad you're finally admitting it," Jake chuckles.

Pete narrows his eyes at our mate and Jake responds with a wink and a soft chuckle.

"Are you ready for us, sweetheart?" Jake whispers to me before planting a kiss on the bite mark he gave me on the opposite shoulder.

"Always." I smile at him over my shoulder and he rewards me with a sloppy, desperate kiss.

"You're up, Pete." Jake squeezes lube onto my lower back, making me flinch from the chill. "Sorry, babe." He drags a slick finger down the seam of my backside and begins to massage the puckered opening again. I scoot forward on my knees and rise, preparing to impale myself on Pete.

"Ugngh," he hisses as I raise and lower myself onto his hips. "So good, little flower. So good."

Jake is now working two fingers in and out of my ass as I whimper and moan.

"Jake, hurry, she feels too good," Pete groans.

"I know." He leans forward and plants a kiss on my back. "Relax, beautiful. It's going to feel like heaven when we're both inside you."

"It always does." I lean forward and press my weight onto Pete's chest, letting him support me. I'm even more exhausted than before.

I don't want to move.

I don't want to think.

I only want to feel.

I want to be dragged screaming and moaning into the mind-blowing orgasms only my lions can give me.

I suck in a deep breath and release it slowly as I feel Jake press into the part of me his fingers just vacated with a burst of sweet pain followed by a sweet release of hormonal pleasure that makes me shudder.

"Oh, my god," I murmur into Pete's chest. "Oh, my god."

"How do you feel, baby? Talk to us."

"P . . . p . . . perfect," is all I can say. I relax and feel boneless as Jake pumps into me from above and Pete from below. I don't know if minutes or hours pass before I feel the first climax roll over me. It's quickly followed by another and another. I'm squealing and shuddering while being crushed between them. The clamping and rippling of my muscles sets off a chain reaction. Jake grips my hips and pushes himself into me until he clenches and spends his release into my channel, his loud growls filling our bedroom.

He pulls out and flops onto the bed, his chest heaving. Pete rolls me onto my back and pushes into my swollen cunt again. His pupils are wide and dark, limned with golden brown irises, remnants of his lion bubbling beneath the surface. His pace quickens and the power of his thrusts increase. It hurts so much but it feels so good and though I didn't think it was possible, I'm coming again and again. My eyes are squeezed shut and I feel tears rolling down the sides of face.

"You're so beautiful like this, little flower," Jake whispers. I open my eyes to find my face inches from his. He begins to stroke my cheek as Pete climaxes above me.

"Jesus fucking Christ," he pants on the other side of me. "You're going to be the death of me, Dawn."

"I could think of worse ways to go." Jake yawns and kisses my shoulder before he climbs out of bed.

"Stay put, gorgeous. Do you want something for the pain?" Pete asks. I nod before he kisses my nose and follows Jake into the bathroom, giving him a sharp slap on his sculpted ass. The bathroom door is left open again but there is no way I'm leaving this bed. I'm not really sure if I can.

They return after a few minutes, again smelling of soap and mint. Pete is carrying a washcloth and Jake is holding a glass of water and a bottle of Tylenol. I usually take Advil but I assume it will have the same effect on my sore limbs and aching sex.

I drink the water and swallow the pain relievers while Pete kneels between my legs, cleaning me and inspecting me for damage. When he's satisfied, he climbs into bed where Jake has already folded me in his arms and I'm drifting off to sleep.

"Hey," I say sleepily. "Why did you give me Tylenol instead of Advil?"

"Because you can't have Advil anymore." Jake is wearing his trademarked sexy, silly grin and it confuses me.

"What? Why not?" I furrow my brow and blink, trying very hard to stay awake and focus. I would remember if I'd suddenly developed some weird allergy to ibuprofen.

"We've known for a couple of weeks, pretty girl. You smell different," Pete says.

"You definitely taste different," Jake adds with a yawn. "We were waiting for you to tell us."

"Tell you what?" I glance between their sleepy smiling faces.

"You're pregnant, Miss Washington." This is what Pete calls me when he wants to tease me about my sluggish wedding planning. We haven't even set a date.

"What?" I sit up. Strong arms settle me back down onto the mattress and cradle me. "Are you sure?"

"Yes. We definitely know what a pregnant female smells like. Now, go to sleep, gorgeous. We'll talk about it in the morning."

I'm pregnant.

It seems too incredible to be true, but it has to be. My lions have what my best friend Chellie jokingly calls "super shifter senses." She is married to a bear shifter, after all.

Jake and Pete can smell my every emotion. They're so accurate at predicting my period—there's always a pint of Mama Palakiko's homemade mango or lilikoi ice cream in the freezer two days before it starts—that I stopped keeping track.

I am really pregnant . . . with a lion shifter cub.

Pete and Jake and I will have a bond stronger than fate or love or lust.

"Jake?" I whisper.

"Yeah, babe?"

"What's the Hawaiian word for family again?"

"'Ohana," they whisper in unison and tighten their arms around my body.

"But you already knew that, gorgeous," Jake says with his lips pressed onto my shoulder.

"I did," I say in a sleepy giggle, "but I love hearing you say it."

"Not as much as we love hearing you say it," Pete grins at me and I can't help kissing him one last time before exhaustion takes me.

"'Ohana," I repeat before closing my eyes and drifting off, dreaming about lion cubs.

WHO IS LIKE YOU?

Sara Taylor Woods

"Tell your brother I say hi."

"What?"

"That's who you're texting, right?"

"Why would you assume that?"

"Because you're not texting me; I'm sitting right here. And if you're not texting me, it's Eitan."

"Shut up." Tirtzah swatted at me without even looking up from her phone.

I grinned, dodging her flailing arm. "I never will."

She rolled her eyes but couldn't quite bite back her smile. "You're exhausting."

"You're exhausting," I retorted. "So what's—"

She held one finger up: wait. Not the finger she usually showed me when I gave her a hard time.

I was happy to wait: she was sitting cross-legged at the opposite end of the couch from me, barefoot and in yoga pants and an oversized cropped T-shirt with the sleeves rolled up just shy of her shoulders. Her short hair was up in a tiny ponytail, a dark little floof at the crown of her head. She could never get it all up, not at that length, and the pieces that frustrated her by coming loose fascinated me, tracing the sharp lines of her cheekbones and jaw, making her neck look a thousand miles long.

Yeah, I was happy to wait.

After another minute, she put her phone facedown on the arm of the couch and turned to me. "Okay. So Eitan—shut *up*—is hosting Pesach this year. You're coming, right?"

"Sure," I said. "I'll put in my request for that night off."

"No." Tirtzah waved a hand between us, as if to erase my misunderstanding. "The whole week."

"Oh." I blinked. "Wow, that's—really gracious."

"So you're coming, right?"

Tirtzah and I had been close for years, but we'd never been to a Seder together. Her family usually went to one of those all-inclusive Pesach retreats, in Florida or Mexico or Arizona, and I ended up at synagogue-sponsored Seders, surrounded by strangers, trying not to make an ass of myself over four glasses of wine. "I'll have to see if I can get the whole week."

"If you can't, that's okay. But we'd love to have you."

"Is your whole family going to be there?"

She listed who was going to be there, ticking them off on her fingers, siblings and in-laws and nieces and nephews and grandparents, and *man*, that sounded nice. Surrounded by strangers, but not really. Not the same kind of strangers.

Still, I said, "I don't want to intrude."

Tirtzah got up on her knees and came close enough to take my face between her hands, locked her blue eyes on mine and said, very slowly, "He. Specifically. Invited. You. So cope."

I laughed and pulled away from her before she could feel how warm my face was. Because she was my best friend and her thigh was pressed against mine even though it didn't have to be and she was smiling big and bright and she was my *best friend* and I was just probably in love with her was all.

Six weeks later, Tirtzah and I were flying along I-77, windows down, Hayley Kiyoko up louder than the screaming wind. My hair was irreparable the minute we hit the interstate, but Tirtzah's got perfect mutant hair. I knew what would happen when we got out of the car: she'd shake her head and run her fingers through it and smile at me, and I'd die a little inside. Just like always.

(Then I'd pull my massive tangled bun down, try to make it wind-tousled and sexy but immediately give up and resecure it, and mutter about how I should just cut off all my hair like she did two years ago, and she'd say *no, no, Ev, I love your hair,* and sometimes she'd touch it, and smile at me, and, well. I'd die a little inside.)

When we pulled into the wide circular driveway, it was already half full of cars. And we were a day early.

"Are you sure there's enough room for everyone?"

She shut the car off and shook her head and ran her fingers through her hair and smiled at me (cue: me dying a little inside) and said, "Nope."

It was evening, and it was morning: the first day.

The bed we shared was too small and we slept back to back, spines curved toward each other like Pisces. I knew this because I woke up first, and because there was no way I could be in a bed with Tirtzah Spalter and *not* be aware of exactly where her body was at all times.

I listened to the house wake up around us (Tillie's delighted squeals down the hall; Raizel's boys wrestling downstairs with an indulgent uncle; the white noise of the shower next door; the clatter of dishes being put up) but didn't get out of bed. I edged my way onto my back and pillowed my head with my forearm so I wouldn't elbow Tirtzah awake. I lay still and watched the wind run its fingers through the trees and tried to think about anything besides Tirtzah's warmth so close to me.

And I was almost successful until she sighed and rolled over, pressing her shoulder into my ribcage and her cheek into my biceps, and focusing on anything else officially became a losing battle. Not when her hair was splashed across the pillow like paint and her pulse was thumping in the hollow of her throat.

Fuck I needed to get out of this bed.

Voices moved down the hallway, past our door, and I leapt up like I'd been caught doing something wrong. The still-steamy bathroom next to us was unoccupied, and when I got back to our room, Tirtzah was lying on her stomach, scrolling through her phone. She glanced over her shoulder at me when I opened the door, depriving me of the time to *really* look at her legs, at the parabolic curves of her ass and hamstrings and calves in those shorts (those shorts she slept in all night, *right next to me*, good lord).

"Morning," she said brightly, completely unaffected by her own legs.

"I didn't mean to wake you."

"You didn't. Eitan texted me."

I snorted. "You both know you're in the same house, right?"

"He didn't know you were awake," she said. "And he didn't care if I was."

"Were you?"

"After he texted, yes."

So I guess she slept through my breath catching when her bare skin brushed against mine. I guess she slept through that.

"Anyway," she said, rolling out of bed, "there's breakfast downstairs. So put on some clothes, you hussy."

Her shorts were around her ankles and I could see her striped panties before I could point my eyes anywhere else, and I could have sworn my entire face was on fire. I changed as quickly as I could and fled.

The whole downstairs was bustling, the kitchen noisy with the sound of chopping vegetables and already rich with the smell of roasting chicken. I retreated to the French doors that lead to the backyard, just trying to stay out of the way and hoping someone would take pity on me and bring me coffee. A bang on the glass behind me scared the hell out of me, and when I looked back there, Tirtzah's teenage brother Asher was staring at me.

He said something. About apples?

I squinted at him. "What?"

"Do you. Like. Apples?"

"Yeah, why?"

He slapped a Krispy Kreme napkin against the glass pane and said, "I got donuts; how d'you like them apples?"

I clapped one hand over my mouth like my laughter would upset someone, and Tirtzah appeared next to me murmuring, "*There* you are," and she grabbed my hand and tugged me out the door, onto the deck, to the table stacked high with Krispy Kreme boxes. All the kids were out there already, fingers and faces sticky with sugar glaze.

"You've got until 11:08," Eitan said through a mouthful of "Hot Now" glazed donut, then groaned. "Lord, how are these *real?*"

Tirtzah's grin was mischievous, infectious, as she waggled her eyebrows at me. "Better get on it," she said. "It looks like too much, but I can guarantee it won't be enough."

So I did. Family members filtered out one and two at a time, and we ate the donuts on the deck in the sun and the breeze and I couldn't remember the last time I'd felt so satisfied.

* * *

The thing about Seders is this: two glasses of wine in, half the table is drunk. I sat between Tirtzah and her brother Chaim, and she and I elbowed each other all night, only half by accident. We all stayed at the table long after the birkhat hamazon, the grace after meals, talking, laughing, swaying, and I was smiling so hard my cheeks hurt.

Tirtz and I tapped out at midnight. I couldn't stop watching her calves flex under the hem of her dress as we climbed the steps. When we reached the top, she glanced back at me with this shy smile, like she *knew*.

I'd spent a lot of time thinking about kissing Tirtzah Spalter, but nothing knocked the wind out of me like that little smile. That little smile made me want to pull her into our room and kick the door closed and kiss her and more than kiss her.

I didn't. We took our turns in the bathroom, and when I came back in, she was under the covers, the kosher lamp next to the bed throwing a soft glow across her face. It was just enough light to see her watch me walk across the room. To see her watch me get into bed.

We lay there, silently, my wine-soaked blood crashing through my veins. She twisted the shade on the lamp closed, leaving us in pitch darkness. The mattress shifted as she settled back in next to me but my eyes hadn't adjusted yet, so I didn't know if she'd turned her back to me or if she was facing me, lips parted, waiting for me to make the move that I've been wanting to make for— Gd—so *fucking* long.

"Ev." That one syllable, barely a breath, and no, she wasn't facing away from me. Her voice was so close, so still and small in the dark. "I didn't tell you before, but—you looked really good tonight."

I wanted to read into it, but I refused to. Friends compliment each other all the time. *We* compliment each other all the time.

"Thanks. You, too."

She didn't respond immediately. It was so quiet I could hear her lips part right before she said, "No, I mean. You looked really. Good."

When she said that, when she said those two words, *really* and *good*, her fingers dragged down my arm.

Probably a mistake, I tell myself. She was just moving around, trying to get comfortable, and this was a small bed and it was nothing, it was fine, this was all very regular.

But her hand didn't move away.

It wasn't a mistake.

I turned my face to hers, too scared to shift my whole body. Too scared to commit to that much. But she was so close already, her breath brushing my mouth, that I thought: *fuck it.* Tirtzah was my best friend, and I was either going to make things much better or much worse. But I had to *do* something.

So I did the thing I'd been wanting to do for months, for years: I let my fingers find her jaw in the dark, and let them slide back toward her neck, and I pulled myself closer to her, and I kissed her.

I kissed her like I'd never kiss anyone again, like air was secondary, like all we needed to breathe was each other.

And, *baruch Hashem,* she kissed me back.

Until she didn't.

Until she said, "Wait."

Until she said, "We can't."

I didn't wait for an explanation, I just disentangled my fingers from her hair and rolled back to my side of the bed and stared up at the ceiling and breathed.

"Sorry," was all I could say, once I caught my breath. "Sorry," and, "I can sleep somewhere else."

"No," she said. "No."

I snorted. She was right; there were no more beds. This was it.

"Ev." Her fingers found my arm again, uncertain in the darkness.

"It's fine," I said. "I'm sorry I misread the situation."

"You didn't."

I stopped breathing. She may have, too. All I could hear in the silence was my own pulse.

She said, "You didn't, Ev. It's just—we're drunk. And I—" She shifted restlessly, the whisper of the sheets like bursts of static in the silence.

"If anything happens between us," she said carefully, "I want it to be because we both want it. Not because we're drunk. Don't you?"

I couldn't process what she was saying. I couldn't—was she saying she wanted something to happen between us?

I guess I took too long to answer, because she said, "Ev? Don't you?"

"Yeah," I said. "I mean, no. I want it to be because we want it."

Then she was quiet for too long. "Do you?" I asked her. "Want it?"

Another beat of silence, and she said, "Yeah. I do."

It was evening, and it was morning: the second day.

Eitan's neighbors hosted the Seder that night. There were more people than the night before, and so much food there was barely room for table settings. My arm was pretty much pressed up against Tirtzah's throughout the whole Seder, and my entire body felt like it was on fire.

Her fingers dragging against my thigh every time she rearranged her napkin on her lap didn't help, and when charoset juice slid down her chin, I nearly reached out to sweep it away with my finger because I wanted to taste the cinnamon-honey-wine of it across my tongue.

The wine was buzzing in my head and I knew if I didn't drink a gallon of water before I went to bed I was going to be hungover in the morning but it was so hard to care when Tirtzah was leaning laughing against me, and *fuck*, why did I agree to not kiss her until we were both sober?

It was late when we got back to Eitan's house. Tirtzah and I crawled laughing into bed and she slid the lamp closed and the room fell into darkness and then we weren't laughing anymore. We lay facing each other, waiting for our eyes to adjust, because even knowing that nothing would happen between us that night, we still needed something, some affirmation to quell the rising anxiety of *Did I imagine that conversation? Has she changed her mind?*

But I didn't know how to touch her and stop. I didn't know how to lie here in the dark, her bare legs so close to mine, and not kiss her. I didn't know what I was doing and I didn't know how to handle that.

She saved me. She reached across the space between us and touched my hair, sliding one of my curls around her finger.

I just forgot how to breathe entirely. That's all.

"I love your hair," she said softly.

It's weird how compliments strike you in different situations: every time My Best Friend Tirtzah has said this, I've rolled my eyes and deflected and said, *ugh, whatever, it's a nightmare*—but now that we were here, sharing a bed, in this sexual-not-sexual situation and she'd said it, the only feeling I had was happiness, maybe a little smugness, a little more like, *yeah you do, you're fucking welcome.*

Somehow we'd gotten closer, Tirtzah playing with my curls. I reached out and touched her arm, let my fingers slide up her forearm, over her biceps, around the point of her shoulder. As my fingertips crossed the ribbed strap of her tank top, tracing the slash of her collarbone, she inhaled so sharply she twitched. Her hand in my hair froze and I stopped touching her, but I did make a mental note.

She said, "Ev."

"Did I do something wrong?"

She swallowed and shook her head as well as she could on the pillow. "No."

Smugness increasing.

"But maybe—I don't know. It's a lot. It's maybe too much for . . . just this. Tonight."

"Sure," I said, "I didn't mean—"

"I like touching you," she said, and my pulse stuttered, "but I want to go to sleep."

"Those things aren't mutually exclusive."

She smiled, her teeth flashing in the dark. "No, I suppose they aren't."

It was evening, and it was morning: the third day.

I woke up to the whispered words, "We're not drunk anymore," and Tirtzah's soft mouth pressing against my throat.

"Shit" was somehow the only thing I knew how to say. But my body took over, my hands curling into her hair as her lips dragged up my jaw and settled on my mouth, her tongue lazy as the morning light.

The bed was small, but not so small I couldn't push her onto her back and climb on top of her. I wrapped my hands around her wrists, pressing them into the mattress. Her eyes were heavy and lidded, her cheeks flushed pink. Sunlight scattered across her face like diamonds.

I remembered the sound she made when I touched her collarbone, and I had to hear it again, the hitch in her breath, the unfiltered physical reaction she had to me.

To *me.*

I lowered my head to kiss her again, but didn't let go of her wrists. She tried her best to meet me halfway, and this time nothing was lazy—it was aggressive, pointed. Hard, like the harsh slant of the afternoon sun.

I let go of one of her wrists and grabbed her face, my fingers and thumb pressing into her jaw. I bit her lower lip—no pretense of a kiss—and swallowed down the guttural little noise that escaped her.

I didn't lift my head, just let her see my gaze linger on her lips before I said, "You need to be quiet."

"You bit me," she said.

"You want me to stop?"

And *there* it was, that sharp little inhale from the night before. She didn't answer immediately, so I waited. Because if she told me to stop, I would. But I didn't think she'd tell me to. I didn't think she wanted me to.

Gd knew I didn't want to.

Finally, she said, "Ev, I—"

I let go of her face, her wrist. I pushed up over her and waited.

"It can't be anywhere anyone will see."

I sucked my lip between my teeth to keep this Cheshire Cat grin from curling all the way up to my hairline. "Deal," I said. "But tell me any time I get too rough."

Her lips parted at the end of my sentence, at *too rough*, and I suspected no matter how rough I got with her, it wouldn't be too rough.

"You haven't yet." Her leg curled up over my calf and I had to swallow before I could speak.

"Can I kiss you again?"

She smirked up at me. "You better."

So I did. I meant to be soft, but I guess I didn't have any restraint left. My hand slid off her jaw and down her throat, over her collarbone, to the wide expanse of her chest. Her hands hovered at my waist, barely touching. Nervous, almost. Like we were both waiting for the other to give the under-the-clothes green light.

One way to solve this: I sat up and pulled my top off. I wasn't wearing a bra; why would I have been?

The way she said *Jesus* sent a hard thrill through me, like she'd never seen anything like this, anyone like me. Her eyes were clear as glass in the white morning light, her lips pink and parted and swollen. Her hair perfectly tousled, like always.

I wanted to say something, something sexy or provocative or bossy, but nothing came to mind or mouth. She lay there, waiting for direction, and, well, maybe I wasn't the only one taking notes during all those conversations about hypothetical preferences.

I slid one hand under the nape of her neck and pulled her up to sitting. Her breath was warm against my breasts, and I wanted more than just her breath there. I dipped to bite her bottom lip again, hard, and watched her eyes flutter shut. Thumb replaced teeth, and I rubbed the sting away. Or rubbed it in, judging by her sharp inhalation. I let her go, let her run her hands up my waist, her thumbs following the wishbone slope of my ribs until they met between my breasts. I let her press her lips to my skin. Like I was doing her a favor.

Her breath was warm but her mouth was *hot*, her tongue dragging up the curve of my breast. She hadn't even touched my nipples, and I was fucking dying. She moved so *slowly*, with absolute deliberation, one hand sliding down my waist to stroke my stomach where the elastic of my shorts sat.

A scream pierced the silence, and we jerked apart. The scream broke into giggles, the sound of a delighted six-year-old being tickled or held upside down or chased.

Tirtzah covered her face, laughing quietly. Then I was, too, because what the hell were we doing in this house full of people?

It didn't matter, though, because she stripped her shirt off, still laughing. I raised my eyebrows and she shrugged and I laughed harder, but sure, she was right, I could not have possibly given less of a fuck about anyone else in the house when I had Tirtzah looking at me like I was all that mattered.

I pushed her back down to the mattress and kissed her again, holding myself up on my hands while hers went wandering—up my arms, over my shoulders, through my hair. When she tipped her head back, I dragged my lips down her throat, letting her feel the scrape of my teeth, letting myself feel how she shuddered. Her fingers were wrapped tight around my forearms, so tight I thought she'd leave bruises. So tight I *hoped* she'd leave bruises.

Breathless, she said, "Floor."

I stopped what I was doing, pulling back a couple of inches. "Yeah?"

"Dude, this bed is really fucking loud."

I hadn't noticed, and I should have. The surprise must've been all over my face, because she started laughing again.

"There is no way it sounds like anything but people banging."

"Fine," I said, hoping to hide my embarrassment—my Gd, did anyone hear us?—"then get on the floor."

I raised up on my knees so she could slide out from under me, but didn't wait for her to get onto the floor. She was still standing, facing away, her back foot barely off the mattress, when I fisted her hair in one hand and sandwiched her against the wall. She gasped at the cold plaster, so I put my hand over her mouth.

"I thought you said you could be quiet." When she didn't respond, I asked, "Can I take your shorts off?"

She nodded.

"Can I touch you?"

Her breath rushed out of her nose, over my knuckles, and she nodded again, slower this time.

"Thank fuck," I murmured. I took my hand from her mouth and hooked my fingers in her waistband, tugging her shorts down. She didn't move anything but her feet so her shorts wouldn't get stuck around her ankles.

I rested one hand on her hamstring, which tensed and released under my palm. The anticipation was making her jumpy, and her jumpiness was making me grin. Her subtle effort to relax was so delightfully unsubtle I couldn't help myself—I scratched short nails up the back of her leg, I bit the strong slope of her shoulder.

Her breathing turned harsh. I was smiling. I again couldn't help myself.

"My goodness," I said, my lips against her ear, "and I haven't even touched you properly yet."

She leaned her forehead against the wall.

I slid my hand around her hip, pressing my palm into her belly, and I felt her breath stutter. I felt my own stutter.

This whole thing felt *momentous* in a way that sex didn't usually for me. Because it couldn't just be *good*—it had to mean something. I needed her to walk away knowing there was no one who could make me feel this way, no one like her in the whole world.

The hallway floor creaked just on the other side of the wall. We both froze, like we'd been caught already. The bathroom door opened and shut.

Tirtzah was barely breathing as my hand slid down her stomach, a centimeter at a time. I thought she'd stop me. I was surprised—at both of us, to be honest. That I started, and that she didn't stop me.

Water ran through pipes and the bathroom door opened and shut again. The footsteps faded. There was hardly a second of stillness after they disappeared before Tirtzah's hand was in my hair, pushing my face into her neck. My mouth opened and it took every ounce of self-control I had not to close it again, to wrap my teeth around that flesh and bite down until her knees buckled.

I wasn't going to do it there, but I knew I'd do it once we got home, which was consolation enough. So instead of biting her, I slid my hand down the front of her underwear and between her legs and *fuck*, I could not believe how wet she was.

For *me*.

I cursed, probably because I couldn't think past the heat against my fingers as they followed the contours of her labia, sliding against the slickness that soaked her underwear. My knees almost went out, because, Gd, how many times had I gotten myself off thinking about this, about her pussy swelling against my fingers, her pretty throat pressed against my lips?

She pushed her ass back against me, and I grabbed her hip like a handle in one hand, the other cupping her cunt possessively.

I wanted this, I fucking *wanted this*, but I needed to see her face the first time she came for me.

I turned her around but pressed her to the wall again, nosing her face to the side so I could kiss her throat, so I could feel the thunder of her pulse against my mouth. I touched her everywhere I could reach, but watched her face. I watched the way her lips parted, the way her eyes tracked the movement of my hand. The way her hair fell in her face and how she couldn't be bothered to tuck it away. When I touched the top edge of her underwear, she sucked her bottom lip between her teeth.

I wanted to make her wait, but I didn't want to make myself wait. My finger trailed down the elastic band in the crease of her thigh. Her hand hovered near mine, like she wanted to help, but

I wrapped the fingers of my other hand around her wrist and guided it away. Every gasp, every little hiccup of her breath pulsed through me, pounding like blood, and making me feel it behind my eyes, in my hands, between my legs.

It wasn't slow when I pushed her panties to the side, and it wasn't particularly gentle. It was desperate, reckless almost, and the heat of her cunt nearly burned me. Her muffled groan as she pressed her forearm to her mouth sent a bolt through me, so sharp I swore I was bleeding.

My fingers slid slick between her lips, but not inside, not quite, and she pulled her arm away from her mouth again so she could watch, so she could see how my hand disappeared. Her breath was shaking, I could feel it against my shoulder, and Gd, *Gd*, I could not wait to see her come.

My thumb found her clit and her hand found my arm, grabbing, fingers squeezing, letting go, dancing up and down my arm like she couldn't decide where she wanted to hold on or even if she needed to. And then she needed to, her short nails digging into the soft skin inside my elbow. She was panting, and I pushed two fingers inside her, three, and then her face crumpled and her mouth opened wide and her head tilted back against the wall, the whisper of her hair against the plaster barely audible over the sound of my fucking her.

"Ev—"

"Can you give me another one?"

She swallowed and nodded and it barely took any time at all before her cunt was squeezing my fingers and she was pressing her teeth into her forearm again to keep from crying out.

I slid down the wall with her, pulling my fingers out of her, feeling the air cooling the wetness on them, letting them drag down her thighs. Her eyes were bright, her cheeks flushed, her lips swollen pretty.

The knock on the door shocked us like gunfire. I nearly swallowed my tongue. "Coffee," Leah said.

Tirtzah slapped a hand over her mouth, her eyes squeezed shut, shoulders shaking.

"Thanks," I called back. "We'll be down in a minute."

The footsteps we didn't hear approach retreated, and when Tirtzah finally uncovered her mouth, her smile was as big and bright as the noonday sun.

A MODEST WOMAN

Lin Devon

A modest woman. The phrase hung in the center of Adaure's mind like a cat toy just out of reach. And it irritated to no end. Modest woman. A woman who understood the value of restraint. Rich chocolate skin but a plain vanilla spirit. A woman in whom the adventure gene had been bred out. The fact that these words had come from the man who had been walking out on her made them all the more abrasive. Not painful, not really. But grating because it was the truth in many ways. It was the image she had crafted for herself. A proper African princess. She couldn't be hurt that it was how she was seen. It was just that Calvin's exit held up a mirror for her, and she no longer admired the woman she saw there. That he hadn't either was no great surprise.

Alone with her thoughts, she found she didn't actually miss him. She thought she would. The immediacy of him as a lover, as handsome arm candy at social functions. He'd been someone to see the world with and, notably, a deterrent to her mother's constant matchmaking. She rubbed at her bare ring finger, surprised to find that despite all that, she was relieved at the absence of the massive engagement ring. The loss of pressure to be a woman she didn't really like for a man she couldn't really say she knew was strange. She'd lived with it for so long. She might have shed the stiff, cultured persona months ago and likely would still be engaged right now, but she hadn't wanted to shed it then, not for him. The sense of freedom was complete because it was freedom from Calvin too. That revelation left her somewhat in awe. She felt naked on the precipice. Anything at all could happen next.

She nibbled at the complimentary cheese plate and sipped the wine but could not relax. A modest woman. It rankled. All that quiet polite lovemaking came to mind. Always a lady. He'd pleaded with her to embrace spontaneity, but she'd had an army of etiquette generals shaping her path. Brought up in London, the only daughter of a Nigerian billionaire, she had been raised to fit a mold, one that had only grown tighter in adulthood. She carried the reputation of her family name and her nation's pride on her shoulders. Never a toe out of line. That she had slept with Calvin at all had felt like wicked indulgence. He hadn't been her first, of course. That title went to the head groundskeeper's son at the family estate back in Lagos. Calvin had been the first her family had approved for the contract of marriage. It was no small consolation that she had never actually loved him.

Adaure watched the world whipping by outside, felt the gentle rocking of the massive segmented metal serpent as it slid effortlessly along the tracks. Just outside the pane the French countryside streaked by in vivid hues of Kelly green, magenta, canary yellow, cornflower blue. The rich palette of Matisse, of Renoir, the wit of Voltaire, the lily soft intimacy of Chopin echoed through the scene, all of it bathed in the buttery afternoon light that had made this region famous. It was decadent in a way store-bought treasures could never be. The sun on the hills seemed to melt and run in gleaming quicksilver rivers in the crevasses between hills.

Everything rising and opening to the heat of the day, perfuming the wind that bowed the grasses nearly double.

Though she'd made this trip many times before, she was usually in meetings on the phone or her laptop. As her father's head of marketing, she was never without a lengthy to-do list. Today she had purposefully left her devices in her bag and, as a result, this was the first time she felt she'd ever truly seen the landscape. Shadows pooled like secrets beneath the raised skirts of the trees, warm even in their shade. The mystery in those warm shadows seemed to call to her, to whisper across the back of her neck. Something deep in her belly stirred to respond.

Adaure set down her glass of rare Chardonnay and let her fingers drift to her collar. Without thinking any more about it she unfastened the top button on her blouse, then another, until she had revealed a deep vee of flesh. Eyes on that sumptuous scene outside the window, she let her fingertips trail the smooth skin from clavicle to sternum only interrupted by the pearl clasp of her bra. She got to her feet with only the mute and coaxing country-side to see. With deliberate slowness she pulled her shirt from the waistband of her skirt and let the fine mulberry silk drift from her shoulders. She took a moment to cup her breasts gently, one in each hand. The delicate Parisian lace was fine as spiderwebs, perfectly molded to the shape of her. Lavender over mahogany. She slipped free of it.

The sensation of standing there in bright sunlight in her modest woman's guise with her modest woman's nipples hardening at the tips of her modest woman's teardrop breasts was immediately thrilling. She watched the ghostly image of herself reflected in the glass, the gentle bounce of her breasts moving with the jostling train, her lips slightly parted and her eyes gleaming. A modest woman she might have been, but only by design, not by desire. To hell with all of it.

She walked up to the window, all that country outside, both pristine and riotous, beckoning her to play, and leaned against the glass. If there were people out there, they would see. Farmers in their fields. Fishermen returning from the river. Let them see. Let them know. She watched as her breath steamed the glass a moment before she pressed her kiss to the image of the wanton woman she saw reflected there. The woman in her reflection kissed her back.

Adaure slid her cashmere pencil skirt up around her waist. She let her hands explore the finely shaped flesh of her own upper thighs. Above the wide lace garters of her stockings her skin was smooth and warm. She was reminded of the way he had coiled his arms around these thighs and held her under the work of his talented tongue. Not the fine-boned and well-bred, perfectly manicured fiancé, Calvin, but Thomas. A groundskeeper's son, he'd held no illusions about the power dynamic between him and the heiress he seduced. He just didn't care. The young man's image danced in her mind's eye, the way he'd looked on his knees between her thighs and gazing down on her, stroking his meaty offering in one work roughened fist. He'd laughed when she'd pleaded for more. The memory sent a thunderclap rippling through her taut belly, a downpour to slick her lips. She hooked her thumbs inside the lace of her panties, slipped them down to her ankles, then stepped out of them.

Her senses sang with the cool air whistling over the neatly trimmed curls of her heated sex. A hand slipped reflexively to cup and discovered how easily fingertips might pop between ready lips fairly coated with slickness. Why, a person could slip and fall right in! She smiled at the joke he'd used all those years ago. A lifetime of instructors, and the teacher she valued most was an uneducated young lothario who couldn't ever seem to get enough of her. It was his measure against which she gauged her own adventurousness. He would not be happy to have seen her in her fiancé's bed.

Sprawled out like a flayed chicken uttering mouselike encouragement to the man who pumped the day's aggression out in the glove
of her body. He would, however, be smiling now.

Adaure slid her skirt back down her thighs, silk lining cool
against her hips. She slipped her blouse back on, buttoned and
tucked it in. In her wavering reflection she watched the way her
nipples danced under the fabric. It was impossible not to see her
nakedness. She slipped the wad of panty and bra in a pocket of her
travel case on the shelf and took a moment to steady her nerves.
The truth was that her lifetime of training had served her well in
most ways. She corrected her short curls and reapplied a thin coat
of mulberry lipstick. She knew how to work a room, how to flatter
the powerful, convince the affluent austere, make a head-turning
entrance. There were countless society dinners, museum galas,
ladies brunches, yachting weekends, every one a strategic rung on
her social ladder. But there was always a plan, which left no room
for adventure. To explore the far reaches, a person has to leave the
familiar. And she did, more than anything, want to explore. Her
heart was a trip hammer, but it beat for the thrill of the unknown.

Adaure pulled the door aside and stepped out into the hall.
Plush carpet muffled the staccato of her heels. To her left stood
the doors to the first-class cabins, to her right a bay of windows.
Vertigo struck her as she walked in one direction while the world
outside flew by in the opposite. She staggered a bit on unsteady
legs, but didn't hit the wall. In the moment it took her to register
she was being held by someone, steadied, her calculating mind
had already listed the facts. Large hands, expensive watch, off the
rack suit two seasons old, clashing cologne and aftershave. One
higher end than the other, but neither anything special. A hint
of rare scotch on the breath grazing her neck, fine cigar smoke
somewhere in the threads of his suit, but not on his breath. And
he was here in first class. The boss's protege no doubt, a young

up-and-comer eager to prove himself to men who would otherwise look down on him. Something to see, someone to watch. He was holding on too long. The barest squeeze on her waist, the smallest hint of a greedy little embrace that pressed her just an inch too tight against him.

Adaure turned in his arms and moved backward a step, palms pressing his chest. He was a finer specimen than she had anticipated. He had a short dark cap of wavy hair and eyes as blue as sapphires in the warm sun-kissed caramel of his skin. He smiled down at her from half a foot above, blinking in naked adoration. Her mouth went dry. This close she was sharply aware of her nakedness, of the thin fabric that kept her from this man's sight. His eyes drifted from her face to the long expanse of her throat, the silk that shimmered with the jostling flesh beneath. She felt a moment of unease at her own brazenness. He could see her nakedness and he was blocking the path back to her cabin. She turned and hurried the rest of the way down the hall and onto the next car.

She found solace in the first-class lounge and bar, but only for a moment. Groups of overstuffed leather chairs were gathered around small tables with views out the windows, but she wouldn't be able to take one without joining an existing party. A group of four silver-haired men in expensive suits turned to watch her walk in. A young man smiled, but his girlfriend did not. Three older women giggled drunkenly and poured more wine, tourists making a show of her. The bartender, never one to make a guest feel unwanted, gestured with a smile to the empty stools at the bar. She had only just slid onto one of the padded leather stools when someone, a man, came to sit beside her. She knew it was him before she looked. Her blue-eyed stranger was seated there, grinning to himself but looking only at the bartender.

Adaure found herself at a crossroads. She lowered her lashes and stole a quick peek. He was fit, tall, quite handsome, certainly reeking of eager virility. He wanted her, clearly, but she hadn't decided yet if it was mutual. He ordered scotch and soda, and she heard his British Indian accent fill the words with poetry and foreign spice. The bartender offered her wine and she nodded, demure. She graced him with a quick curve of her lips and he beamed, but walked a few paces off to give the two of them some privacy. First class was nothing if not discreet. She watched him, though, and every so often he returned the favor. Not the blue-eyed suit, the bartender. He had the kind of sweet country face under a mop of shaggy chestnut hair that inspired country maids to wickedness. Long nose over sculpted lips between sun-bronzed outdoorsman's cheeks. If she'd been a country maid in his sights, she'd have done any wickedness he'd asked.

She stretched her shoulders and peered out the window, catching a glimpse of the silver-haired masters of industry still sneaking glances, murmuring to themselves. The four of them, each seeming ready to devour her like dogs on the scent, each wearing a gleaming wedding ring. The young couple were immersed in a passionate kiss across their little table of beers, but the woman was still glaring daggers at Adaure over her beloved's shoulder. She had her choices, and they were slim.

Her randy Brit tilted his head toward her and she peeked up at him. He said in a voice rich as dark coffee, "You should come in here at night. It's amazing. Like drifting through space, no lights out there but the stars." He laughed to himself at her blank expression. "I see. You probably don't even know what I'm saying. London. Me. English."

He placed a hand on his chest, still smiling. She smiled back but said nothing. This would be very telling indeed. He wet his lips with the pointed pink tip of his tongue. His eyes drifted. Under his seeking gaze she was reminded how exposed she was. Her long legs were in full view now that she'd sat down. Her skirt had slid several inches up to expose a hint of the fine lace at the top of her stockings. He stared at the divide in her shirt, the shadow of her breasts clearly free beneath the fabric. He made no secret of his thoughts, communication barrier be damned. He turned toward her on his stool so that she found herself now seated between his spread knees. He leaned forward and crooked a finger for her to lean in too. She glanced at the bartender, who was watching closely now, and leaned closer. The Brit angled his face as if to whisper something in her ear and inhaled deeply an inch from her neck. Her expensive perfume was doing what it promised.

He murmured beside her cheek, "You smell absolutely delicious. I could hollow you out with my tongue."

Shock rippled through her, but she forced herself to maintain her guise. Restraint training did come in handy on occasion. She smiled sweetly, noncommittal.

He licked his lips again and looked into her eyes to ask, "May I buy you a drink?" He mimed sipping a cocktail and she smiled back, lifted her full glass, and sipped. He laughed, nodded. "Of course. Forgive me. I guess I'm nervous. I can't remember the last time I was so close to such a beautiful woman. So sensual, I think you must be a dream. I wish you could understand me. I wish you'd know what I was saying when I say that I could look at your face all night."

Adaure squeezed her crossed legs together, sending jolts of pink electricity coursing from the crux. He sighed and shook his head, his eyes on the long lines of her legs. He was on the edge of his seat. "You have such a beautiful body. Maybe I'm glad you don't understand me. This way I can tell you how hard you're making me, just being this close to you." He smiled sweetly, belying his raunchy words. "I can tell you how much I wish we were alone so that I could bend you over this bar and open up that tight body.

I wonder how much you'd let me do. A woman like you is just the kind of weekend I've been needing. I could set you up at the Seasons in Paris and not come up for air for three days and nights. Twice a year when I'm in town, hm? Or I could just take you back to my cabin right now, make an Olympic event of that arse and you'll never see me again. Nobody to know. No paper trail at all. Nadia can't bitch about what she doesn't know. And my bosses over there would be so deeply impressed. Mm, I like that option."

Stuffed shirts were the same all over. This one sounded like a cheap version of the last one, the one she'd almost married. Looking for a fantasy to relieve the stress of the corporate world, but not a woman to worship the way she craved. Another time she might have responded well to the anonymity. But now some face-less Nadia was between them, and the pig bosses too. When he bent to lay a kiss on her shoulder, she swiveled in the other direction and left the car. She made her way back to her cabin alone, thinking that she might have better spent her time just chatting up the bartender.

The knock came to her door not five minutes after she'd entered. She rolled her eyes and made no move to answer it. She reclined on the padded bench, gazing out the window annoyed and frustrated. The voice from the other side of the door was deep, but also soft, apologetic, and French.

"*Mademoiselle? Je suis désolé de te déranger, mais . . . cet homme allait te suivre et . . . je . . . je l'ai eu confiné dans sa chambre. Il ne te dérangera plus. Je pensais que tu devrais savoir.*"

Adaure leapt from her seat and opened the door a few inches to find a familiar face, but not the one she'd been dreading. Green eyes danced with humor from under the shade of thick chestnut eyebrows. The bartender stood there, a crooked smile on his pensive features.

"You had him confined to his room?"

He looked surprised, then laughed at her ruse. He nodded and responded in heavily accented English, "Yes, he was going to follow you. You seemed to be done with it, so I intervened. You do speak English. And French?"

"*Oui,* and a few others. I should thank you. *Je voudrais te remercier.* Do you have to get back right away?"

He glanced back down the hall, shook his head. "Lunch break."

She smiled broadly, opened the door, and took his hand to draw him in. Confused, hopeful, sweet as a schoolboy, he swallowed audibly when she locked the door. She leaned against it and took the sight of him in. Still wearing the white button-up, thin black tie, and black vest, he looked gift-wrapped. His eyes traveled southward, taking in the way her fingers slipped each remaining button through its corresponding hole on her shirt. He made a low moan in his throat as she slipped free of the silk but made no move to touch her. In fact he stepped back a foot, but the French curse he uttered under his breath was complimentary.

She walked past him and leaned her back against the window, her bottom resting on the gleaming brass bar beneath. As he watched she slid her skirt higher and higher up her thighs, revealing at last that she wore nothing under it. The shy invitation of her lips was visible behind the neat pelt of curls. She raised one high-heeled foot and placed it delicately on the bench, then slid a hand down to hide her sex again, playful. He licked his lips. She could see his chest rising and falling from across the room.

He managed to rasp, *"Puis-je vous montrer l'effet que vous avez sur moi?"* and passed a hand over the growing mound straining his zipper.

"*Oui,*" she purred. She certainly did want to see the effect she had on him. "Show me."

He held her gaze as he unfastened his pants, slid them to his hips, and drew himself free. He was watching for her reaction, that crooked smile still on his lips. This country boy was packing a heat-seeking missile. Her thighs flinched at the size of him, but she resisted the urge to snap them shut. Rosy pink and throbbing with snaking veins, he was shaped like a battering ram. The room seemed to shrink. She was so desperately hungry, so needy she thought she might pass out or shake apart if he didn't come and touch her.

He walked to her, that monstrous beauty bouncing freely from his fly, a creature sniffing out the burrow she hid in her belly. He placed gentle hands on either side of her face, caressing her hair. He angled his face and kissed her butterfly light on either side of her mouth. A more intimate form of the Frenchman's greeting. He kissed her jaw, opened his mouth on her throat, her bare shoulder, his hands roaming to her breasts. He was moving slowly to his knees. He looked up at her and kissed the fingers that hid her from him. His palms slid along her belly, her hips, her thighs. He wrapped his tongue around her index finger, glistening with the dew of her want, and drew it deeply into his mouth.

"Mange moi. Dévore moi." She cooed as she stroked his hair. To be eaten alive by this sweet, deviant, somehow reverential man was exactly the treasure she'd sought.

"With pleasure," he replied.

He slid his hands up the back of her thighs and squeezed her bottom at the same time he took her finger in his teeth and cast her hand aside. Like the starving to a feast he went at her. He used his leverage and pressed her bodily to his face, burying his mouth between her lips. His tongue was a wonder, rippling and flicking across her folds, cradling and then lashing her clitoris. He looked up at her, a wicked light in his eye as he slipped his index finger inside her to the knuckle. She made an involuntary little whimper and he joined it with his middle finger. She clenched around the intrusion, which encouraged his talented mouth to deepen his kiss. He drew the tip of her sensitive button between his lips and suckled it as he worked his hand at a steadily quickening pace. Caught between pursed lips, her tender nub sang under the onslaught of relentless tongue work. She barely registered that he had flung her legs over his shoulders and now held the bar instead of her bottom for leverage. She was squeezed between the cool window and his hot mouth as she felt the rush of the oncoming wave. She might have called out, might have moaned loud enough for the passengers at the far end of the train to hear, but she wouldn't have heard. There was only the rushing pulse in her ears, the rush of the train, the rush of the orgasm that carried her fast and far away from herself.

He kissed her open thighs, her quaking belly, traveling north to find her breasts heaving and her nipples like pebbles under his lips. He held her pillowy softness in both hands, traveling to and from to alternate gentle nipping, playful tonguing, and blowing cool breath across wet nipples. The act sent aftershocks through her still pulsing pussy.

He drew himself up, kissing her clavicles and her throat. She looked up at him, eyes glassy, adoring. He cupped her face, one gentle hand stroking her hair, her fine-boned chin, his thumb caressing her lower lip. He trailed his index finger across the tip of her wet tongue and she tasted her own flavor on his skin.

"*Vous ette une belle reve.* I cannot possibly be truly awake." His heated cock pressed a fat line across her belly. So close and much, much too far away. He searched the pocket of his slacks and came up with a condom. He grinned. "Marry me now and I'll throw this away."

She laughed and opened the packet, taking his steely piece and unrolling the sheath over him. "Just today then? Is this all I can have of you?" He pressed her to the window and nestled narrow hips between her still vibrating thighs, planting juicy kisses across her throat. She hadn't answered his question. She didn't know what the answer should be. He reached between them to grip his cock and said, "I'll have to make myself memorable then."

He opened his mouth to hers, the taste of her own heady scent still lingering on his tongue. She was lost to this wanton sensuality, this careless openness. Without preamble his pulsing cock met her waiting vacancy and he plunged inside. He swallowed her gasp in his kiss. He pressed her to the window and took the twin mounds of her bottom in his kneading hands to hold her wide. He spoke in his native French and in his heavily accented English of her unsurpassed beauty, her legendary loveliness, and of his own unworthiness, his own gratitude for the gift of her. Poetry, of the kind all young French men know, and the kind that invariably worked. She laughed in glee at his sweetness, and moaned into his sex-scented mouth as he rolled his hips to drive himself deeper, harder inside her. He held her hips and pulled her body down to meet his thrusts, bouncing her on the monument of him. His girth was incredible, his pace relentless, and in this position she was fully at the mercy of his machinations.

"Ah, plus serré, mon cherie. Plus humide por moi." He growled. Wet, yes. Hot, yes. He drew her hard against him, pounding her depths with vigor. How he took up every spare inch of her, how he fit so deeply it ached, how gentle his words and how rough his work. She came. He was unrelenting. She came again and still he offered more. She held him, hearts hammering so close together, and rode him to his own overdue climax. He groaned words in French she couldn't understand, grinding his pelvis to her as he convulsed and exploded inside her. Hot jets of emission that might otherwise have drenched and filled her still-quaking passage were caught and held. His sweat coated her.

In her mind's eye she saw her Thomas, enigmatic professor of bodily pleasures, as he'd been the last time she'd had him. In the big mirror in her bedroom she'd watched him over his shoulder, marveling at the way his high round bottom had clenched and swung in a steady rhythm, the soft, dark flesh of his balls pressing tight against her. She'd watched him dig for depth, as this man had, pressing hard until he'd found her limits and then pressing for more. He'd been sweaty and streaked with dirt from the job, his boots caked in soil. The mud stains on her bedsheets had been difficult to explain to the maid. He had uttered the most beautiful words in her ear as he'd had his filthy way. She understood now that it was this juxtaposition she'd loved so much. She'd been wearing pearls, she recalled, pearls and a cashmere sweater yanked high over her bare breasts. It seemed she'd always been a caste rebel.

She looked at this young barman as he carried her on shaking legs back to the bench to sit with her. The ethnic difference between them was less interesting to her than the social difference. He kissed her delicately, easing them both down from the peak to lazy postcoital rapture. He was sweet and generous and eager to be lodged permanently in the memory of this privileged woman. A woman in whom the adventure gene was paramount. Because she could have anything she wanted. And she wanted him. She recognized her reflection in his eyes. A wanton woman. She smiled and kissed his cheek, feeling at last like herself again.

"We've done things a little backwards, but may I know your name? I am Mathieu." She knew the answer to his earlier question now. Her father had put her in charge of the Florentian estate's new renovations. More importantly, the expansion of the Parisian house. Between Florence and Paris she would need to ride this train quite often. She could see him again. But another thought occurred to her as images of the grounds she would oversee in Paris floated through her mind. Aside from her secretary and estate manager, she might require a personal valet. She watched Mathieu stand and correct his clothes and hair, grinning, adoring her. She took a card from her bag and slipped it into his pocket. "You can call me Adaure, and if you want to leave the train to work under me in Paris you'll call me soon."

It was imprudent, certainly, and immodest to keep her collection on display. Thomas was now her personal chauffeur. He'd be more impressed than jealous, but could she really do this? A woman like herself was taught to put legacy above all personal desires. A woman of such high breeding knew exactly what was prudent. She knew about reserve, restraint, and, above all, modesty. And she paid it absolutely no mind.

WICKED RIDE

Corrina Lawson

Beth tugged Alec into the sparse, colorless room, closed and locked the door.

"Okay, I don't get it." He ran a hand through his thick, dark hair. "A white padded room? You think I need to be locked up? Is that your big surprise?"

He smiled, but Beth could telepathically sense his unease.

Argh. She'd already started wrong. She laced her hand in his. "No, no, Alec." She smiled. "I've never been afraid of you."

The tension in his shoulders eased. The confusion on his face did not. "Then what's this all about?"

Beth leaned against him. Alec took the hint and folded her into his arms. Despite the jokes from his friends about "fiery" firestarters, Alec was one of the most patient men she'd ever met. He'd listen and consider what she asked.

The problem was all on her end. She's spent so much of her life denying her telepathic abilities, telling herself they weren't needed, that they were dangerous, that they could hurt people.

Or that her abilities were wrong, which meant *she* was wrong.

Alec never had any such doubts about his telekinesis or his ability to call fire. He loved his gifts. Reveled in them. She needed to learn how to be like him. And what better way than to play like this? To have him all to herself, to meld, to merge, to make love in a fantasy world they created.

She breathed in the faint, clean smell of his aftershave, felt the muscular chest under his cotton T-shirt, and wrapped her hands around his waist, letting them slide lower, to his tight ass. Desire crawled into her, hardening her nipples, making her skin as sensitive as a cat's whisker.

An erection stirred under his jeans.

"Beth," he breathed out, "I'm not complaining but this doesn't seem a very romantic room. Though," he tilted her chin so she'd look at him, "the walls are padded. That seems helpful."

She laughed and almost, but not quite, had to rise on tiptoes to frame his face with her hands. "Alec. I've been thinking that I should emulate you."

"Mmmm . . . I still don't understand but keep going."

"Bear with me a little bit longer. Can you call fire in your hands?"

"Sure."

He stepped back, and a flame appeared above his palm in the next instant, all with an ease that she envied.

But he frowned. "You don't want me to, uh . . . burn . . . you, do you?"

"No, pain doesn't appeal to me as it does to some people." She was fumbling this still. "I wanted to watch you call fire because it's so natural to you."

"It is natural." The flame vanished. He clasped her hand and kissed the inside of her palm, sending shivers down her spine. Would she ever stop looking at him and wanting to get naked? Probably not.

"Aha. I get it," he said. "You still think your telepathy is unnatural? We've talked about this. You don't scare me either, babe."

"I scare myself," she admitted, curling her hands around his waist this time. "I knew you'd understand, so that's why I want to try this with you and . . ."—*go for it, go for it*—"and I wanted to try it with us, with sex, because, well, what's more enjoyable than that? Why shouldn't we use our powers for a hell of a good time?"

He laughed, picked her up, and spun her around the room. "This is going to be awesome. I'm so in."

She kissed him, and, as their tongues entwined, the bond between them, a near-physical energy that always accompanied their intimacy, snapped into place. If her nerves could have erupted into song, they would have.

They had a special bond. She amped up his TK and firestarting. He amped up her telepathic ability. They'd need both today. And that was why she'd set up this room—to keep the outside world safe from whatever they did.

The last time they'd joined this fully, it'd been a literal fireball.

"We should sit down," she said.

He sat, spread his legs, and pulled her between them, leaving her butt directly against his erection, with her back resting against that ripped chest. He cupped her breasts, teasing them with his fingers through her cotton blouse.

If she'd doubted he would be up to this, well, now there was proof he was definitely up for this.

"I've been practicing something new with my telepathy." She cleared her throat. "Alone." Creating the fantasy by herself had been, well, orgasmic. But not as satisfying as it would be with company. She guessed. Hoped. Desired.

"I'm sorry to have missed that." He slid his hand under her blouse from the back and unhooked her bra. Why was that act such a sensual move? Never mind the reason. It was.

"Now it's time to do it together," she said.

"Absolutely."

He pushed her hair back and kissed her neck at the curve where it met her shoulders. His TK snaked down her skin, stroked her breasts under the bra and tickled her nipples. She swallowed hard, her heart threatening to beat out of her chest.

The TK rolled down her stomach and stroked the inside of her upper legs. Wetness flooded her underwear. A single flick of TK against her clit sent her moaning, almost squirming in his arms.

"Wait." She reached behind him and grasped his hips. "I haven't even started yet."

"All evidence to the contrary," he whispered.

"I'll show you," she whispered.

She closed her eyes and reached for his mind. An initial burst of thought, desire, need, love, and ecstasy raced through her, overwhelming all sense of touch, pushing her even closer to the edge of orgasm. She saw herself through his eyes, a short woman with dark eyes, dark hair, and shining with love, with desire, all overlaid with his trust in her.

Everything a woman dreamed about.

No, no . . . *control it*. Send, not receive.

She threw her mind into telepathic stream, sending her thoughts back to him. Her images showed Alec in motion—the quick smile, the luxurious hair that demanded touching, the blue eyes that missed nothing, that easy way of moving, almost floating, and how he cocked his head while listening, paying attention.

Alec was a man who always paid attention.

"Is that how I look to you?" he tipped her head back and held her gaze while his TK sent feather-light touches down to her toes.

"That's what you are." She ran a finger down his nose. Damn, she was even in love with his nostrils!

"I like it when you share with me."

"This is only the beginning." All right, she'd taken control of the thoughtstream, accepted his thoughts, sent hers back to him, even while . . . well, distracted. As her body hummed under his hands and TK, she'd been able to maintain control of the telepathy.

He ran his hands down her arms, licked her neck with his tongue, teased her clit with his TK.

"It's hard to think when you're doing that," she whispered.

"It's hard, period, Beth. Let me. C'mon."

Not yet!

As you wish.

His TK faded. Through their link, she sensed he was on the verge, his penis so ready to release all that pent-up desire and lust. The urge to turn around, rip off her skirt, push him to the floor, ride him while he gripped her hips tight, while he played her clit with his TK like a virtuoso . . . almost overwhelmed . . .

She'd regroup after and . . . .

No, she was procrastinating again.

Orgasms and making love with Alec were amazing. This would be next level.

She laced her fingers through his, closed her eyes, and joined their minds again. A punch of desire that soaked her underwear happened between one breath and the next. Another beat of their hearts, a flash of her telepathy, and her creation began to come into being.

Haha. She'd thought *come.*

At first, they stood together in an utterly white space, holding hands.

"Whoa. Are we inside your mind?" Alec asked.

"We're inside each other's minds. Essentially, we're one mind."

"And soon, one body?" He grinned in that lazy way of his.

"Bodies moving together, for certain."

She filled the world around them.

A blue sky, sun shining, appeared above. Below, solid ground, blacktop. There, now, add in setting. An amusement park midway, full of various games, food stands, and park visitors. To the left, beyond the midway, roller coasters and massive swings rose over the buildings.

Alec grinned. "Is this a telepathic virtual world?"

"Shush. Not finished yet."

One more long breath to add sounds to their tableau: the laughs of children, the screams of riders on the coasters, and the general, constant hum of people.

Scents now: ice cream, pizza, fried dough, a faint overtone of sweat. Heat from the summer sun but, wait, a cool breeze as well.

She held that scene, birthed it into being, and walked hand-in-hand through their new world with Alec.

"Wow," he breathed. "How did you do this?"

"I pulled a memory from my past, stepped into it, and pulled you into it with me."

"It's amazing! I've always wanted to go to an amusement park! But there was never time . . ."

Alec had been raised in isolation, partially because his fire-starting could have been dangerous to others before he developed solid control and partially because his late guardian wanted him isolated and dependent.

"Joined like this, we can go anywhere I've been," she said to him as she turned them down a lane. "Anywhere you've been, too, in theory."

"How real is it? The people? The rides?"

"As real as we make it."

"But they really can't see us, right?"

"We could make them react to us, if we wanted. Like, if you wanted to play a game, we could have the person running it interact with us."

"This is the best game of all!" He pointed from him to her and a wicked grin grew on his face. "You wanted to test this with me to see how long and how clearly you could hold the world inside your head?"

"Our head, and how much, um, distraction I can take."

"Distraction, huh? Can you hold the fantasy while I do this?"

He kissed her, lifting her off her feet. She clung to his broad shoulders and wrapped her legs tight around his waist. She felt his TK stroke her clit, move just so . . .

She nipped at his neck, licked his ear, stuck her tongue inside it, bit his earlobe. He moaned, and his TK pressure on her clit grew more insistent, faster, but also more tender and careful. She ground against him, from her jeans to his, her desire melding into his, so close, no need to wait . . . she had to come now or . . .

Or nothing. Come now.

Fireworks, literal fireworks skyrocketed overhead, booms that echoed along with her shattered cries. He nipped at her lips as they came together, his come staining his light blue jeans. She wriggled free, off him, seized with a need to touch, to be closer, to make him hers in every way. She yanked open his pants, licked up the come that'd gathered around his penis, as his orgasm reverberated and combined with her own. He grew hard again, almost instantly. She licked his balls, pushed his jeans down to his knees to expose the long, wonderful length of him.

Around them, the crowd kept walking, riders still screamed on the coasters, the midway game hosts still barked for more customers.

"Is this real or am I imagining it?" he breathed out.

"Yes, and yes," she said as she took him into her mouth.

As he ran his hands through her hair and rocked his hips, she lost track of whether she was the one licking, sucking, and bringing him to orgasm or if she was the one who felt each tiny flick of the tongue, each light scrape of teeth, each stroke of his balls . . .

He came again, a long spurt that she swallowed. He stood, breathing heavily, silent, before falling to his knees opposite her. He kissed her, his tongue seeking to meld with hers, as if they could absorb each other whole. Become that one person.

Maybe they already had.

Finally, her shudders ended. Or his did. She rested her head on his shoulders.

"Beth?" he asked.

"Yes?"

"This was an excellent idea. I couldn't tell where . . ."

". . . you ended and I began. That was all right?"

"That was spectacular." He grinned, then stood, pulled up his pants, and helped her up.

But when he went to buckle the jeans, she pointed a finger at his crotch and said "Abracadabra!"

The jeans buttoned themselves.

He laughed. "So, are we naked or clothed in the real world?"

She laced her fingers through his. "For us, for now, *this* is the real world."

He buried his face in her hair. "Oh, wow, I love this surprise."

"It's not over," she whispered, regaining more of herself. She studied the park around her. Oh, wonderful, she'd managed to keep it intact through even that, even as she lost her mind. On her own, she'd never managed to hold an imaginary world past the orgasm. She'd been right! It'd taken their merging, both of them, to maintain the reality during intense emotions.

He draped an arm around her shoulders. "I was going to say that I thought it would be weird that they were around us but . . . it wasn't," Alec confessed as they moved through the crowd.

"Maybe there's a bit of the voyeur in you."

"In us. We built this together, right? You could have picked a scenario with just us. A beach or a mountain top or something."

"Oh, I hadn't considered that! Maybe we can work new scenarios in the future. But stop distracting me now."

"Oh, then, lead on!"

They walked toward the coaster. She still felt as if they were floating, sliding through this world, rather than simply strolling. She briefly wondered if they still sat on the floor, her back to his chest, in that white room.

Stop worrying about that. Enjoy this.

"Glad you're so into it," she replied, slipping a hand in the back pocket of his jeans.

As they turned a corner, the main attraction loomed. A roller coaster rose in the air above them.

"Whoa," he said. "Sign says it's called the Wicked Cyclone."

"You've always wanted to ride a roller coaster," she said. "We're going to do that. Our way."

"Our way is excellent."

She pressed against him, slipped her hands under his T-shirt, felt his rumble of pleasure as she explored the hard muscles of his back.

"So the Wicked Cyclone will live up to its name?"

"Oh, you just wait and see!"

The Wicked Cyclone was a whirl of movement, a circular, spinning coaster over a track that moved smoothly over orange rails, turning riders upside down at least twice and twisted them this way and that.

"Oh, yeah," Alec said after watching it go. *You don't do things by half, Beth. How did you get such detail in the coaster?*

It's a real coaster. I've ridden it a few times. And I watched videos over and over so I could duplicate it for us.

"Tell me about it." Alec said it out loud because he loved when Beth became passionate talking about something and she'd obviously put a ton of effort into this . . . experience? Creation? Sexual adventure?

Fun covered it all nicely.

"Okay, so there's three thousand three hundred twenty feet of track!" She pointed above them. "It integrates wood and steel, to give it a bit of an old-school feel but the steel allows the ride to be smoother overall than a wooden coaster."

"How high is it?" He shaded his eyes to look up and realized Beth had perfectly recreated the light of a sunny day.

"It reaches ten stories. The first hill is one hundred nine feet, and you hit a high speed of fifty-five mph on the way down." She tugged him into the entrance. "But the best part is that it has a two-hundred-degree stall and two zero-g rolls."

Zero-g sex?

That day when we first really merged, we had sex in mid-air. I wanted to try something like it. But maybe safer than that time.

"Let's ride!"

He pulled her with him along the path, pushing past the waiting crowd. Oh, man, sex on board this thing? He could use his TK to augment the zero-g and they'd be upside down and . . . he sent her an image of them spinning, naked, upside down, his head between her legs.

She laughed. "I was thinking me sitting on top of you . . ." The image she sent had her climbing on top on him, in the same seat, rocking together as they rolled.

"Won't you hit your head?" He was so rock hard again. Hell, half the time around her, he was either hard or could be in an instant. This headspace intimacy jacked that up, big-time.

Hah! But it's our fantasy, Alec. I'll make sure there's, um, headroom.

Wicked! But can we try it my way the first time?
It's our fantasy, after all. And this is your treat . . .
Our treat.

"That might be a good experiment too, see how well *you* can manipulate this world," she said out loud.

"Experiment, hell. I think it'll be fucking fun. Literally."

They cut in front of everyone waiting for their turn. She'd made it so realistic that some riders actually bitched at them but, by the time they reached the loading area, the front car was empty and waiting.

The loudspeakers around them sounded a warning about "a cyclone coming in" and fake newspaper headlines telling of killer storms decorated the walls of the coaster loading area.

"Do you want the people gone?" she asked. "I can do that."

"Where's the fun in that?! Let's hear their screams around us. Can you do that?"

"*We* can do that!"

Hand in hand, they climbed into the front car and buckled in. Warnings sounded about keeping one's hands inside the car.

Oh, yeah, he wanted his hands inside something. He reached to slide his fingers under her pants. But she waved a hand as the roll bar came down and, zap, they were both naked.

"We don't need clothes."

"We sure as hell don't," he agreed.

The gears caught the car and they began the ascent. "One hundred nine feet??"

"Yes."

Nothing but blue seemed to be in front of them.

Click, click, click, sounded the gears. He slid his fingers inside her wet, willing opening. Her hand reached for his rock-hard cock but he shook his head.

Ladies first.

His thumb stroked her clit. Half his hand slipped inside her. Damn, she was so open for him. Her hands holding the lap bar grew white with the force of her grip.

Click, click, click.

They reached the top of the hill.

He leaned over and whispered one word in her ear. "Go."

The gears released the cars. They raced down the hill, his fingers inside her, her eyes wide open. Her moans were lost in the screams, but she came all over him as they rounded the first turn, laughing, rocking, and, yeah, screaming, as her orgasm squeezed his fingers tight.

"Holy fuck," he muttered.

They screamed around the first turn but the cars slowed for a few seconds while they ascended a smaller hill. He pulled his fingers out and licked them, tasting all that was wonderful and unique about her, all that was his.

She gasped, leaned back, rolled her hand in her own come, and grasped his erection, sliding her hand up and down with her self-created lube.

He screamed this time as they descended, wanting to hold back, wanting to make it last forever. The world blurred, the cars corkscrewed, nothing pulled against them, and he came with a scream as they zipped out of the zero-gs.

"Holy fuck," she muttered.

"Should we . . ."

She pulled him into a kiss. "Hold on. Think of the coaster. Stay with me. I want to finish the ride. We have to hold onto this creation until the end."

Another corkscrew—hah, aptly named! They laughed as they hit zero-gs again, with the breeze caressing their naked skin, and in what seemed like an instant later, they rolled to a stop where they'd begun.

She waved a hand. Their clothes returned. But the scent of come and sex and joy remained.

He laid his hand over her heart, beating as fast as his own.

"Wanna ride again?" he asked.

"You bet," she said. "But maybe once we can go through it as a ride?"

"A regular ride, you mean? Sure." He took her mouth once again, hungry, excited, not nearly ready to give this up. "And then we ride *my* way."

"Deal," she whispered.

Best surprise ever.

I dunno. Maybe we'll try this with skydiving next!

BROKEN BARS

S.P. Jaffrey

I walk into the reception hall to the sound of music. I don't know anyone here except for your immediate family and that's okay. I'm always on the outside. Everyone is celebrating your return, there's laughter and joy. They've all had the chance to see you already, to hug you, to give you a kiss to welcome you home. I haven't seen you yet and part of me is nervous. It's one thing to see a woman once in a blue moon in a room with bars under the watchful eyes of the prison guards. Of course, she will look beautiful and desirable. It's another thing to see that same woman outside, one of a hundred guests, all dressed up in your honor.

I see you standing with your friends, your hair is short but styled and your beard is trimmed. You're in a suit, a white shirt, and a tie. The last time I saw you was in the visiting room. There was a cartoon mural on the wall and a corrections officer with a gun leaning against the garishly painted Woody Woodpecker. You were wearing baggy, regulation khakis which contrasted sharply against the red, plastic chairs we sat on. Our chairs faced each other just a foot apart, close enough for you to hold my hand gently but far enough that the explicitly sexual exchange between the couple in the chairs next to us intruded on our space. You tried not to laugh in embarrassment as the woman, in her long schoolmarm skirt and sensible shoes, began to pant quickly and quietly next to me, a performance art for her man, whose eyes were fixated on the show.

But I don't want to think about that now. I don't want to remember that world. I just want to think about you standing in front of me. This gift that none of us expected and could not even dare to hope for after the judge sentenced you to die as an old man in prison. We couldn't believe then that one day you'd be out again, the lies that took you away from us exposed at last with the surprise confession of a jailhouse snitch. My wedding ring weighs heavily on my finger, admonishing me for my lack of faith, my inability to believe in the impossible. I should leave. I know I should. I don't belong here. I don't belong to you anymore.

But then I see you laughing and everything stops. I see you like I've always seen you. And even though your hair is more silver than black, you look the same as you always do to me. You're still the twenty-two-year-old boy who lay on top of me and buried his face in my neck all those years ago. Before my marriage, before your incarceration. When it was just the two of us stealing a private moment in my parents' old townhouse. I make a move toward you but then I stop for a minute, wondering if I look okay. I decided to wear a sari, a maroon one with a thin gold border. The blouse ends just below my chest, the back held with interlaced ribbons, offering a full view of the curve of my waist. I wonder if you'll like it or if you'll think it's too much for the conservative community we come from. But then I remember, this is who I am. And you accept me as I am.

At that moment, you look up and your eyes light up. It's the same look I saw on your face across the hallway when we were kids. It's the same look you would always give me when I came to visit you secretly in that fortress of barbed wire that kept you locked away from me for almost two decades. It's a look of recognition, far deeper than just a normal hello. It's a look of belonging. You smile and walk quickly over to me. Before I can say a word, you pull me in a hug, your one hand gripping the bare skin at my waist, your other hand holding me tight. I throw my hands around your neck and you lift me up off my feet.

We speak but I don't remember what we say. It doesn't matter. We never run out of things to say anyway. I greet and hug your other loved ones and I know they must have spoken to me too. But I don't remember. The only person I feel in that crowded hall with colorful, dancing bodies is you. You're making your rounds talking to everyone as is your duty. But I'll look up and see you looking at me and you'll smile a smile just for me. One only I can understand.

Sometime late in the evening, the music starts to slow down. The fast-paced dancing is over and now the DJ is playing slow songs for the few couples that are still on the dance floor. I stand by the table watching them when I see you walking over to me.

"Come on," you say, holding your hand out.

"What?" I ask, looking at your parents standing nearby.

"Come on," you say again, taking my hand and leading me onto the dance floor. I follow you self-consciously, feeling eyes on me, wondering who I am and why you are with me. I glance back and see your mom smile at me, the diamond pin in her hijab winking at me in encouragement. So I keep following you. I always follow you.

"People are going to talk," I say, as you put your hand on my waist and hold the other one against your heart. "You know how Pakistani people are."

"I don't give a fuck," you say and we both laugh. You hold

me close, my arm around your neck, our heads leaning into each other, fitting perfectly like a puzzle piece. I can't remember the song but I know I don't want it to end. Because at the end, I'll have to give you back to everyone who has a claim on you. So, I move with you and just breathe in your cologne.

"When did you get here?" you ask me quietly.

"Just today," I respond in your ear.

"You're staying with your aunt?"

"That's what I told your mom." You look at me, surprised. "I have a hotel not far from here. I didn't want your family to think anything weird if you met up with me tomorrow. I thought saying I had a hotel might put ideas in their heads. Good Muslim girls don't stay in hotels with their husbands at home, especially when they're going to visit their ex."

You start laughing. "You're slick. But why only tomorrow? Do you have plans tonight after this?"

I look up at you; I'm the surprised one now. "I thought you would have to go home after the party with everyone. I just figured you'd meet up with me tomorrow."

"I didn't wait all this time just to sleep alone in my bed when you're nearby," you say, and my heart flutters a little. But then you look at me seriously. "Unless that's not what you want."

"It's what I want," I whisper in your ear without hesitation. You lean into me again and I can feel your breath hot against my neck. "I'll leave early and wait for you. It'll give me a chance to freshen up and change out of this sari, anyway."

Your hand tightens on my waist. "Leave the sari on. I'll take care of it when I get there."

I feel my cheeks get hot and the song ends. You kiss me on the cheek and walk away to speak to someone. I start getting ready to leave as the first guests start making their way to the door. I leave you the hotel's address as I say goodbye.

It's a short drive. Back in my room, I wait, wondering how long it will take you to leave everyone and come to me. I pull out the pins in my hair and let the waves fall around my shoulders. I take out the safety pins that hold my sari securely in place. The chiffon slips down my shoulder slightly as I hear the knock on the door. Without hesitation, I open the door.

You take my hand in your own and your other hand goes into my hair, cupping my cheek. You kick the door shut behind you and walk me backwards into the room. "You're so beautiful," you say, your forehead against mine. "I'm yours," I respond, and your lips come down on mine.

Our kiss is gentle at first, as we rediscover each other. Both your hands are cupping my face and my hands slide up your back, feeling the muscles. Your lips move to my jawline, your teeth lightly grazing my skin. As your lips move to the soft area near my ear, your hands move lower, sliding off the silky fabric on my shoulder.

I gasp as your lips move to my neck and your hands fall to my breasts, your thumb running lightly over my nipple, sending a shiver down my spine. My hands move to your waist and I pull out your shirt from where it's tucked in. You look down at me and grin before your mouth comes down hard on mine, your tongue exploring, remembering.

My hands fly up to your hair as I meet your kisses with my own. I feel you pull on the fabric of my sari, which finally comes undone and cascades down to the floor. Your hand clutches my rear and you laugh at how much more of it there is than used to be. I reach down and start unbuttoning your shirt, pushing it off of you just as we bump against the side of the bed.

You push me down gently and lie on top of me, your face buried in my neck, your tongue moving up to my earlobe as I run my hands across your bare chest and down to your belt and the buttons of your pants. Your mouth moves back to mine and your hands begin to undo the hooks in my blouse.

Slowly we undo all barriers to each other until it is just you and me. Your hands slide down my sides and lift my legs around you, holding you close. And we move together, closer than before but still two people discovering each other. Your mouth trails down to my breasts and I can barely think as you take one and then the other in your mouth, still moving against me. When I can't take it anymore, I push you onto your back, climb on top and kiss you hard. Slowly, I work my way down, past your jawline, then your throat, to the muscles of your shoulder and your chest and then the muscles in your abdomen.

When I reach your penis, the part that is you, I let my tongue roll over the tip and I feel you shudder as your hands come into my hair. "Do me one favor," I say, my tongue still working around you. "Don't come into my mouth." I hear you groan as I take you between my lips, working you softly and then harder while your hands guide me to what feels right.

I listen to your moans and your hands go back to your head as you let yourself enjoy. But then your breathing gets faster and you suddenly pull me up by my shoulders, pushing me back onto the pillows, climbing back on top of me.

"My turn," you say, with a wicked smile. And then you do the same. Your lips trail lower as your hands and tongue touch my breasts and then work down to my belly button and then lower to kiss the inside of my thigh. You take my fingers and kiss them before moving them down to that most private part of me. "Show me what you want," you say softly.

I close my eyes and touch myself, showing you what feels good, feeling no self-consciousness with you. For a brief second, I think of my husband. Of the many nights I lay next to him touching myself, thinking of you as he snored peacefully beside me. But the thought is quickly chased away as you move my hand and replace it with your own. I suddenly start to feel heat rising up my body. And then you replace your fingers with your tongue, and I can't speak or breathe. The pressure builds as you continue and then when it feels like I'm about to lose my mind, it's like an explosion of stars, making me yell out and shudder with pleasure uncontrollably.

Your mouth is suddenly back on mine as I continue to tremble and then you're inside of me for the first time in our long relationship. And it's like we fit perfectly, like we were always supposed to be one. You move inside of me, slow and then fast, and I follow your movements with my own in perfect rhythm. Your forehead is resting on mine and you smile at me as the momentum climbs.

I dig my nails into your back and sink my teeth into your shoulder, as a moan comes out of me. Then another and another, mixing with your own grunts of pleasure. My legs cross behind your back, pulling you closer, and you hold onto my thighs. Finally, you yell out and collapse on top of me, both of us sweaty and satiated. You lift your head and kiss me gently on my lips and then my nose and finally on my forehead before settling down to put your head on my chest, over my heart.

I keep my legs around you, holding you close to me so we can't see where I end and you begin. And I stroke your head as you lay against my heart. We both close our eyes and finally rest as our heartbeats return to normal.

Tomorrow, we both know that we'll go back to our lives. But for tonight, there are no barriers or obstructions. Finally.

BEFORE AND AFTER

Kristine Lynn

I traced my finger along the pink, raised scar. It ran north and south across my chest, another smaller scar bisecting it where my nipple should be. The longitude and latitude of my diagnosis, treatment, and recent reconstruction made for a topographical map of the past two years, four surgeries, eighteen cytotoxic visits. I was the sole navigator of this new landscape, though. Not even my husband has been granted access to the latest version of my body.

I heard him in the bedroom, rooting around in his dresser drawer as if the clothing had somehow shifted in the night. Every morning it was the same, despite the fact that not a pair of socks had been put away differently in more than two decades. I sighed, closed my eyes against the image.

Beneath my fingers, the scar felt manageable, smaller than Dr. Kline had promised. I tried to imagine what it would look like through Richard's eyes, feel like beneath his calloused fingers.

Richard. My grocery shopper when the smells of the produce aisle made me retch, chauffeur to chemo appointments, the man who would leave bed half-naked in the middle of winter and fetch me a new bowl to vomit in when the first was full.

My husband of twenty-seven years. I'd spent longer with him than without him.

By all accounts, he was the model partner—the support I needed, the man I loved. When I lost my hair in tufts, finally relenting control and taking a Bic razor to the remaining patches of thinning dull blonde, he never shaved his head in solidarity, though, a subtle sign the support extended only so far.

My hair loss also coincided with when he started kissing me on the cheek at night, much as he did his eighty-three-year-old mother. His hands no longer sought my hips in the pale light of morning, his lips no longer grazed my bare shoulder before bed, hoping for more than either of us had the energy to commit to.

He was supportive, chivalrous, diligent. But days became weeks, weeks stretched into months, and months gave way to years. Cancer and romance were mutually exclusive.

To him, anyway.

At month four, when my energy returned but my hair had not, I pretended to be sick twice a week. I would lock myself in the guest bathroom, turn on the shower, strip out of my sweats and panties, and press my pelvis against the handheld shower nozzle. Two trembling fingers would glide along my clit, using the warm water as a lubricant, the metal head as a vibrator.

I came alone, shuddering against the shower bench Richard had installed for his father's visits before he passed away. Hot, salty tears would stream down my cheeks, falling on the nightshirt I was too horrified to remove. One breast was gone by then, the other on borrowed time.

But I didn't know that yet. Not that it would have mattered. Two minus one still equaled zero.

He was in the closet now, selecting a button-down from one of three designs. His morning routine was a study in ritual. In less than three minutes he would knock on the door and tell me he loved me, that he hoped I had a good day, that he would see me when he got home. In that order.

Like the socks, not much had changed in over twenty years. I shook my head free of that thought, and the dozen others like it. I'd never asked Richard to join me in the shower, and he'd never tried. A faux pas two years in the making, a misunderstanding of need that plagued me, even now.

I cupped my new breasts, let my thumbs slide down the dimpled skin. I squeezed the altered, added flesh, surprised at how different they felt. The only truth to them were the hashtag of lines on my skin, marking the change below. I bounced them, keeping them cradled in my palms.

They felt more firm, less . . . *real.*

But of course. They're *not* real. They're a construct designed to make me feel more like the woman I was *before.*

The same bisecting scar that slashed my chest divided my life into two equal parts: before the diagnosis, and after.

Before. Whole. Unscathed. Healthy.

After. Scarred. Monstrous. Malignant.

I knew it was coming, but still, the knock surprised me. I looked up at the door, expectant.

"Love you, hon. Have a good day and I'll see you when I get home."

Clockwork. A marriage of pattern, molded and designed. Surely, I'd helped create the tessellated day-to-day life, but I couldn't recall how or why I'd let it become so stagnated. Maybe it was just easier this way. The door shut silently behind him, only the soft thud of the furnace changing the pressure in the room letting me know he'd gone.

I released both breasts simultaneously, surprised at the uniformity of them. Before—*that word again!*—my right breast had hung heavier than the left, a parting gift from my daughter who could only breathe out of one nostril when she breast-fed, and therefore only successfully fed from the right. After, there wasn't any give to either side, just stretched skin over muscle.

Then—*now*—full, new, uniform globes, vastly unlike their original counterparts.

The loss of connection with my daughter when the old ones were surreptitiously carved from my body ached like a phantom limb. Only memory, scar tissue, and dead nerves remained.

But they looked good. So, at least there was that.

I could wear the silver top Richard bought me to celebrate our silver anniversary. I could fill my old bras. I could fondle my chest as I played with my clit, even if I could only elicit pleasure from one of those gestures.

The sensation in my breasts had vanished along with the fatty tissue, with the extrication of my cancer-ridden nipples. Still, in those lonely, water-soaked moments of ecstasy, I'd longed to be able to cup my own bosom, pinch my nipples between my thumb and finger, feel the sting of pleasure that erupted when the flesh protruded from between my fingers.

No, that was a lie. That particular iteration of my desire was my backup plan, my second string. I wanted Richard. I ached for his hands, once the workhorses of his career as a plumber, to grab me by the hips, to turn me around and rub his erection against my backside before slipping inside me. I wanted those rough fingers to stroke my new breasts.

My pussy throbbed with need, my skin burned in each place I imagined my husband's skin tracing mine. More ghost pains of a time before.

My breath suspended in my chest, the whir of the furnace

like a jet engine in the silence. If I was desperate enough to satisfy myself, imagination my only link to my other half, what was I willing to do about it? I had little to lose. He'd never leave, he'd shown me that much. So, if I asked him to touch me, to see me for who I'd become, to make love to that new person and he said no? Well, then the decision lay in my hands for how to proceed.

But if I did nothing . . . then I was a willing participant in the decay of our union. Longing for touches, caresses, kisses I hadn't asked for would just be cruel to both of us.

Okay, then. It was settled. I'd attempt to seduce my husband that night, before I lost my nerve. As if on cue, my teeth chattered, and my hands shook. I was nervous, yes, and who wouldn't be? But the risk was worth the potential reward. Before, I may not have had the courage. I even lacked it after. But now? Now I knew what I needed to do, and so I set to work on a foolproof plan to get my husband to sleep with me.

That evening, donning the silver V-neck top and my tight black jeans from before, I put the finishing touches on the room before closing the bedroom door and walking downstairs. Candles and music to keep the phantoms at bay.

My hair was still short, cropped to right below my chin, and ramrod straight since it had grown back in. I styled it for the first time in months, adding body and curl to the bob that highlighted my jawline. Quite literally the only benefit to the cancer was the loss of the extra thirty or so pounds I'd carried before.

I felt the loss as I sauntered downstairs, not nearly as uncomfortable in the jeans as I thought I'd be. If anything, they were a little loose around the waist. I couldn't suppress the smile that crept up my lips when I heard the garage door open. I had just shy of four minutes for Richard to gather his books—he ran his own plumbing business now, but no longer did the work himself—and make his way inside, where he'd shed his shoes and jacket in the mudroom off the garage.

I shook my head, ran my hands through the tight curls, loosening them. My breasts barely moved despite an ample portion of them peeking out of the push-up bra I'd purchased that afternoon. I counted down his entrance in my head, clamping my teeth to prevent them from chattering again.

Absently, I ran my hand over my chest, which, under the two thick layers of fabric, felt normal, pleasant even. I repeated the mantra I'd established on my shopping trip earlier that day.

You have nothing to worry about. Richard loves you. You're beautiful.

That last part tripped me up each time I whispered it in the vacuum of my car, thought it as I fingered a silky bra and panty set in a store populated with twenty-somethings and perky, untouched breasts.

Was I?

Even if I believed it, would he?

Too late now.

The door to the mudroom opened, its ever-present squeak the clock by which I governed my afternoons. Before the creak, I was runner, artist, woman-who-worked-in-oils. After, I was wife, chef, cancer survivor.

Not tonight.

Tonight, I would be Mary, wanton mistress. I'd never played this role, not before, nor after. I wondered if I'd recall the lines I needed to say when they mattered most. If he'd slip a reminder under his breath to help if I stumbled.

I shuffled my feet that ached in the wedges I found lonely and unused in the back of my closet. I was desperate for a stance that didn't come off as too needy, too uncomfortable. I entertained the idea of grabbing a dish from the sink, washing it so my hands had something to do other than tremble. But Mary, the wanton mistress, didn't wash dishes. Not in this dress anyway.

One moment, I was alone with my racing thoughts, my heart pounding so loudly I was afraid he'd hear it in his short walk from the mudroom to the kitchen. And then, he was there, standing in front of me with a look of confusion etched on his soft features. The move to the front office had eliminated his work on new construction, the lifting of heavy equipment, the manual labor of the trades. It was easier on his body, yes, but the tradeoff came in the loosening of his jowls, his midsection. Not that I minded. I saw the man I married underneath all those years, injuries, pounds.

"Mary," he said. The way his voice lifted at the end, my name became a question. It was as if he doubted the authenticity of the woman his gaze took in, from the styled hair, to the painted face, to the wrapped package below the neck.

I only nodded, afraid of my own voice and its ability to convey anything other than abject terror. I wanted this, wanted *him,* too much to mess it up now.

He set his leather satchel down beside the dining table and took a hesitant step toward me. My pulse sped up. I was too old for this. I was going to have a heart attack and I'd arrive at the hospital looking like I was trying to nab a man twenty years my junior. If the heart attack didn't kill me, the mortification surely would.

"You, uh, wow." He raked his hands through his hair. The years had been kind to him in that regard. Aside from some distinguished gray patches, he had the same head of hair as the day I'd met him. "You look incredible."

A tentative smile pulled at the corners of my lips.

"Thank you." *There.* I'd said something and survived. I could do this.

His face reddened and his brows pulled together as if a problem had just occurred to him and he needed to solve it immediately.

"What's wrong?"

"It's just, I, um, well . . . did I forget our anniversary or something?"

The nerves rattling around in my chest took flight up my throat, where my feeble tongue was powerless to stop them. They burst through my mouth in a fit of laughter that echoed off the tile surfaces in the sterile kitchen.

After I'd calmed down, and Richard's face had gone from concern back to confusion, I smiled. I felt better now, knowing he was as unsure of how to do this as I was.

"No, sweetheart, you didn't. I just thought it was time."

The creases on his forehead deepened, the corners of his mouth worried between his teeth.

"Time? For what?"

"For us," I told him, moving away from the safety of the breakfast bar that held me upright and closing the distance between us.

It was that moment, that one honest moment where I knew what I wanted and the knowledge dawned on him, that I wish I would have captured on camera.

The way the color drained from his forehead and pooled in his cheeks.

How his lips parted, and his smile revealed the small gap between his front teeth.

How his hands uncrossed from his chest and hung at his sides, palms open and facing me.

"Oh," he said, chuckling. "Well, okay then."

When neither of us moved, and the sound of our synchronized breathing filled the room with a pregnant pause, he chuckled again.

"How do we do this? Should I take you to dinner first?" he asked. Another laugh bubbled up from my chest, each one lightening the weight I'd been carrying in my heart for months, years.

"Afterwards, I won't complain about a decent meal. But I'm a sure thing, Rich. No need to impress me with seafood."

It was his turn to laugh at my reference to our first date three decades ago, an airy a sound as I'd ever heard him make. Who needed music and candlelight with a laugh like that? No ghosts of our pasts would dare come near us tonight, I was sure of it now.

And that was the last thing I could recall with vivid clarity.

His hands clasped my waist and pulled me tight against him. When his lips touched mine, my mind went blank.

I parted my lips to let his tongue, gentle and tentative, seek out mine. When our tongues touched, any hesitation on Richard's part vanished. He became a beacon of need, thrusting his tongue deeper inside my mouth, his lips widening to cover mine. His hands, rough but strong, fisted in my hair. My own, softer hands pulled at the button-down tucked into his pants, sliding up his exposed flesh when the fabric finally gave way. He groaned against my mouth, a feral sound that soaked my panties. In response, I ground my hips against the stiffness pressing against his jeans.

Just the thought of my husband's hard cock—another gift from his youth that had never waned—took whatever moisture lined my panties and doubled it.

He pulled his head back just enough to take my bottom lip between his teeth. His groan became a growl and in the infinitesimal space between us, I could see the need, the ache, the desire I'd amassed reflected in his eyes.

His hands moved south along the nape of my neck, across the expanse of my shoulders, down my waist until they reached my hips. All the while, his mouth peppered mine with kisses that were nothing like the chaste pecks that had punctuated our nights until now. When his hands tightened around my waist, lifted me up and into his arms, only a whisper of surprise escaped my parted lips.

"Take me to the bedroom," I commanded as he carried me out of the kitchen.

He nodded, a smile curling only the left corner of his mouth, adding to the mischief that danced in his eyes.

Gazing up at him, feeling weightless in his arms, suddenly I was neither the woman before or after the diagnosis. I was Mary, the young woman who met Richard at a college hockey game. I'd cheered loudly for the other team the whole second half, despite wearing a sweater for their rivals, my and Richard's alma mater. Later that night, the same look of desire and playful abandon in his eyes, he'd approached me and asked why I'd done that.

"Because it didn't seem fair that no one was cheering for them," I'd replied, as serious as cancer. "Even the losers need some love every now and then."

Just two months later, he'd proposed. In the dim light of morning after celebrating our engagement by making love into the night, he'd kissed my neck and whispered that he knew in that moment, at the game, that he'd marry me, that he'd love me forever.

In his own way, he had.

He kissed my neck again now, setting me down upon the bed as gently as he would a newborn child. He slid my wedges from my feet, placing them beside the bed like little soldiers guarding our tryst, then undid the button on my jeans, carefully removing them. His breath hitched in his chest when his gaze settled on the lace panties I wore. We were halfway there, and neither of us seemed inclined to stop now. I lifted my arms in the air, an invitation if he dared accept it.

This was the moment of truth. When he would lay eyes on my new body, my new breasts. New did not equal flawless, though, and so when my hands shook above my head, I wasn't at all surprised. I was petrified but turned on at the same time. A flood of emotions coursed through my veins.

He knelt in front of me, nestled between my legs. His cheeks were flushed, and when he licked his lips, my pulse raced. He wanted me, too. That had to count for something.

When his hands slid up my sides, pulling the shiny, silver cloth over my head, he breathed in deep, his chest filling the space between us. He moved slowly, intentionally, methodically. So very Richard. As the top lifted over my head, he dipped his lips to my chest, decorated in the same delicate fabric that covered my soaking pussy. He trembled, kept his distance for a moment.

"I'm not fragile, Richard," I said, cupping my breasts over the lace. He groaned, put his hands over mine and squeezed.

"I know you're not. Hell, you're the strongest woman I know. Fuck, Mary, I just wish I'd have seen that sooner. I've been so afraid the past two years, I never stopped to consider that you might be okay, that we might be okay." His voice trembled with those last few words. "It's just," he started, running his hands through his hair. "It's just every surprise we've had in the past few years hasn't been a good one. The lump. The scans. The blood tests. Shit, even the first reconstruction almost didn't take. I just don't want to rush this surprise, since it's the best damn one I've ever had. I didn't think you'd ever want me again after I pulled away. You have to know it's just because I was scared I was going to lose you. It won't happen again, Mary. I promise."

My heart swelled at the sentiment, and my breasts, what was left of them, felt heavy with desire. It was so new a sensation, so different than the past, it caught me off guard.

"Shhh," I told him. "I want you. I want you to make love to me like you used to."

That was all the permission he seemed to need. He lifted my ass and like he really was the man I'd met eons ago, tore my panties off in one deft movement.

I squealed with delight. *This. This is what I needed.*

When his lips grazed my skin, trailed below the border of the lace into scarred territory, my heart threatened to stop altogether. Richard pulled the straps down, trapping my arms, but freeing my breasts. They didn't move, and neither did Richard. He smiled.

"They're different."

"I'm different."

"You're beautiful. They're amazing." His mouth closed over where my nipples should be and my thoughts fogged, evaporated. He sucked my newness into him, running his tongue along the scars as his other hand cupped my second breast.

I purred. It was exactly like I'd imagined. Richard pushed me back against the mattress, his eyes glittering in the candlelight. His head ducked between my thighs, spreading my knees to get closer to my sex, which throbbed with need.

Yes, I wanted to cry.

Please, I wanted to beg.

When his tongue ran along my slit, then dove inside my folds, thrusting and fucking my dampness, I almost came.

But I couldn't. Not yet. I also wanted to relish this moment, savor the feel of my husband's lips as he sucked on my clit, took me into his mouth at the same time he slid a finger inside me.

I gasped.

He pushed another finger inside, pulled at my sex while he licked me from ass to cesarean scar. Good God. Had it ever been this good? Surely not, or we never would have left the bedroom.

My hands fisted in his hair, pulled his face closer to my body. I wanted to devour him, have him eat me from the inside out. When I could feel the crest of an orgasm building, worried that I might pass out from the sheer thrill of it, I pushed his head up. He let me guide his head to my stomach, which he peppered with kisses, his tongue blazing a path up to my crisscrossed chest. He sucked and nibbled at the bottom of my right breast as if he wanted to give me a hickey, and I laughed. He growled again, this time with lust and mischief, throwing his head back in a howl. Who was this man? He was different, too. Though I didn't mind this change as much as I did my own.

His fingers still fucked me, but he slowed his pace, gliding them in and out of my swollen center with expert ease. It didn't hurt that I was wet enough to fill a swimming pool with my desire.

He performed the same move on my left breast with his tongue, and I giggled. When his fingers slid out of my pussy, I immediately felt the loss. The ache returned, this time worse now that my body knew what it had been missing.

"Fuck me, Richard," I whispered. He nodded against my chest, his fingers tracing the scars lovingly.

"Yes, ma'am," he said, his breath hot on my skin. Keeping one hand on my chest, he used the other to shimmy out of his jeans, unbutton his shirt, and shrug out of it. His smile was fuckable, as was the erection that was now freed and right where I wanted it. I sat up, cupped his ass in my hands, and pulled his cock to my mouth before he could protest. I ran my tongue along his crown, tasted the saltiness of the day and precome on his tip. If I could only feast on this flesh, this flavor for the rest of my days, it would be enough.

His growl became a throaty groan as his hands wrapped around me, his arms resting on my shoulders. My mouth closed over him, taking his girth as far back in my mouth as my throat would allow. I sucked and teased his tip with my tongue, only briefly allowing my teeth to gently nip at him. My lips went taut as I rode his cock. He rocked his hips, forcing himself beyond what I thought I could take. I loosened my throat, took more of him in. God, he felt good, his hands in my hair, his hardness fucking my face, his ass in my hands. He shuddered in my grasp, the only warning before he released a short burst of come, hot and creamy in my mouth. Swallowing, I licked him clean, swirling my tongue along his length before laying back against the bed and looking up at him. A thin sheen of his come glistened on my lips and I left it there, a treat for later. I'd never liked giving Richard head before, but now I felt the power of the control I had over him course through me, heady and all-consuming.

I slid a finger inside my pussy, then put it to my tongue, tasting what Richard just had. We didn't taste that different, both salty, briny, like we were made of the sea. Richard just stood there, watching my every move. I squeezed my breasts as I had that morning, the thick flesh spilling from between my fingers.

"Fuck, Mary."

"Yes, please," I said, smiling. Richard met my smile, and I was pleased to see that what we'd just done hadn't hampered his erection. He settled on top of me, placed his tip at the entrance to my pulsing sex. His eyes asked an unspoken question, wondered whether, after all this time, he was welcome there.

I nodded my consent, anticipation at having my husband inside me after so long causing my skin to erupt with goose pimples. Yes, he was welcome, missed, loved.

With permission granted, Richard thrust his shaft inside me, filling every molecule of space I offered. He rolled in and out, his hips grazing mine, his stomach rubbing against my concave abdomen. Every time he rocked, he went deeper, further inside until I wondered what other secret compartments I had to give him access to.

"I'm close," he whispered, his lips brushing my earlobe, tickling it.

"Come, baby. I want you to come inside me."

Twice more he thrust, harder each time, before his arms went rigid, his ass clenched in my hands. His breathing came in short bursts and beads of sweat framed his brow. My own release built, and as his shaft pumped once more, I rode the wave of my own orgasm, feeling it wash over me, making me as new as the breasts that rose and fell with my ragged breaths.

He collapsed next to me, turning me on my side so that his cock stayed buried inside me while I faced him.

"That was fucking incredible," he said.

"It was." That, of course, was a gross understatement. My world had shifted when he'd kissed my breasts, had gone completely off its axis when I came at the same time as Richard. It was no longer a dichotomous world, before and after as two separate entities, two separate parts of my existence.

As Richard kissed my forehead, his hand tracing circles on my chest, down my arms, I fused those worlds, rejoicing as I became Mary, simply Mary once again.

LIONESS

Theo de Langley

You ask me, again, if I'm sure. This time you use your voice. But you've been asking all evening, over and over, through the first careful kisses during dinner, to the later, less careful ones. I find your thoughts so easily, easier than anyone else's, and I want to be annoyed. But we haven't seen each other in so long, and you want me so badly, that I make a rare concession to charity.

"You've asked me that"—some quick calculations—"three times already."

"But," you say, looking down on me with your strange eyes, shot through with gold, "this is the first time I've asked it out loud." You know I'm being kind to you, and that's not what this encounter is supposed to be for.

"And my answer is still the same," I say, still forgetting to be sharp. You stare at me like you're the one tied to this bed, like I could run you through and you'd thank me for it. "*Yes.*" Oh, yes. Yes, yes. I see the instant the matter's settled, and hear it, too, resonating like a bell in your mind. "Now, don't keep me waiting." I settle my head against the green velvet cushion you bought me, because you hate showing up empty-handed.

"Never," you promise, and we both know that's bullshit. But I've still got the taste of wine on my tongue, and you kiss me with that hot, ready mouth, and I'm willing to believe it.

Well, almost. "Never? Hmm." I catch myself before I enter that particular maze. *Focus.* That's the first lesson you learn, if you don't want the magic to rip you apart from the inside. I was twelve when I learned it. *Focus on what you can control.*

"You can make this tighter," I say, pulling against the ropes that you spent so long tying with those practiced hands. You know this rope—waxed so the blood from your trophies doesn't seep in—and the knots better than you know yourself. The truth is, any tighter and it'll hurt; but I've always been good at pain. It's why I excel at my craft.

"It's fine."

Oh. For the first time, my sense of balance wavers. I say your name. Normally that's enough for you to yield. Not this time.

"I thought," you say, drawing off your black gloves, "the point was that I give the orders, little Witch." In the candle-shadows, you're a menacing figure: your beautiful features harsh and obscured, your eyes gleaming like hot coals.

Anyone else would be afraid of you, but you're so *delighted*, I can hear it, in your voice and your thoughts, so very delighted to be in this position, for once—or maybe just surprised. Our lives have so many surprises, and most of them are bad. "Very well, Huntsman." The word is delicious on my tongue. "You give the orders."

When I close my eyes, I feel the tension bleed from me for the first time in years.

For a moment—two, three—nothing happens, but I feel you looking at me. I want to say something, make some quip, but I fight the impulse. You must see it in my face, regardless. You order me to be quiet. I pluck restlessly at the ropes, but say nothing.

I promised myself I wouldn't listen, but you're thinking through the logistics, finally. I can hear the keen efficiencies of your mind, honed by years of hunting. The sharpness of it skims across me, and I feel myself growing hot. First your hand slides up my thigh, proprietary, and slips the white silk off. I memorize the calluses on your palm, your five fingers with their blunt, gentle nails. You withdraw your hand and I can't stifle the sound of anticipation. It wouldn't be the first time, or the tenth, that you've had me with my clothes on.

Your knife comes out. I hear its thin song as it's unsheathed. I hear your silent apology to the gown I'm wearing, and my eyes open of their own accord.

Your eyes gleam as you fix me with that hunter's stare, and the blade, which you've used so often it's practically part of you, flashes in your hand. I know now the last thing your prey sees.

You wait, watchful, poised on a razor-edge. *Are you sure? Are you sure?*

Yes. For you, yes. Always, *yes.*

Your face clears, changes a fraction. "Closed," you say sternly, and there's a swooping sensation between my hips. I close my eyes—possibly the first time in my life I enjoy being obedient.

When the air hits my skin it's a shock. Even with the fire in the hearth and the candles on the table, it feels almost cold. My bodice peels away in one long slow slide of the knife. The edge brushes my body, just a whisper of steel, and I'm reminded of how your finesse sits so tightly inside the brutality of your vocation. The skirt, you do with your hands, tearing through the layers of silk as though they're nothing. Suddenly I'm naked, like I have been so many times before for you, but this time feels different. The hair on my arms stands on end.

I expect you to take your knife to the last of my clothes. I spent a small fortune on silk underthings especially for this occasion, though I'd never tell you that. But you hesitate, and I want to tell you to forget it, just do it, *for gods' sake, hurry up and have me.*

You don't. You're doing it to torture me, which is the point of this exercise; for a brief, dizzy moment I wonder if you've been able to read my thoughts this whole time, and simply kept it secret. (Secrets, of course, aren't in your nature.) I resolve myself, keep calm, keep still, but there's a slow fire spreading through me. I might ignite the very air if you touch me, and so I will you to touch me.

I feel your kestrel-shadow fall across my face. Your fingers wind through my hair, not quite gentle, and twist, until I have to bare my throat to you. The velvet ribbon around my neck pulls tight. Your hand, gripping my jaw, until I can't move, and then you kiss me, the scrape of your stubble against the soft skin behind my ear. You breathe in the scent of my perfume, my hair, as though you want to fill every cell in your body with it, as though the soul they say you don't have floated on your breath, against the contours of my neck. I offer myself up to it, and you kiss me again. The kiss turns to a bite; the points of your canines make themselves felt. I gasp, turning toward it. *You're going to leave a mark,* I think, and then groan in sublime pain.

I imagine the mark blooming, hot and red, as you stroke your fingers across it. You're worried that I'll try to hide it. Instead I'm going to wear my hair up for a week.

You move away from me. Your thoughts trail behind you like smoke. I can feel them eddy in the corner of my mind's eye. I will you, again, to hurry up and have me, though by now I know that's not how you want this to go.

A hand—the right, I think—the killing hand, rests again against my throat. I wait for pressure. It doesn't arrive. *Aren't you just full of mysteries?* But then: your killing hand trails lower, precise and slow. You caress my breasts, each in their turn, as though you're touching something fragile and rare. Then your touch turns fierce. You're pressing your advantage, finally, I realize, as you squeeze my nipples. I sigh without meaning to and clutch at the ropes.

Apparently, this is all the encouragement you need. You *pinch,* hard, on the left, and an ozone spike of pain flares through my body, chased immediately by a rush of pleasure that pools between my legs. You do the same on the right, and the space between the pain and the pleasure disappears. I'm balanced on a forked tongue of lightning. All at once, you turn tender again; those long soothing strokes of your hands diffuse me. You repeat this process, again and again, until I lose track of time. I want you to stop, and I hope that you never stop. On one particularly keen squeeze, a sound scrapes out of my throat before I can contain it.

You stay silent, but your thoughts take on an amused lilt, filtering through mine like water through stones. *So that's the kind of mood you're in, hmm?*

I seldom wish you could read my thoughts—who knows what you'd think of me—but right now I'd make all manner of unsavory bargains to give you that ability. But there's no help for it: I yield.

"Yes," I whisper, hardly louder than an exhale. My voice sounds strange to me.

I flinch in surprise as your voice caresses my ear; I hadn't realized I was that far gone. "You know what they say," you whisper, your voice dark and warm against my ear, "about calling the wolf in from the woods." Your teeth find my neck again, always just on the edge of too much. "Here he is."

Another noise I can't contain, and you laugh at me. *Bastard.*

You step away for what feels like a long time, though it's probably only a minute or two. Your footsteps are slow and deliberate: a Huntsman, staking out the territory. I shiver, and I don't care if you see it.

You stop, level with my left hip, and run a considering finger across the silk that's stretched taut across my hips. I wonder if you've finally decided to dispatch them the way you did everything else, and at this point I'm silently begging you to.

Instead your hand spreads out: your fingers form a tender brand in five parts. Your thoughts lose their contour of predatory amusement and take on a softer shape. You marvel at me, shamelessly, pouring out praises and sweet words as though you've been saving them up for months. Probably you have. You love me. You do. That makes me quake more than any little trick you might do with your body. You kiss each hip in turn, and the scrape of your stubble makes me laugh.

I feel you smile against my skin, pleased that your message got through, and then you stand again. You think something devious, too quick for me to catch. As I'm trying to parse it, your fingers move down, between my thighs. I gasp, moving them wider apart, before remembering myself. I go as still as sleep.

You grip each thigh, forcing them apart. I know it isn't how the game is supposed to go, but we both know how I feel about following all the rules. I push against your hands, trying to close my legs again, fighting until my body shakes.

"No. Open."

You knew I was testing you, judging by the harsh note in your voice. I go slack. My blood sings in my ears and I wait. I wait.

Your fingertips skim down my thighs, then up again, slowly, by fractions. You're calculating—something. The longer this goes on, the more I can hear what you're thinking, and the more overwhelming it is: a rush of wind across a wheat field, and I bend to it. You finally reach the spot I've been begging for and my breath leaves me. I go silent.

You take this as a challenge. (It is.)

You move your thumb, just barely, feeling out my response.

Then, you begin to stroke slowly and insistently, with all that finesse I usually love, without actually giving me *enough*. The downside of having someone know another's body, as you know mine, is that they then have the power to drive one completely mad.

I haven't been embarrassed by my body in years. Decades. And I'm not embarrassed now, as I feel myself soaking through the fine silk you've been so careful of. My brain is frothing, surf against rocks. All I know is that I'm going to scream very, very soon if you don't *touch me*.

You continue, unperturbed. Suddenly, I feel it: the tingle that starts in the soles of my feet, as though I'm about to fall from a high place. Or fly. My nerves light up like signal fires and . . .

And you stop. My breath hisses through my teeth. I feel the sweat on my forehead, making my hair cling to my face.

"Mm, not yet," you say. That's a voice you've never used with me before, the kind you use to taunt your quarry. "I think you can handle more than that." More tenderly, you add, "Then you can have as many as you can stand."

You're maddening. You're *maddening*. My nerves are still crackling with the need for some kind of release, and the magic rushes forward to offer it. I bare my teeth, a beast, yes, and feel the power pulse out from my body into the room. Behind my eyelids, the light flares. The fire roars in the hearth.

Your thoughts go very still. Then, a frisson of cruel delight reaches me. *Now, that's an idea*, you think. I hear you move to the table, move the empty wine bottle, pick up a candle.

Oh. I start in surprise, and a lingering trace of magic sizzles at my fingertips. My eyes shoot open. There's a faint singed smell.

"Careful," you say, pleasantly. "Or you'll burn through the ropes. And probably most of this inn, too." You stay where you are, a blood-red candle burning in your hand. You're waiting for me to decide.

"Bastard." I put as much venom into it as I can muster without raising my voice above a whisper. I release the ropes and relax.

"In more ways than you can imagine." You smile at me, taking it for the *yes* that it is. I want to smack you. I want to kiss you.

"Don't open your eyes again. At least . . . not until the end."

You think something filthy as you look at me, and then you tip the candle.

The first three drops hit my left thigh. I drag air in through my clenched teeth, and then breathe it out again, slowly, the way my old teacher once taught me, when I was new and the magic still blistered my skin. I regain mastery of my breath, but barely. If I was balanced on the lightning before, I'm very close to falling off. But not yet.

Let me help you with that. Your thought flows hot like wax across my mind, and I can't decipher what you mean. Then your free hand reaches again between my legs, pressing harder than before, faster, closer to what you know I like, and I understand. I make a small, undignified moan.

That moan was, apparently, your cue. A line blazes up my body as you draw a long red path from my navel to my heart. I can feel the tendons in my neck standing out as I throw my head back and let myself give a full-throated howl of pleasure and pain.

The heat from the wax is still pulsing through my body when you pull the silk to the side and finally slide two wet fingers inside of me. I gasp in relief and let my knees fall wide. For a flash I feel what you feel as you move inside me—molten, silken—and the sweetness of it licks up my spine like a flame on a wick. I squirm against your fingers and finally allow myself to make all the noises I've been wanting to make all evening. I shut my eyes tighter.

You let a drop fall. It lands on my flank, where the skin is thin and sensitive. At the same time, you press your fingers in more deeply, and withdraw them as the wax cools. Again and again you do it, pushing into me each time a drop falls.

There's no stopping it. The change in my body is irrepressible. My nerves sing, anointed, galvanic, from the soles of my feet to the curve of my throat.

"Open your eyes," you say, and you sound even more wrecked than I am. "I want to see."

A trembling overcomes me. I clench around your fingers as the heat pulses from between my legs up through my body, that molten, silken feeling from before surging over me. I open my eyes wide and cry out hoarsely as my body spasms. Half the candles in the room extinguish. Through a pink haze I watch you lick the taste of me from your hand.

My head falls back as I try to catch my breath. The room goes in and out of focus. My ears ring, but I can still hear the sounds of you frantically removing your clothes at the foot of the bed. You sound almost clumsy in your haste.

I want to look at you, to relearn that body that I love so well, with all its beauty and all its scars, but I can't make myself lift my head. Later. I'll do it later, when my hands are free.

Sounds from the bedside table make me turn my head to watch you as you tip the contents of a small amphora into your palms and then wrap them around your cock. A faintly sweet smell hits my nose. You must have spent a king's ransom on that oil.

My eyes drift open, closed, open. I hear my own panting breath, like a lioness exhausted from the hunt. My body feels light, like I would float away if I wasn't tethered here by your ropes. But then, that's how it's always been with us.

You pull the much-abused silk down my legs, suddenly careless. And then you marvel. You're love-drunk and aching and barely holding on, and still you take the time to praise me, and that goes through me hotter than wax or flame, or even magic.

You crawl on your hands and knees from the foot of the bed and settle between my thighs. The look on your face forces the breath from me. I bite my lip, suddenly wide awake.

Your eyes shine, even in the heavy shadows, as you take my right ankle and press your lips to it. You do the same to my left, and then put them on your shoulders. You pull me toward you until my arms stretch above my head. You touch me again. I'm slick and hot and sensitive, and I shiver in anticipation. You drop your chin; you watch me with a Huntsman's eyes as you enter me.

For a moment, the whole horizon of the world contracts into the bright, fevered point where our hips meet. Your tremor echoes in me. I see you close your eyes against the feeling. You take a deep breath, then another, and set your jaw. Then, at last, you start to move. My eyes go unfocused as you build a deliberate, measured rhythm. Too soon, though, you falter. You stop, breathing hard. I watch you push the hair, which is normally so tightly pulled back, from your face.

I can't help the cry of frustration. The last waves of my release had just begun to ebb as the new ones were building. I'm overwrought; it's almost painful and I want more of it. If I were free, I would probably leave a few new scratches along that lovely back of yours.

"All right," you say, swallowing. You grip my calves and rise higher on your knees, until I'm pulled completely taut, until there's no give in the rope at all.

This time, you don't stop.

It happens faster now, and more forcefully. I know this, from years of experience (with you and people less skilled than you; we both know there is none more skilled, except perhaps, me), but it still surprises me. There's a starburst in my head and I call you every endearment I can think of, in the secret language of my kind. You aren't supposed to hear them—no one is—but you deserve them.

You follow me closely. Your eyes roll back and your body flexes as you let out a long breath that ends in a groan. I watch your chest heave and feel a stab of pride. A Huntsman spent and out of breath, and by my own doing.

I feel sweet drowsiness overcome me and could quite happily fall asleep right here, despite the shell of red wax covering my body. So, it seems, could you, judging by the languidness of your movements.

You stand, weak-kneed, and make your way carefully across the room. You pick up your belt from where you threw it. You withdraw your knife again and hold it up.

None of it makes much sense to me, in the dim rosy warmth that's enveloped me. "Hmm?" I ask, or at least mumble something approximating it.

"Hold still." Your voice is even rougher than normal. I watch you with sleepy curiosity as you make your way back over to me. You kneel beside me on the bed, and then press the flat of the blade against me.

The realization of what you're asking makes my heart jolt. "Oh." We've never done this before; I've never let anyone . . .

Your eyes are so patient and sweet, so careful. I exhale. I close my eyes. I bare my throat again to you. And your knife.

I hear your breath and your thoughts falter. You weren't expecting it. You thought I'd want to do it myself. Even after all this time I catch you off guard, and it makes me smile to myself.

The blade sighs against my skin, peeling away the wax. Your touch is achingly gentle: the blade's edge, the hand resting on my hip, the lips that press against each newly revealed sliver of skin. You're painstaking and penitent. Despite the stiffness in my arms, I want this to go on for hours.

Soon, though, it's over. I wait for you to stand and undo the knots. Instead, you put away the instrument and bend your head to kiss my belly. You move downward, lift my legs, and kiss the backs of my knees, then move up again to kiss the insides of my thighs.

"What . . ." I begin, blearily, when I feel the tip of your tongue press into me.

You lift your head, just enough to speak. "I promised you as many as you could stand, remember?"

For some reason I start to laugh, a giddy, delirious sound of joyous exhaustion and raw pleasure. It becomes a whimper as you put your mouth on me again and let your gifted tongue do its work. You always make such sweet little sounds when you do this, I'm afraid to tell you how much I like it, in case you grow self-conscious.

You're scrupulously soft, but I still feel every flicker and movement with startling intensity. This time it only takes a few minutes. My vision whites out around the edges. I wrap my legs around you and dig my heels hard into your shoulders as my body seizes up one more time. My spine curves off the bed.

"*Fuck!*" It's the first real scream I've allowed myself. The whole upper floor of the inn probably heard it. Good. A series of diminishing tremors moves through me. You slow your tongue, but don't stop, until the pleasure twists into full pain, and I push you away with my heel. Now I see why you left my legs free.

You stand, coltishly unsteady, to catch your breath. Your mouth is red and swollen, and your hair is wild. If only you understood how beautiful you actually are. But you don't want to hear that, either.

You untie me. My wrists are adorned with smarting pink lines, a rope-kissed testament of our time together. I'm almost boneless as you place my hands gently on my belly and then encourage me to sit up. You bring another cushion for my head and a silver cup filled with cool water, sweetened with herbs and honey. My very favorite. I let you give me water, like a child, making grateful noises as I drink.

When I've had my fill, I nod, and watch as you drink deeply, too. Your throat works as you tip your head back and swallow, and you're so pretty that I want to bite you.

You put the cup aside and kneel beside the bed, massaging my wrists and arms until the marks begin to fade. It's enough to send me nearly into a trance, and I can't do much besides blink slowly at you.

You pause at the scar that follows the branching veins in my forearm, which I've covered with a tattoo: a river, running to the sea. You've never asked how I got it, but you're perceptive enough that you've guessed most of it anyway. Most of us don't survive that first year. I almost didn't. That, I know, your kind also understands.

Your thoughts turn vicious for a moment, a dark bristling hum in my head as you swear vengeance on the past.

That, out of everything, is my final undoing. I blink hot, wild tears and don't bother wiping them away as I look at you.

You say my name, soft and worried, and I can't answer. I just pull you to me. You rise from your knees and let yourself be pulled, falling easily, into the riot of sheets and ruined skirts. I climb on top of you and hold you as tightly as I can. Somehow you manage to wrestle a blanket free and cover us. Your heartbeat is a steady, sure drum, and yet you, too, are trembling as you stroke my hair.

I lift my head, eventually. "You're crying."

"Am I?" you ask, as though your cheeks aren't streaked with tears.

"I thought your kind never cried. That's what the songs say."

"Mm, we paid the troubadours off. Got a reputation to maintain."

I laugh, shifting a little, and run my fingers through your hair. It's softer than it looks, but that's no surprise. It's you, after all. I let my hands wander, exploring your body for no other reason than that I missed it. You are a strange book of curves and angles, a bestiary, with a lifetime of scars illuminating your story. I know all of them, and all of them make my heart ache.

All of them except one.

"This is new." It's ugly, almost a crater, with crude stitches holding it closed. A dragon, maybe. You flinch.

"Boar," you say, tersely. "A week ago."

"A *boar* did this?"

"Lususian boar. Mean bastards."

A boar the size of a draft horse. And it just missed your kidney. My blood runs cold.

"Every time," I say, struggling for breath, "I see you . . ." I can't finish.

"What?" you ask, puzzled.

I bite my lip so hard it might bleed. Then I take a breath. Your life is one of the two things I can't fix (my life is the other), but I can fix this.

"Here," I say, smiling, as I pick up your kind knife. "I can do a better job than whatever half-wit did those stitches."

"I did those stitches."

Of course. Probably poured some hideous liquor on it and did it with a sharpened twig, knowing you.

"You really ought to take more care. It's a pity to ruin such a fine canvas with shoddy work."

Your mind turns around that, and while you're distracted, I slice through the sutures. The wound reopens. There's a lingering stench of corrupted magic to it.

You swear in surprise. But I push your hand away and press my own to your side, drawing out the infection. It stings. I could say the standard healing spell—probably should, given how tired I am—but I opt instead for the stronger one, making the boundary of each word precise and keen. There's fire between my teeth and lightning in my throat, and I push it into you. Your flesh mends, purified and whole. All that remains is a pale pink mark.

"It might still scar," I say, winded. "But you'll hardly notice."

You look at me with wide, boyish eyes. "Thank you." Your mind reels like stars.

I'm too tired. I deflect you with a kiss. "We could both use a bath," I say, settling against you.

You close your eyes. "In the morning."

"And what about my new dress? This one cost me two hundred gold pieces."

"I guess I'll have to kill quite a few boars."

I laugh. "I suppose so. But please, just . . ."

"I'll be careful. I wouldn't want to, mm, mar the canvas you like so well."

It's as much as you can give me, and I take it, thankful. "Good," I whisper, and I watch you sleep until the candles all burn out.

PRIVATE LESSONS

Penny Howell

Just four lessons in and Bunny Henderson couldn't stop fussing with her hair, trying to get it to sit exactly right under her silk scarf so her finger curls didn't look a fright as she drove across town with the top down on her new Buick. Bunny wasn't sure why she cared so much what Henry, the young, square-jawed piano instructor, thought of her messy hair, but something about the way he rolled up the sleeves of his linen shirt to press gently on the smooth keys resting just above her thighs unnerved her. The flexing of his thick forearms alone was both gratuitous and captivating. But it was just the motivation she needed to put a little extra time into her appearance.

In Henry's presence, Bunny felt like she had on her honeymoon, ages ago—an embarrassing number of years ago, really. A percolating wave of excitement and fear crashed through her sexagenarian body, followed by a hitching of her breath as she momentarily forgot how to breathe, overcome with a jittery anticipation.

The lessons, along with the new-used convertible and cherry

blossom lipstick (a classic, timeless shade) were all new additions meant to revive and upgrade Bunny's mundane life.

On a Sunday morning, while flipping through the thin local newspaper, a small advertisement in the classifieds had caught her attention.

Piano Lessons

Fill your life with the gift of beautiful music. Beginner and advanced students welcome.

It was one of those strange, serendipitous moments when the reality of the world outside you rises to meet the notions you've quietly pondered in your head. Bunny didn't even stop to think about the logical implications of such a commitment. She simply leaned over, picked up her phone, and dialed the number at the bottom of the advertisement. Her stomach swirled and knotted as the line trilled, and that's how she knew she was making the right decision. She hadn't felt that way in such a long time. It woke her up, renewed her, jarred her back into existence. Just the idea of doing something new could do all that, hold all that power. How could she resist going through with it?

The voice on the other end sounded young and sweet. She'd be surprised if he was more than thirty. *Thirty*, she thought. She couldn't even remember what her thirties were like. It was an entire lifetime ago.

"You're my first student," he said, jovial and elated. "Well, from the ad, I mean. I've had other students before."

Bunny liked being called a student. It made her feel young again, like it wasn't so silly that she needed to start her life over. At first, Henry offered a morning slot the following Sunday, but impatient Bunny couldn't imagine waiting a whole week. She'd waited long enough to really live her life, and she feared seven days was enough time to talk herself out of it.

"Would you have any availability today?" she pushed back.

"Ah, an eager one, I see." Henry considered the request and accepted.

Bunny had just a little over an hour to prepare herself. Dressing, she felt as though she were floating. She'd spent nearly two years mourning the loss of her husband, mourning the loss of the life they used to have—a life she had, frankly, grown to resent. Though this resentment hadn't made itself known to Bunny until after her husband, the anchor to that life, had passed away. The resentment had been as unexpected as the accident that took him from her. At first, she'd denied it, playing it off as her just not wanting to think of their life together because it would only make her more despondent. But ultimately, she couldn't fight it off forever. It wasn't that they weren't happy together. They'd raised children and hosted barbeques with friends in the summer. They'd drank wine on their back porch in the evenings as they shared their highs and lows from the day. They'd vacationed in a little beach house every August. But Bunny was ready for something different. To live a life according to her whims. A life that was all her own. Her own wants, desires. Each decision her own without compromise.

"Nice ride," Henry said from his porch on the morning of their first lesson. The summer sun kissed his face. He held a hand to his brow to shield his eyes from the brightness of the day.

Bunny explained that it had been her dream car. The kind of car her father didn't think was appropriate for a young lady to have to tool around town. A few years later, it wasn't a practical choice for a young wife to cart around three children in. She settled for a sturdy, reliable station wagon, the kind of car her older sister, the perfect wife, used to shuttle her children back and forth from school or soccer practice. That had been the pattern of choices throughout Bunny's life: stability and comfort over excitement and adventure.

Mourning behind her and many years left in front of her, Bunny promised herself that she would start loving her life the way she saw fit. She traded in her sedan for a big boat-bodied, cherry red convertible, curvy and seductive like she had been at nineteen when she met her husband. A siren of the road. She permed her hair and paid for professional color instead of the cheap box dye that had ravaged her frayed ends, morphing from a mousy brunette to a vibrant blonde bombshell like in the movies she'd obsessed over as a young woman. And then Bunny sought out these piano lessons, a longtime dream of hers.

Henry rented a small house near the college campus, where he was a doctoral student in sociology. During their first lessons, she learned he had played in a small quartet in the city. She wondered what would make a young man leave behind such a vibrant, vivacious locale for the sleepy suburbia of a small college town.

"The city's not all it's cracked up to be," was all he offered her. She suspected a broken heart.

"Alright, Bunny, let's get started. Shall we?" Henry said, motioning grandly to the small upright piano with its worn bench and stained keys.

Nerves kicked in and Bunny clutched her purse, holding it tighter against her body. And then, there was Henry, sliding up alongside her, gently easing his hands under the purse chain, slipping it off her bony shoulder and lightly pulling the purse away from Bunny's body. Vulnerable and shaky, Bunny took a seat at the piano. The instrument, with its long row of identical keys, bewildered her. How did these simple black and white things create such beautiful music? How was she expected to turn nothing— air and wires and pieces of wood—into something? She felt silly, suddenly, thinking that she could do it, that she would turn these basic keys into noises that were grand and wonderful and pretty.

Henry approached her from behind. Bunny felt the heat

coming from his chest, could make out one fragrant note of his cologne after another as he stepped closer. Vanilla. Sandalwood. Bergamot. Ginger. Bunny swallowed deeply, her mouth suddenly dry. And then Henry's hands cupped her shoulders. Bunny stopped breathing. Her eyes widened as a shock ran through her body. With smooth movements and even pressure, Henry pulled Bunny's shoulders back. Her breastbone cracked as her posture opened.

"Good posture is very important," Henry said. "Did I hurt you?"

Bunny shook her head. "No. Not at all."

After Henry joined her on the bench, he showed her scales. He turned on the metronome to keep the beat. He showed her a short, childish song of only a couple notes repeated over and over again, followed by a nursery rhyme. It reminded her of her now-adult children, which only reminded Bunny of her age. She wasn't the nubile young thing she wanted to be. Piano wouldn't undo thirty years of regret.

"This is so silly," Bunny said with a blush, meaning both the song and the idea that a woman her age could change.

"Ah, but it's not," Henry said. "Keeping beat is very, very important." His voice mimicked the beat Bunny played to. "You start small and then when you master that, you move onto harder things." Bunny cleared her throat, thrown off by the way he said *harder*, as if with emphasis. She could've sworn he smirked at her. *Did he do that on purpose?* she wondered.

"There you go," Henry whispered. "Just like that. Softly."

When his palms slid over the backs of Bunny's hand, she caught another whiff of his cologne. Bunny's stomach knotted from the electricity in his touch and the embarrassment of how young and fresh his skin looked on top of her opaque and spotted flesh. She had kept much of her figure in shape as best she could for having birthed three sporty boys, but it had never occurred to her to pay closer attention to her hands. Her eyes, her neck, and chest had commanded most of her attention for upkeep. Bunny cleared her throat and pulled her hands away from his, dropping them to her lap.

He didn't apologize, not that she had expected him to. Not really, anyway. Apologize for what, exactly? No lines had been crossed; she'd simply been caught off guard by her own vanity. What did it matter if she had spots on her hands? She displayed signs of aging because she was older than him—by several decades. It was simple fact, not something to be quite so ashamed of.

At the next lesson, Bunny found herself taking an extra twenty minutes to carefully apply powder and overline her lips in a way she'd seen Sophia Loren do once in a movie. Finished with her task, Bunny smiled at herself, pleased with the results. She was feeling so good, she pulled out a pair of fine black stockings and matching garter belt, relieved when the thing still fit. She sat on the edge of the bed, one leg draped over the other. It surprised Bunny when she caught herself running her hand up her calf, admiring her smooth skin and hard muscles, sculpted from years of only wearing pumps. She'd always had great legs. When Bunny was younger, she'd made it a point to wear skirts exclusively.

Bunny leaned forward, guiding the stocking's cuff around her toes, those delicate but meaty things. The stocking engulfed her foot and took her leg all the way in its mouth, stopping at the top of her milky thigh. She snapped the top to the belt and then repeated with the other. After, she eyed herself in the mirror. Palms on her waist, she modeled the lingerie, shifting hips and shimmying her shoulders, channeling the pin-up girls from the pocket calendars that the boys from her teenage years used to keep in their trucks.

She thought she looked great when she left the house, and confirmed it when she checked herself out in the flip-down mirror of her car's visor. But when she excused herself to the bathroom, Bunny gasped at the foolish woman staring back at her from the large mirror. What had gotten into her? With a tissue, she wiped away the excess red, leaving bare and blanched lips begging for moisture.

When Bunny returned beside Henry on the bench, she could feel him looking her over.

"You took off your lipstick," he observed.

"Yes, well, I don't know what I was thinking this morning."

"I thought you looked nice," Henry said.

Bunny fought back a blush. "Please," she said. "I looked like a trollop."

"What's so bad about acting like a trollop every once in a while?" Henry teased.

There was something about his voice, a change in affectation revealing a growl that lurked beneath the words. Bunny recognized it like bumping into an old friend, a slow sense of familiarity: flirtation. This young man—her piano teacher—was flirting with her.

That night, Bunny struggled to fall asleep, panged by a deep longing throbbing between her legs, wanting something so badly, and suddenly fully aware of knowing what that *something* was. Yet she was afraid to acknowledge it. The power this desire had claimed over her in just a few weeks, with such a great, consuming force, was nothing short of astonishing.

Bunny looked around in the dark as though someone might be watching her, judging her. She blushed as the satin strap of the nightgown slipped down her shoulder. She rejoiced as the cool cotton of her sheets touched her bare skin. Blood rushed to Bunny's face, her flushed cheeks turning hot. She imagined Henry shirtless at the foot of her bed, studying her nakedness with a greedy, expectant smile stretched across his face. Bunny pressed her legs together, creating a delirium of pressure at her center, as a tiny moan released from her parted lips, jarring her back to reality, back to the dark room where she was naked and alone waiting for that familiar shiver of guilt to work its way over her body.

In the middle of Bunny's fourth lesson, the music was finally coming together. The counts made sense. The mathematics she'd feared for all these years became hypnotic and rhythmic, allowing Bunny to lose herself in the tune.

"You're a very quick learner," Henry purred from behind her.

He pressed his palms onto her bare shoulders and her fingers worked the smooth keys, making the chords inside the piano's large wooden body sing out. The air and energy between student and teacher shifted as he leaned down. Then suddenly, Henry's hot breath tickled her clavicle and the peach fuzz on her earlobes as he spoke softly.

Bunny gasped at the sight of her nipples clawing at the delicate fabric of her dress. The soft cupped lace bra she'd purchased only days ago did nothing to stop the intrusion on her lesson. She moved her biceps closer to her breasts, attempting to shield them. And then, as though her body moved separately from her brain, she dropped her arms completely and pushed her chest out further, hopeful Henry would take the bait, seeing down the top of her scoop neck to admire the curvature of her large breasts sitting perkily in the first nice bra she'd ever owned.

It hadn't occurred to her that he might actually lean down and press his lips to her neck—or that such a sudden and jarring moment would cause such delight to ripple within her. Or that she'd unconsciously knock her head back against his stomach, giving the young man better access to whatever he wanted of hers.

His kisses trailed down her neck to the tops of her breasts. His tongue took a dip in her clavicle. Bunny reached for his belt loops, sitting low on his hips, to steady herself on the piano bench. Henry palmed the front of Bunny's dress, tracing every curve. In this moment she was thankful she had decided against the girdle, instead letting the wool of her dress cling to every dimple and curve of her body. She had earned every stretch mark and if Henry thought her body didn't have such imperfections, he would've been a stupid and naive boy. But Bunny sensed he wasn't either of those things.

There was no need to hide herself anymore. He wanted her all the same, making her feel forty years younger but without the confusion and lack of confidence. Bunny was all woman. And Henry could have all of her.

Bunny moaned into Henry's kiss, letting herself go. Henry spun her on the bench, so she sat lengthwise on the surface, parallel to the piano. Their moans and the squeak of the bench echoed in the otherwise quiet house. Henry gently pulled Bunny's legs apart, one on either side of the bench, ripping at the panties beneath her dress, tearing them from her. Bunny squealed with unabandoned delight.

She'd never experienced such chaos and energy. She and her husband had made love with a dim lamp on, barely enough light to see each other's bodies. Never in broad daylight. Never in the middle of the living room with the curtains open. Now, her lady parts were on full display, alive with freedom and desire. Henry grabbed her behind the knees and pulled her down the bench closer to him, where he now waited on his knees for her.

She hiked up her skirt for him, bunching the pink wool at her hips, exposing more of herself, feeling his overjoyed breath against the delicate skin he found there.

"I always knew you were a dirty girl, Bunny."

Bunny's eyes rolled back in their sockets as Henry dove his face between her legs, carefully lapping her outer lips, and then sucking on the perky nub he found between the folds. She convulsed against his mouth, and then harder with shock as his tongue found something sweeter in a place she'd never imagined his mouth would explore. She clenched her backside together, but Henry gently peeled her cheeks apart once more, as if telling her, "It's okay. This is a fine thing for us to do."

He lapped at her puckered sweetness once again. Bunny pinched her own nipples, causing her cries to deepen and her hips to sink lower on Henry's tongue, which had flattened against her sex now, burrowing itself deeper and deeper while maintaining as much contact as possible.

And then, Bunny could take no more. Her heart raved, beating against her rib cage, fighting to get out and finish the job. Her hips bucked under the pressure building between her legs. She ground against Henry's tongue, eager for more. A gush of warm water burst from her as she arched her back, soaking her dress and the bench beneath her thighs.

In the wake of release, Bunny's body lit up as a heady delirium consumed her. Emanating from her hips, a heated tingle coursed through her, all the way up to her cheeks and tiny nose. In its wake, her skin turned rosy and her muscles went limp.

It was as though a fire inside her had years ago dwindled to smoldering, expectant embers without her even noticing. A gradual fade that was only apparent now because of the way the fire had so suddenly been relit. Only now could Bunny recognize and name the absence that she had quietly carried inside herself all these years: desire.

She had experienced the joys of sex with her husband, of course, but now in the glow of Henry's fiery tongue, it was clear that pleasure had always come second in Bunny's marital bed. Their intimacy could best be described as practical and perfunctory, not the unbridled bodice-ripping Bunny had read about in novels. She had never been seduced by her late husband, had never been taken by him or tossed across the room onto the bed in a moment of sexual urgency. She had certainly never been savored quite so devoutly as she was in this very moment. He would have been appalled by the way her passion had manifested itself, erupting from her body so violently and unexpected. Bunny blushed and turned her head, cringing as she awaited the repulsed gasp from the man between her legs.

Henry lifted his drenched face. A delighted though reddened face met Bunny's horrified expression. Henry burst out laughing, not in a teasing way, in a madman kind of way, relishing her astonishment.

"I take it that's never happened before," Henry finally said.

All Bunny could do was shake her head. Was she supposed to apologize? Search for a towel to clean up the mess? But Henry really didn't seem to mind. It finally sunk in that, perhaps, that is what he had wanted the whole time he was exploring her with his mouth. Henry leaned in, a salty yet perfumed scent to him now, his body hovering just over hers. Him fully clothed and Bunny exposed from the waist down.

Elated with the ability to make a man utterly weak for her and gleefully ready to harness this newfound power over and over again, Bunny quietly said goodbye to the meek little thing she had unknowingly allowed herself to become. Splayed across the piano bench, the warm afternoon sun shining down on her from the nearest window, she had finally let go of years of pent-up frustration and all the confusing baggage from a happy but mundane marriage. As the last drops dripped from her sex, Bunny agreed to put herself first from here on out.

"I wonder what other kinds of firsts we can explore for you, Bunny. Any requests? We still have fifteen minutes left in today's lesson."

Bunny thought for a minute, carefully weighing her options, and then whispered in his ear. In response, Henry bit his lip and nodded quietly, anxious to get to work.

ABOUT THE AUTHORS

GWENDOLYN J. BEAN is an erotic writer who likes to think, "What if?" and then turn it into a story about sex. This is her first story. She lives in a small town outside of Toronto, Canada, with her family.

ANN CASTLE lives in central Illinois. Her previous erotica has appeared in *Nasty: Fetish Fights Back* and other anthologies.

THEO DE LANGLEY lives in the Netherlands with her spouse and her cat. She writes mostly in secret. She knows how to use a sword and is only slightly a witch.

LIN DEVON has been reading and writing erotic lit longer than was appropriate. She is an established artist with degrees in Fine Arts and Library Science reflecting a lifelong polyamory for art and for books. She is of African American and European descent and identifies as pansexual. Her stories span a wide spectrum.

LUCY EDEN (lucyeden.com) is the *nom de plume* of a romance-obsessed author who writes the kind of romance she loves to read. She's a sucker for alphas with a soft gooey center, over-the-top romantic gestures, strong and smart MCs, humor, love at first sight (or pretty damn close), happily ever afters, and of course, steamy love scenes.

INGA GARDNER (ingagardner.com) lives in New Hampshire, US, with her family. She is also the author of *The Reunion*, a novel, and *Just a Casual Thing*, a novella.

ADRIANA HERRERA (adrianaherreraromance.com) was born and raised in the Caribbean, but for the last fifteen years has let her job take her all over the world. She loves writing stories about people who look and sound like her people getting unapologetic happy endings. She's a social worker in New York City, working with survivors of violence.

PENNY HOWELL (pennyhowellbooks.com) lives by a simple motto: a little love and a lot of sex make for a very happy person. When not writing, you can find her making gin cocktails and obsessing over her three fur-babies. Though a born-and-raised New Englander, she hates the outdoors and cold weather.

S.P. JAFFREY is a Pakistani-American writer and educator, with a background in international journalism. Her writings have been featured in international news outlets and anthologies and are focused on culture, religion, and social justice issues.

GABRIELLE JOHNSON is a nonprofit professional by day and a romance writer by night. When she's not consuming all things romance across television, film, and literature, you'll find her wherever strong drinks and cute animals are. Or, on Twitter, @geminianxiety.

ANGELA KEMPF (premeditatedworder.com) is a radical sex revolutionary and parent of two living in Denver, who can most often be found with her nose in a book, eating tacos, or smashing the patriarchy. She ghostwrites for sex workers, sex therapists, and erotica writers around the world.

KIM KUZURI is a nonbinary butch queer who has ridden in cattle drives, worked in strawberry fields, done the barista thing, and ultimately ended up in the SF Bay Area. For fun, Kim lifts weights, collects geeky tattoos, and draws thirsty fanart of their latest media obsessions. @kimkuzuri on Instagram.

CORRINA LAWSON (corrina-lawson.com) is an award-winning newspaper reporter, a former bookstore manager, and co-founder of GeekMom.com. For more of Alec and Beth's adventures, try their novel, *Rise of the Firestarter*. For more erotica, try the award-winning *Love's Inferno*.

ANGELINA M. LOPEZ (angelinamlopez.com) writes sexy, contemporary stories about strong women and the confident men lucky to love them. Her first two books in her Filthy Rich series, *Lush Money* and *Hate Crush*, received rave reviews from *Entertainment Weekly*, NPR, and *Booklist*. She was a newspaper journalist and magazine writer before focusing on her true love, romance writing.

KRISTINE LYNN lives in northern Arizona, where she teaches English by day and writes erotic short stories and novels by night. Her first two novels, *Mountain Treasure* and *Forbidden Treasure*, are out in print and ebook format with Cobblestone Press. You can find her erotic short stories published on Bellesa.com.

ERIN MCLELLAN (erinmclellan.com) is the author of the Farm College, So Over the Holidays, and Storm Chasers series. She writes happily ever afters that are earthy, emotional, humorous, and sexy. Originally from Oklahoma, she currently lives in Alaska and spends her time dreaming up queer contemporary romances.

VELVET MOORE has appeared in *Orgasmic: Erotica for Women*, *Best Women's Erotica 2011*, and *The Mammoth Book of Best New Erotica 10*. She currently lives in Ohio and makes a living as a corporate writer.

JOANNA SHAW is a young writer from Pennsylvania with a short resume and a long list of ideas. Although currently recovering from a serious illness, she hopes to get to work sometime soon. She can be found writing or crafting in the meantime.

HOLLEY TRENT (holleytrent.com) is a bestselling and award-winning author of contemporary, paranormal, and science fiction romance. As a southern transplant to the Rocky Mountains, she pens stories that blend the adventure of the west with the sultry heat of the southeast.

SARA TAYLOR WOODS writes erotic romance and contemporary fantasy. She's the author of two-time HOLT finalist *Hold Me Down*, as well as contributor to erotica, fantasy, and horror anthologies. She lives with her family in South Carolina.

ABOUT THE EDITOR

RACHEL KRAMER BUSSEL (rachelkramerbussel.com) is a New Jersey–based author, editor, blogger, and writing instructor. She has edited over sixty books of erotica, including *Coming Soon: Women's Orgasm Erotica; The Big Book of Orgasms: 69 Sexy Stories; Come Again: Sex Toy Erotica; Dirty Dates: Erotic Fantasies for Couples; Cheeky Spanking Stories; Bottoms Up; Spanked: Red-Cheeked Erotica; Please, Sir; Please, Ma'am; He's on Top; She's on Top; The Big Book of Submission, Volumes 1 and 2; Lust in Latex; Best Bondage Erotica of the Year, Volumes 1 and 2; Anything for You; Baby Got Back: Anal Erotica; Suite Encounters; Gotta Have It; Women in Lust; Surrender; Orgasmic; Fast Girls; Going Down; Tasting Him; Tasting Her;* and *Crossdressing,* and is Best Women's Erotica of the Year series editor. Her anthologies have won eight IPPY (Independent Publisher) Awards, and *The Big Book of Submission, Volume 2, Dirty Dates,* and *Surrender* won the National Leather Association Samois Anthology Award.

Rachel has written about books, culture, sexuality, dating, and other subjects for *AVN, Bust, Cosmopolitan, Curve,* The Daily Beast, Elle.com, *Fast Company,* Fortune.com, *Glamour,* The Girlfriend, The Goods, Gothamist, *Harper's Bazaar,* Huffington Post, *Inked, InStyle, Marie Claire, MEL, Men's Health,* NBC News THINK, *Newsday, New York Post, New York Observer, The New York Times, O: The Oprah Magazine, Penthouse, The Philadelphia Inquirer, Publishers Weekly,* Refinery29, Rewire, *Rolling Stone,* The Root, Salon, *San Francisco Chronicle, Self,* Slate, Time.com, *Time Out New York,* and *Zink,* among others. She has appeared on "The Gayle King Show," "The Martha Stewart Show," "The Berman and Berman Show," NY1, and Showtime's "Family Business." She hosted the popular In the Flesh Erotic Reading Series, featuring readers from Susie Bright to Zane, speaks at conferences, and does readings and teaches erotic writing workshops around the world and online. She blogs at lustylady.blogspot.com and teaches writing classes and consults about erotica and sex-related nonfiction at eroticawriting101.com. Follow her @raquelita on Twitter.